THE BRIGHTER BUCCANEER

FOREWORD BY
IAN DICKERSON

THE ADVENTURES OF THE SAINT

Enter the Saint (1930), *The Saint Closes the Case* (1930),
The Avenging Saint (1930), *Featuring the Saint* (1931),
Alias the Saint (1931), *The Saint Meets His Match* (1931),
The Saint Versus Scotland Yard (1932), *The Saint's Getaway* (1932),
The Saint and Mr Teal (1933), *The Brighter Buccaneer* (1933),
The Saint in London (1934), *The Saint Intervenes* (1934),
The Saint Goes On (1934), *The Saint in New York* (1935),
Saint Overboard (1936), *The Saint in Action* (1937),
The Saint Bids Diamonds (1937), *The Saint Plays with Fire* (1938),
Follow the Saint (1938), *The Happy Highwayman* (1939),
The Saint in Miami (1940), *The Saint Goes West* (1942),
The Saint Steps In (1943), *The Saint on Guard* (1944),
The Saint Sees It Through (1946), *Call for the Saint* (1948),
Saint Errant (1948), *The Saint in Europe* (1953),
The Saint on the Spanish Main (1955), *The Saint Around the World* (1956),
Thanks to the Saint (1957), *Señor Saint* (1958), *Saint to the Rescue* (1959),
Trust the Saint (1962), *The Saint in the Sun* (1963),
Vendetta for the Saint (1964), *The Saint on TV* (1968),
The Saint Returns (1968), *The Saint and the Fiction Makers* (1968),
The Saint Abroad (1969), *The Saint in Pursuit* (1970),
The Saint and the People Importers (1971), *Catch the Saint* (1975),
The Saint and the Hapsburg Necklace (1976), *Send for the Saint* (1977),
The Saint in Trouble (1978), *The Saint and the Templar Treasure* (1978),
Count On the Saint (1980), *Salvage for the Saint* (1983)

THE BRIGHTER BUCCANEER

LESLIE CHARTERIS

SERIES EDITOR: IAN DICKERSON

THOMAS & MERCER

The characters and events portrayed in this book are fictitious. Any similarity to real persons, living or dead, is coincidental and not intended by the author.

Published by Thomas & Mercer, Seattle

www.apub.com

ISBN-13: 9781477842706
ISBN-10: 1477842705

Cover design by David Drummond, www.salamanderhill.com

Printed in the United States of America.

To H. W. Shirley Long,
But for whose persistent
salesmanship these stories would
certainly not have been written,
and I should have been saved no
end of hard work

FOREWORD TO THE NEW EDITION

I first met the Saint in the late 1970s. From September 1978 to March 1979, I avidly watched every single episode of *Return of the Saint* every Sunday evening, annoying my parents—who had to reschedule bath time—but making the following day at school a whole load more bearable. I was nine years old.

I've always been a voracious reader, so when I discovered that one of my brothers had some books about a character called the Saint it was pretty much a foregone conclusion that said literature would find its way from his bookshelves to mine (and has stayed there ever since . . . sorry, Andy!). One of those books was *The Brighter Buccaneer.*

So maybe that's why I've always loved this book. After all, it helped inspire me to go and track down every other Saint book, join the Saint Club, meet Leslie Charteris, and ultimately become series editor of these reprints.

No, I think it's more than that. It is, partly, the uniqueness of getting fifteen different Saint adventures in a shade over sixty-eight thousand word. Fifteen Saint adventures! In one book! No wonder my nine year old self was happy . . . It's also the location(s). These are classic Saint adventures, set in England before the Saint went on his travels with the team of Simon, Patricia, and more often than not dear old Claud Eustace—and perhaps there's also an element of the fact it remains immune to the retitling that all the other early Saint books have suffered.

Nope, still more than that.

This book was published at a time of remarkable productivity for the Saint and Leslie Charteris: *Getaway* (a.k.a. *The Saint's Getaway*) was published in September 1932, *Once More the Saint* (a.k.a. *The Saint and Mr Teal*) in January 1933, and this one followed a month later. Three books in six months. Charteris was hungry, he'd found a market for his work, and was determined to make the most of it.

The fifteen stories herein were in fact first published in late 1932 by a now defunct Sunday newspaper entitled *Empire News*. Its fiction editor, Bill McElroy, had been looking for someone to write a weekly short story for the newspaper, and H. W. Shirley Long, who was then working as an assistant to Charteris's agent Raymond Savage, persuaded McElroy that the Saint and Leslie Charteris were the men for the job. They were swiftly hired, and from August to November that year, Charteris wrote a weekly Saint story.

This book and its cousin—*The Saint Intervenes*—are unique, for although Charteris dallied with full-length novels, novellas, and short stories, he never quite managed to squeeze as many Saint adventures into so few words ever again.

These adventures show the Saint and Leslie Charteris at their very best: fifteen tales full of Saintly mischief, each one plotted and delivered in just a handful of pages. Many of them took inspiration from real life: Sir Joseph Whippelthwaite, "The Appalling Politician," was based on the then British Cabinet Minister Sir Samuel Hoare; whilst "The Unpopular Landlord" was based on a landlord that Charteris's mother was having problems with. And in "The Unblemished Bootlegger," we meet Peter Quentin for the first time. Peter is a new recruit to the Saint's cause and would go on to appear in several further Saint adventures.

This was Charteris's fifteenth book, his eleventh about the Saint. He was twenty-five years old when this was first published. What an astonishing output—even today with the advent of the Internet you struggle to find any twenty-five-year-old who's written so much, so successfully.

I often think his skill as a writer has often been overlooked; his full length novels are bona-fide thrillers, packed with tense scenes and wonderful characters. And for him to then turn round and deliver such finely plotted amusing short tales (and in some cases, very short tales) is the mark of a great story-teller and writer.

That's more like it.

I have read and reread the adventures of the Saint. Sure, they're dated now, but the quality of the characters and the writing shines through. Just don't take them too seriously, this is fun, life-affirming, escapist entertainment told by a master story-teller.

—*Ian Dickerson*

THE BRIGHTER BUCCANEER

THE BRAIN WORKERS

"Happy" Fred Jorman was a man with a grievance. He came to his partner with a tale of woe.

"It was just an ordinary bit of business, Meyer. I met him in the Alexandra—he seemed interested in horses, and he looked so lovely and innocent. When I told him about the special job I'd got for Newmarket that afternoon, and it came to suggesting he might like to put a bit on himself. I'd hardly got the words out of my mouth before he was pushing a tenner across the table. Well, after I'd been to the phone I told him he'd got a three-to-one winner, and he was so pleased he almost wept on my shoulder. And I paid him out in cash. That was thirty pounds—thirty real pounds he had off me—but I wasn't worrying. I could see I was going to clean him out. He was looking at the notes I'd given him as if he was watching all his dreams come true. And that was when I bought him another drink and started telling him about the real big job of the day. 'It's honestly not right for me to be letting you in at all,' I said, 'but it gives me a lot of pleasure to see a young sport like you winning some money,' I said. 'This horse I'm talking about now,' I said, 'could go twice round the course while all the other crocks were just beginning to realize that the race had started, but I'll eat my hat if it starts at a fraction less than five to one,' I said."

"Well?"

"Well, the mug looked over his roll and said he'd only got about a hundred pounds, including what he'd won already, and that didn't seem enough to put on a five-to-one certainty. 'But if you'll excuse me a minute while I go to my bank, which is just round the corner,' he said,

'I'll give you five hundred pounds to put on for me.' And off he went to get the money—"

"And never came back," said the smaller speaking part, with the air of a Senior Wrangler solving the first problem in a child's book of arithmetic.

"That's just it, Meyer," said Happy Fred aggrievedly. "He never came back. He stole thirty pounds off me, that's what it amounts to—he ran away with the ground-bait I'd given him, and wasted the whole of my afternoon, not to mention all the brain work I'd put in to spinning him the yarn—"

"Brain work!" said Meyer.

Simon Templar would have given much to overhear that conversation. It was his one regret that he never had the additional pleasure of knowing exactly what his pigeons said when they woke up and found themselves bald.

Otherwise, he had very few complaints to make about the way his thirty years of energetic life had treated him. "Do others as they would do you," was his motto, and for several years past he had carried out the injunction with a simple and unswerving whole-heartedness, to his own continual entertainment and profit. "There are," said the Saint, "less interesting ways of spending wet weekends . . ."

Certainly it was a wet weekend when he met Ruth Eden, though he happened to be driving home along that lonely stretch of the Windsor Road after a strictly lawful occasion.

To her, at first, he was only the providential man in the glistening leather coat who came striding across from the big open Hirondel that had skidded to a standstill a few yards away. She had seen his lights whizzing up behind them, and had managed to put her foot through the window as he went past—Mr Julian Lamantia was too strong for her, and she was thoroughly frightened. The man in the leather coat twitched open the nearest door of the limousine and propped himself gracefully against it with the broken glass crunching under his feet. His voice drawled pleasantly through the hissing rain.

"Evening, madam. This is Knight Errants Unlimited. Anything we can do?"

"If you're going towards London," said the girl quickly, "could you give me a lift?"

The man laughed. It was a short, soft lilt of a laugh that somehow made the godsend of his arrival seem almost too good to be true.

An arm sheathed in wet sheepskin shot into the limousine—and Mr Lamantia shot out. The feat of muscular prestidigitation was performed so swiftly and slickly that she took a second or two to absorb the fact that it had indubitably eventuated and travelled on into the past tense. By which time Mr Lamantia was picking himself up out of the mud, with the rain spotting the dry portions of his very natty check suiting and his vocabulary functioning on full throttle.

He stated, amongst other matters, that he would teach the intruder to mind his own unmentionable business, and the intruder smiled almost lazily.

"We don't like you," said the intruder.

He ducked comfortably under the wild swing that Mr Lamantia launched at him, collared the raving man below the hips, and hoisted him, kicking and struggling, on to one shoulder. In this manner they disappeared from view. Presently there was a loud splash from the river bank a few yards away, and the stranger returned alone.

"Can your friend swim?" he inquired interestedly.

The girl stepped out into the road, feeling rather at a loss for any suitable remark. Somewhere in the damp darkness Mr Lamantia was demonstrating a fluency of discourse which proved that he was contriving to keep at least his mouth above water; and the conversational powers of her rescuer showed themselves to be, in their own way, equally superior to any awe of circumstances.

As he led her across to his own car he talked with a charming lack of embarrassment.

"Over on our left we have the island of Runnymede, where King John signed the Magna Carta in the year 1215. It is by virtue of this Great Charter that Englishmen have always enjoyed complete freedom to do everything that they are not forbidden to do . . ."

The Hirondel was humming on towards London at a smooth seventy miles an hour before she was able to utter her thanks.

"I really was awfully relieved when you came along—though I'm afraid you've lost me my job."

"Like that, was it?"

"I'm afraid so. If you happen to know a nice man who wants an efficient secretary for purely secretarial purposes, I could owe you even more than I do now."

It was extraordinarily easy to talk to him—she was not quite sure why. In some subtle way he succeeded in weaving over her a fascination that was unique in her experience. Before they were in London she had outlined to him the whole story of her life. It was not until afterwards that she began to wonder how on earth she had ever been able to imagine that a perfect stranger could be interested in the recital of her inconsiderable affairs. For the tale she had to tell was very ordinary—a simple sequence of family misfortunes which had forced her into a profession amongst whose employers the Lamantias are not so rare that any museum has yet thought it worthwhile to include a stuffed specimen in the catalogue of its exhibits.

"And then, when my father died, my mother seemed to go a bit funny, poor darling! Anyone with a get-rich-quick scheme could take money off her. She ended up by meeting a man who was selling some wonderful shares that were going to multiply their value by ten in a few months. She gave him everything we had left, and a week or two later we found that the shares weren't worth the paper they were printed on."

"And so you joined the world's workers?"

She laughed softly.

"The trouble is to make anyone believe I really want to work. I'm rather pretty, you know, when you see me properly. I seem to put ideas into middle-aged heads."

She was led on to tell him so much about herself that they had reached her address in Bloomsbury before she remembered that she had not even asked him his name.

"Templar—Simon Templar," he said gently.

She was in the act of fitting her key into the front door, and she was so startled that she turned round and stared at him, half doubtful whether she ought to laugh.

But the man in the leather coat was not laughing, though a little smile was flickering round his mouth. The light over the door picked out the clean-cut buccaneering lines of his face under the wide-brimmed filibuster's hat, and glinted back from the incredibly clear blue eyes in such a blaze of merry mockery as she had never seen before . . . It dawned upon her, against all her ideas of probability, that he wasn't pulling her leg . . .

"Do you mean that I've really met the Saint?" she asked dizzily.

"That's so. The address is in the telephone book. If there's anything else I can do, any time—"

"Angels and ministers of grace!" said the girl weakly, and left him standing there alone on the steps, and Simon Templar went laughing back to his car.

He came home feeling as pleased as if he had won three major wars single-handed, for the Saint made for himself an atmosphere in which no adventure could be commonplace. He pitched his hat into a corner, swung himself over the table, and kissed the hands of the tall slim girl who rose to meet him.

"Pat, I have rescued the most beautiful damsel, and I have thrown a man named Julian Lamantia into the Thames. Does life hold any more?"

"There's some mud on your face, and you're as wet as if you'd been in the river yourself," said his lady.

The Saint had the priceless gift of not asking too much of life. He cast his bread with joyous lavishness upon the waters, and tranquilly assumed that he would find it after many days—buttered and thickly spread with jam. In his philosophy that night's adventure was sufficient unto itself, and when, twenty-four hours later, his fertile brain was plunged deep into a new interest that had come to him, he would probably have forgotten Ruth Eden altogether, if she had not undoubtedly recognized his name. The Saint had his own vanity.

Consequently, when she rang up one afternoon and announced that she was coming to see him, he was not utterly dumbfounded.

She arrived about six o'clock, and he met her on the doorstep with a cocktail shaker in his hand.

"I'm afraid I left you very abruptly the other night," she said. "You see, I'd read all about you in the newspapers, and it was rather overpowering to find that I'd been talking to the Saint for three-quarters of an hour without knowing it. In fact, I was very rude, and I think it's awfully sweet of you to have me."

"I think it's awfully sweet of you to be had," said Simon gravely. "Do you like it with a dash?"

He sat her down with a dry Martini and a cigarette, and once again she felt the strange sense of confidence that he inspired. It was easier to broach the object of her visit than she had expected.

"I was looking through some old papers yesterday, and I happened to come across those shares I was telling you about—the last lot my mother bought. I suppose it was ridiculous of me to think of coming to you, but it occurred to me that you'd be the very man who'd know what I ought to do about them—if there is anything that can be done. I've got quite a lot of cheek," she said, smiling.

Simon slipped the papers out of the envelope she handed him and glanced over them. There were ten of them, and each one purported to be a certificate attributing to the bearer two hundred one-pound shares in the British Honduras Mineral Development Trust.

"If they're only worth the paper they're printed on, even that ought to be something," said the Saint. "The engraving is really very artistic."

He gazed at the shares sadly. Then, with a shrug, he replaced them in the envelope and smiled. "May I keep them for a day or two?"

She nodded.

"I'd be frightfully grateful." She was watching him with a blend of amusement and curiosity, and then she laughed. "Excuse me staring at you like this, but I've never met a desperate criminal before. And you really are the Saint—you go about killing dope traffickers and swindling swindlers and all that sort of thing?"

"And that sort of thing," admitted the Saint mildly.

"But how do you find them? I mean, if I had to go out and find a swindler, for instance—"

"You've met one already. Your late employer runs the J. L. Investment Bureau, doesn't he? I can't say I know much about his business, but I should be very surprised if any of his clients made their fortunes through acting on his advice."

She laughed.

"I can't think of any who have done so, but even when you've found your man—"

"Well, every case is taken on its merits; there's no formula. Now, did you ever hear what happened to a bloke named Francis Lemuel . . ."

He amused her for an hour with the recital of some of his more entertaining misdeeds, and when she left she was still wondering why his sins seemed so different in his presence, and why it was so impossible to feel virtuously shocked by all that he admitted he had done.

During the next few days he gave a considerable amount of thought to the problem of the Eden family's unprofitable investments, and since he had never been afflicted with doubts of his own remarkable genius, he was not surprised when the course of his inquiries produced a possible market which had nothing at all to do with the Stock Exchange. Simon had never considered the Stock Exchange anyway.

He was paying particular attention to the correctly rakish angle of his hat preparatory to sallying forth on a certain morning when the front door bell rang and he went to open to the visitor. A tall, saturnine man, with white moustache and bushy white eyebrows, stood on the mat, and it is an immutable fact of this chronicle that he was there by appointment.

"Can I see Captain Tombs? My name—"

"Is Wilmer-Steak?"

"Steck."

"Steck. Pleased to meet you. I'm Captain Tombs. Step in, comrade. How are you off for time?"

Mr Wilmer-Steck suffered himself to be propelled into the sitting room, where he consulted a massive gold watch.

"I think I shall have plenty of time to conclude our business, if you have enough time to do your share," he said.

"I mean, do you think you could manage to wait a few minutes? Make yourself at home till I come back?" With a bewildering dexterity the Saint shot cigarette-box, matches, pile of magazines, decanter, and siphon on to the table in front of the visitor. "Point is, I absolutely must dash out and see a friend of mine. I can promise not to be more than fifteen minutes. Could you possibly wait?"

Mr Wilmer-Steck blinked.

"Why, certainly, if the matter is urgent, Captain . . . er . . ."

"Tombs. Help yourself to anything you want. Thanks so much. Pleased to see you. Bye-bye," said the Saint.

Mr Wilmer-Steck felt himself wrung warmly by the hand, heard the sitting room door bang, heard the front door bang, and saw the figure of his host flying past the open windows, and he was left pardonably breathless.

After a time, however, he recovered sufficiently to help himself to a whisky-and-soda and a cigarette, and he was sipping and puffing appreciatively when the telephone began to ring.

He frowned at it vaguely for a few seconds, and then he realized that he must be alone in the house, for no one came to take the call. After some further hesitation, he picked up the receiver.

"Hullo," he said.

"Listen, Simon—I've got great news for you," said the wire. "Remember those shares of yours you were asking me to make inquiries about? Well, it's quite true they were worth nothing yesterday, but they'll be worth anything you like to ask for them tomorrow. Strictly confidential till they release the news, of course, but there isn't a doubt it's true. Your company has struck one of the biggest gushers on earth—it's spraying the landscape for miles around. The papers'll be full of it in twenty-four hours. You're going to pick up a fortune!"

"Oh!" said Mr Wilmer-Steck.

"Sorry I can't stop to tell you more now, laddie" said the man on the wire. "I've got a couple of important clients waiting, and I must see them. Suppose we meet for a drink later. Berkeley at six, what?"

"Ah," said Mr Wilmer-Steck.

"Right-ho, then, you lucky old devil. So long!"

"So long," said Mr Wilmer-Steck.

He replaced the receiver carefully on its bracket, and it was not until several minutes afterwards that he noticed that his cigarette had gone out.

Then, depositing it fastidiously in the fireplace and helping himself to a fresh one, he turned to the telephone again and dialled a number.

He had scarcely finished his conversation when the Saint erupted volcanically back into the house, and Mr Wilmer-Steck was suffering from such profound emotion that he plunged into the subject of his visit without preamble.

"Our directors have gone carefully into the matter of those shares you mentioned, Captain Tombs, and I am happy to be able to tell you that we are prepared to buy them immediately, if we can come to an agreement. By the way, will you tell me again the exact extent of your holding?"

"A nominal value of two thousand pounds," said the Saint. "But as for their present value—"

"Two thousand pounds!" Mr Wilmer-Steck rolled the words almost gluttonously round his tongue. "And I don't think you even told us the name of the company."

"The British Honduras Mineral Development Trust."

"Ah, yes! The British Honduras Mineral Development Trust! . . . Naturally our position must seem somewhat eccentric to you, Captain Tombs," said Mr Wilmer-Steck, who appeared to have only just become conscious of the fact, "but I can assure you—"

"Don't bother," said the Saint briefly.

He went to his desk and flicked open a drawer, from which he extracted the bundle of shares.

"I know your position as well as you know it yourself. It's one of the disadvantages of running a bucket-shop that you have to have shares to work on. You couldn't have anything more worthless than this bunch, so I'm sure everyone will be perfectly happy. Except, perhaps, your clients—but we don't have to worry about them, do we?"

Mr Wilmer-Steck endeavoured to look pained, but his heart was not in the job.

"Now, if you sold those shares for, say, three hundred pounds—"

"Or supposing I got five hundred for them—"

"If you were offered four hundred pounds, for instance—"

"And finally accepted five hundred—"

"If, as we were saying, you accepted five hundred pounds," agreed Mr Wilmer-Steck, conceding the point reluctantly, "I'm sure you would not feel you had been unfairly treated."

"I should try to conceal my grief," said the Saint.

He thought that his visitor appeared somewhat agitated, but he never considered the symptom seriously. There was a little further argument before Mr Wilmer-Steck was persuaded to pay over the amount in cash, Simon counted out the fifty crisp new ten-pound notes which came to him across the table, and passed the share certificates over in exchange. Mr Wilmer-Steck counted and examined them in the same way.

"I suppose you're quite satisfied?" said the Saint. "I've warned you that to the best of my knowledge and belief those shares aren't worth a fraction of the price you've paid for them—"

"I am perfectly satisfied," said Mr Wilmer-Steck. He pulled out his large gold chronometer and glanced at the dial. "And now, if you will excuse me, my dear Captain Tombs, I find I am already late for an important engagement."

He made his exit with almost indecent haste.

In an office overlooking the Haymarket he found two men impatiently awaiting his return. He took off his hat, mopped his forehead, ran a hand over his waistcoat, and gasped.

"I've lost my watch," he said.

"Damn your watch," said Mr Julian Lamantia callously. "Have you got those shares?"

"My pocket must have been picked," said the bereaved man plaintively. "Yes, I got the shares. Here they are. It was a wonderful watch, too. And don't you forget I'm on to half of everything we make."

Mr Lamantia spread out the certificates in front of him, and the man in the brown bowler who was perched on a corner of the desk leaned over to look.

It was the latter who spoke first.

"Are these the shares you bought, Meyer?" he asked in a hushed whisper.

Wilmer-Steck nodded vigorously.

"They're going to make a fortune for us. Gushers blowing oil two hundred yards in the air—that's the news you'll see in the papers tomorrow. I've never worked so hard and fast in my life, getting Tombs to—"

"Who?" asked the brown bowler huskily.

"Captain Tombs—the mug I was working. But it's brain that does it, as I'm always saying . . . What's the matter with you, Fred—are you feeling ill?"

Mr Julian Lamantia swivelled round in his chair.

"Do you know anything about these shares, Jorman?" he demanded.

The brown bowler swallowed.

"I ought to," he said. "I was doing a big trade in them three or four years ago. And that damned fool has paid five hundred pounds of our money for 'em—to the same man that swindled me of thirty pounds only last week! There never was a British Honduras Mineral Development Trust till I invented it and printed the shares myself. And that . . . that . . ."

Meyer leaned feebly on the desk.

"But listen, Fred," he pleaded. "Isn't there some mistake? You can't mean . . . After all the imagination and brain work I put into getting those shares—"

"Brain work!" snarled Happy Fred.

THE EXPORT TRADE

It is a notable fact, which might be made the subject of a profound philosophical discourse by anyone with time to spare for these recreations, that the characteristics which go to make a successful buccaneer are almost the same as those required by the detective whose job it is to catch him.

That he must be a man of infinite wit and resource goes without saying, but there are other and more uncommon essentials. He must have an unlimited memory not only for faces and names, but also for every odd and out-of-the-way fact that comes to his knowledge. Out of a molehill of coincidence he must be able to build up a mountain of inductive speculation that would make Sherlock Holmes feel dizzy. He must be a man of infinite human sympathy, with an unstinted gift for forming weird and wonderful friendships. He must, in fact, be equally like the talented historian whose job it is to chronicle his exploits—with the outstanding difference that instead of being free to ponder the problems which arise in the course of his vocation for sixty hours, his decisions will probably have to be formed in sixty seconds.

Simon Templar fulfilled at least one of these qualifications to the nth degree. He had queer friends dotted about in every outlandish corner of the globe, and if many of them lived in unromantic-sounding parts of London, it was not his fault. Strangely enough, there were not many of them who knew that the debonair young man with the lean, tanned face and gay blue eyes who drifted in and out of their lives at irregular intervals was the notorious law-breaker known to everyone as the Saint. Certainly old Charlie Milton did not know.

The Saint, being in the region of the Tottenham Court Road one afternoon with half an hour to dispose of, dropped into Charlie's attic work-room and listened to a new angle of the industrial depression.

"There's not much doing in my line these days," said Charlie, wiping his steel-rimmed spectacles. "When nobody's going in for real expensive jewellery, it stands to reason they don't need any dummies. Look at this thing—the first big bit of work I've had for weeks."

He produced a glittering rope of diamonds, set in a cunning chain of antique silver, and ending in a wonderfully elaborate heart-shaped pendant. The sight of it should have made any honest buccaneer's mouth water, but it so happened that Simon Templar knew better. For that was the secret of Charlie Milton's employment.

Up there, in his dingy little shop, he laboured with marvellously delicate craftsmanship over the imitations which had made his name known to every jeweller in London. Sometimes there were a hundred thousand pounds' worth of precious stones littered over his bench and he worked under the watchful eye of a detective detailed to guard them. Whenever a piece of jewellery was considered too valuable to be displayed by its owner on ordinary occasions, it was sent to Charlie Milton for him to make one of his amazingly exact facsimiles; and there was many a wealthy dowager who brazenly paraded Charlie's handiwork at minor social functions, while the priceless originals were safely stored in a safe deposit.

"The Kellman necklace," Charlie explained, tossing it carelessly back into a drawer. "Lord Palfrey ordered it from me a month ago, and I was just finishing it when he went bankrupt. I had twenty-five pounds advance when I took it on, and I expect that's all I shall see for my trouble. The necklace is being sold with the rest of his things, and how do I know whether the people who buy it will want my copy?"

It was not an unusual kind of conversation to find its place in the Saint's varied experience, and he never foresaw the path it was to play in his career. Some days later he happened to notice a newspaper paragraph referring to the sale of Lord Palfrey's house and effects, but he thought nothing more of the matter, for men like Lord Palfrey were not Simon Templar's game.

In the days when some fresh episode of Saintly audacity was one of the most dependable weekly stand-bys of the daily press, the victims of his lawlessness had always been men whose reputations would have emerged considerably dishevelled from such a searching inquiry as they were habitually at pains to avoid; and although the circumstances of Simon Templar's life had altered a great deal since then, his elastic principles of morality performed their acrobatic contortions within much the same limits.

That those circumstances should have altered at all was not his choice, but there are boundaries which every buccaneer must eventually reach, and Simon Templar had reached them rather rapidly. The manner of his reaching them has been related elsewhere, and there were not a few people in England who remembered that story. For one week of blazing headlines the secret of the Saint's real identity had been published up and down the country for all to read, and although there were many to whom the memory had grown dim, and who could still describe him only by the nickname which he had made famous, there were many others who had not forgotten. The change had its disadvantages, for one of the organizations which would never forget had its headquarters at Scotland Yard, but there were occasional compensations in the strange commissions which sometimes came the Saint's way.

One of these arrived on a day in June, brought by a sombrely-dressed man who called at the flat on Piccadilly where Simon Templar had taken up his temporary abode—the Saint was continually changing his address, and this palatial apartment, with tall windows overlooking the Green Park, was his latest fancy. The visitor was an elderly white-haired gentleman with the understanding eyes and air of tremendous discretion which one associates in imagination with the classical type of family solicitor, and it was a solicitor that he immediately confessed himself to be.

"To put it as briefly as possible, Mr Templar," he said. "I am authorized to ask if you would undertake to deliver a sealed package to an address in Paris which will be given you. All your expenses will be paid, of course, and you will be offered a fee of one hundred pounds."

Simon lighted a cigarette and blew a cloud of smoke at the ceiling.

"It sounds easy enough," he remarked. "Wouldn't it be cheaper to send it by post?"

"That package, Mr Templar—the contents of which I am not allowed to disclose—is insured for five thousand pounds," said the solicitor impressively. "But I fear that four times that sum would not compensate for the loss of an article which is the only thing of its kind in the world. The ordinary detective agencies have already been considered, but our client feels that they are scarcely competent to deal with such an important task. We have been warned that an attempt may be made to steal the package, and it is our client's wish that we should endeavour to secure the services of your own . . . ah . . . singular experience."

The Saint thought it over. He knew that the trade in illicit drugs does not go on to any appreciable extent from England to the Continent, but rather in the reverse direction, and apart from such a possibility as that the commission seemed straightforward enough.

"Your faith in my reformed character is almost touching," said the Saint at length, and the solicitor smiled faintly.

"We are relying on the popular estimate of your sporting instincts."

"When do you want me to go?"

The solicitor placed the tips of his fingers together with a discreet modicum of satisfaction.

"I take it that you are prepared to accept our offer?"

"I don't see why I shouldn't. A pal of mine who came over the other day told me there was a darn good show at the Folies Bergère, and since you're only young once—"

"Doubtless you will be permitted to include the entertainment in your bill of expenses," said the solicitor dryly. "If the notice is not too short, we should be very pleased if you were free to visit the . . . ah . . . Folies Bergère tomorrow night."

"Suits me," murmured the Saint laconically.

The solicitor rose.

"You will travel by air, of course," he said. "I shall return later this evening to deliver the package into your keeping, after which you will be solely responsible. If I might give you a hint, Mr Templar," he added, as the Saint shepherded him to the door, "you will take particular pains to conceal it while you are travelling. It has been suggested to us that the French police are not incorruptible."

He repeated his warning when he came back at six o'clock and left Simon with a brown-paper packet about four inches square and two inches deep, in which the outlines of a stout cardboard box could be felt. Simon weighed the package several times in his hand—it was neither particularly light nor particularly heavy, and he puzzled over its possible contents for some time. The address to which it was to be delivered was typed on a plain sheet of paper; Simon committed it to memory, and burnt it.

Curiosity was the Saint's weakness. It was that same insatiable curiosity which had made his fortune, for he was incapable of looking for long at anything that struck him as being the least bit peculiar without succumbing to the temptation to probe deeper into its peculiarities. It never entered his head to betray the confidence that had been placed in him, so far as the safety of the package was concerned, but the mystery of its contents was one which he considered had a definite bearing on whatever risks he had agreed to take. He fought off his curiosity until he got up the next morning, and then it got the better of him. He opened the packet after his early breakfast, carefully removing the seals intact with a hot palette-knife, and was very glad that he had done so.

When he drove down to Croydon Aerodrome later the package had been just as carefully refastened, and no one would have known that it had been opened. He carried it inside a book, from which he had cut the printed part of the pages to leave a square cavity encircled by the margins, and he was prepared for trouble.

He checked in his suitcase and waited around patiently during the dilatory system of preparations which for some extraordinary reason is introduced to negative the theoretical speed of air transport. He was fishing out his cigarette-case for the second time when a dark and strikingly pretty girl, who had been waiting with equal patience, came over and asked him for a light.

Simon produced his lighter, and the girl took a packet of cigarettes from her bag and offered him one.

"Do they always take as long as this?" she asked.

"Always when I'm travelling," said the Saint resignedly. "Another thing I should like to know is why they have to arrange their time-tables so that you never have the chance to get a decent lunch. Is it for the benefit of the French restaurants at dinner-time?"

She laughed.

"Are we fellow passengers?"

"I don't know. I'm for Paris."

"I'm for Ostend."

The Saint sighed.

"Couldn't you change your mind and come to Paris?"

He had taken one puff from the cigarette. Now he took a second, while she eyed him impudently. The smoke had an unfamiliar, slightly bitter taste to it. Simon drew on the cigarette again thoughtfully, but this time he held the smoke in his mouth and let it trickle out again presently as if he had inhaled. The expression on his face never altered, although the last thing he had expected had been trouble of that sort.

"Do you think we could take a walk outside?" said the girl. I'm simply stifling."

"I think it might be a good idea," said the Saint.

He walked out with her into the clear morning sunshine, and they strolled idly along the gravel drive. The rate of exchange had done a great deal to discourage foreign travel that year, and the airport was unusually deserted. A couple of men were climbing out of a car that had drawn up beside the building, but apart from them there was only one other car turning in at the gates leading from the main road, and a couple of mechanics fussing round a gigantic Handley-Page that was ticking over on the tarmac.

"Why did you give me a doped cigarette?" asked the Saint with perfect casualness, but as the girl turned and stared at him his eyes leapt to hers with the cold suddenness of bared steel.

"I . . . I don't understand. Do you mind telling me what you mean?"

Simon dropped the cigarette and trod on it deliberately.

"Sister," he said, "if you're thinking of a Simon Templar who was born yesterday, let me tell you it was someone else of the same name. You know, I was playing that cigarette trick before you cut your teeth."

The girl's hand went to her mouth, then it went up in a kind of wave. For a moment the Saint was perplexed, and then he started to turn. She was looking at something over his shoulder, but his head had not revolved far enough to see what it was before the solid weight of a sandbag slugged viciously into the back of his neck. He had one instant of feeling his limbs sagging powerlessly under him, while the book he carried dropped from his hand and sprawled open to the ground, and then everything went dark.

He came back to earth in a small barely-furnished office overlooking the landing-field, and in the face that was bending over him he recognized the round pink countenance of Chief Inspector Teal, of Scotland Yard.

"Were you the author of that clout?" he demanded, rubbing the base of his skull tenderly. "I didn't think you could be so rough."

"I didn't do it," said the detective shortly. "But we've got the man who did—if you want to charge him. I thought you'd have known Kate Allfield, Saint."

Simon looked at him.

"What—not "the Mug?" I have heard of her, but this is the first time we've met. And she nearly made me smoke a sleepy cigarette!" He grimaced. "What was the idea?"

"That's what we're waiting for you to tell us," said Teal grimly. "We drove in just as they knocked you out. We know what they were after all right—the Deacon's gang beat them to the necklace, but that wouldn't make the Green Cross bunch give up. What I want to know is when you started working with the Deacon."

"This is right over my head," said the Saint, just as bluntly. "Who is this Deacon, and who the hell are the Green Cross bunch?"

Teal faced him calmly.

"The Green Cross bunch are the ones that slugged you. The Deacon is the head of the gang that got away with the Palfrey jewels yesterday. He came to see you twice yesterday afternoon—we got the wire that he was planning a big job and we were keeping him under observation, but the jewels weren't missed till this morning. Now I'll hear what you've got to say, but before you begin I'd better warn you—"

"Wait a minute." Simon took out his cigarette-case and helped himself to a smoke. "With an unfortunate reputation like mine, I expect it'll take me some time to drive it into your head that I don't know a thing about the Deacon. He came to me yesterday and said he was a solicitor—he wanted me to look after a valuable sealed packet that he was sending over to Paris, and I took on the job. That's all. He wouldn't even tell me what was in it."

"Oh, yes?" The detective was dangerously polite. "Then I suppose it'd give you the surprise of your life if I told you that that package you were carrying contained a diamond necklace valued at about eight thousand pounds?"

"It would," said the Saint.

Teal turned.

There was a plainclothes man standing guard by the door, and on the table in the middle of the room was a litter of brown paper and tissue in the midst of which gleamed a small heap of coruscating stones and shining metal. Teal put a hand to the heap of jewels and lifted it up into a streamer of iridescent fire.

"This is it," he said.

"May I have a look at it?" said the Saint.

He took the necklace from Teal's hand and studied it closely under the light. Then he handed it back with a brief grin.

"If you could get eighty pounds for it, you'd be lucky," he said. "It's a very good imitation, but I'm afraid the stones are only jargoons."

The detective's eyes went wide. Then he snatched the necklace away and examined it himself.

He turned round again slowly.

"I'll begin to believe you were telling the truth for once, Templar," he said, and his manner had changed so much that the effect would have been comical without the back-handed apology. "What do you make of it?"

"I think we've both been had," said the Saint. "After what you've told me, I should think the Deacon knew you were watching him, and knew he'd have to get the jewels out of the country in a hurry. He could probably fence most of them quickly, but no one would touch that necklace—it's too well known. He had the rather artistic idea of trying to get me to do the job—"

"Then why should he give you a fake?"

Simon shrugged.

"Maybe that Deacon is smoother than any of us thought. My God, Teal—think of it! Suppose even all this was just a blind—for you to know he'd been to see me—for you to get after me as soon as the jewels were missed—hear I'd left for Paris—chase me to Croydon—and all the time the real necklace is slipping out by another route—"

"God damn!" said Chief Inspector Teal, and launched himself at the telephone with surprising speed for such a portly and lethargic man.

The plainclothes man at the door stood aside almost respectfully for the Saint to pass.

Simon fitted his hat on rakishly and sauntered out with his old elegance. Out in the waiting room an attendant was shouting, "All Ostend and Brussels passengers, please!" And outside on the tarmac a roaring aeroplane was warming up its engines. Simon Templar suddenly changed his mind about his destination.

* * *

"I will give you thirty thousand guilders for the necklace," said Van Roeper, the little Jew of Amsterdam to whom the Saint went with his booty.

"I'll take fifty thousand," said the Saint, and he got it.

He fulfilled another of the qualifications of a successful buccaneer, for he never forgot a face. He had had a vague idea from the first that he had seen the Deacon somewhere before, but it had not been until that morning, when he woke up, that he had been able to place the amiable solicitor who had been so anxious to enlist his dubious services, and he felt that fortune was very kind to him.

Old Charlie Milton, who had been dragged away from his breakfast to sell him the facsimile for eighty pounds, felt much the same.

THE UNBLEMISHED BOOTLEGGER

INTRODUCTION

What is now called the Prohibition Era in the United States—sometimes, I suspect, in the sentimentally reminiscent tone of voice that is meant to make you think of "old unhappy far-off things and battles long ago"—probably gave rise to more stories per square second than any comparable epoch in history. It was not to be expected that such an intense concentration of stirring events would have left Simon Templar's life altogether untouched. But because most of the stories that stem from this period are fundamentally so much alike, I choose this story of the Saint because it is so different. And also, I must admit, because I myself saw it develop from the beginning.

In the first pages of the story there is quoted a letter "which had been passed on to the Saint by a chance acquaintance."

On reading it over now, I realise that this phrase was nothing but a convenient trick designed to eliminate a longer explanation for which at the time I didn't think I could spare the space.

But I remember very clearly what really happened. The place was Juan-les-Pins; the time, a sultry summer afternoon. I was paddling idly around a lake-smooth Mediterranean, in a canoe, with the man who can claim as much credit as anyone else for the fact that I have been bullied into recording so many chapters of the Saint Saga.

He said, among various other things, "By the way, just before I left London, a fellow showed me a letter that the Saint ought to have a look at . . ."

Because by occupation this man is an editor, and ever since the first Saint story he has never stopped pestering me to dig into my memory for more stories of the Saint. In fact, as you see, he will go so far as to try and initiate them. But the disgraceful thing about this case is that after it was all over—he didn't get the story. By that time I was in the middle of a series for another editor, in which this one somehow became included.

You might think that he could never have forgiven me for a thing like that. But he did. Possibly he had to. For in due course he himself had a lapse, which I have been able to hold over him ever since.

Obviously I can't give his name real name here. But *that* story was told in the book *The Saint's Getaway*, and in it I gave him the name of "Monty Hayward."

—Leslie Charteris (1939)

Mr Melford Croon considered himself a very prosperous man. The brass plate outside his unassuming suite of offices in Gray's Inn Road described him somewhat vaguely as a "Financial Consultant," and while it is true that the gilt-edged moguls of the City had never been known to seek his advice, there is no doubt that he flourished exceedingly.

Out of Mr Croon's fertile financial genius emerged, for example, the great Tin Salvage Trust. In circulars, advertisements, and statements to the Press, Mr Croon raised his literary hand in horror at the appalling waste of tin that was going on day by day throughout the country. "Tins," of course, as understood in the ordinary domestic vocabulary to mean the sepulchres of Heinz's 57 Varieties, the Crosse & Blackwell vegetable garden, or the Chef soup kitchen, are made of thin sheet iron with the most economical possible plating of genuine tin, but nevertheless (Mr Croon pointed out) tin was used. And what happened to it? It was thrown away. The dustman removed it along with the other contents of the dustbin, and the municipal incinerators burnt it. And tin was a precious metal—not quite so valuable as gold and platinum, but not very far behind silver. Mr Croon invited his readers to think of it. Hundreds of thousands of pounds being poured into dustbins and incinerators every day of the week from every kitchen in the land. Individually worthless "tins" which in the accumulation represented an enormous potential wealth.

The great Tin Salvage Trust was formed with a capital of nearly a quarter of a million to deal with the problem. Barrows would collect "tins" from door to door. Rag-and-bone men would lend their services.

A vast refining and smelting plant would be built to recover the pure tin. Enormous dividends would be paid. The subscribers would grow rich overnight.

The subscribers did not grow rich overnight, but that was not Mr Croon's fault. The Official Receiver reluctantly had to admit it, when the Trust went into liquidation eighteen months after it was formed. The regrettable capriciousness of fortune discovered and enlarged a fatal leak in the scheme; without quite knowing how it all happened, a couple of dazed promoters found themselves listening to sentences of penal servitude, and the creditors were glad to accept one shilling in the pound. Mr Croon was overcome with grief—he said so in public—but he could not possibly be blamed for the failure. He had no connexion whatever with the Trust, except as Financial Consultant—a post for which he received a merely nominal salary. It was all very sad.

In similar circumstances, Mr Croon was overcome with grief at the failures of the great Rubber Waste Products Corporation, the Iron Workers' Benevolent Guild, the Small Investors' Co-operative Bank, and the Universal Albion Film Company. He had a hard and unprofitable life, and if his mansion flat in Hampstead, his Rolls-Royce, his shoot in Scotland, his racing stud, and his house at Marlow helped to console him, it is quite certain that he needed them.

"A very suitable specimen for us to study," said Simon Templar.

The latest product of Mr Croon's indomitable inventiveness was spread out on his knee. It took the form of a very artistically typewritten letter, which had been passed on to the Saint by a chance acquaintance.

Dear Sir,

As you cannot fail to be aware, a state of Prohibition exists at present in the United States of America. This has led to a highly profitable trade in the forbidden alcoholic drinks between countries not so affected and the United States.

A considerable difference of opinion exists as to whether this traffic is morally justified. There can be no question, however, that from the standpoint of this country it cannot be legally attacked, nor that the profits, in proportion to the risk, are exceptionally attractive.

If you should desire further information on the subject, I shall be pleased to supply it at the above address.

Yours faithfully,
Melford Croon

Simon Templar called on Mr Croon one morning by appointment, and the name he gave was not his own. He found Mr Croon to be a portly and rather pale-faced man, with the flowing iron-grey mane of an impresario, and the information he gave—after a few particularly shrewd inquiries about his visitor's status and occupation—was very much what the Saint had expected.

"A friend of mine," said Mr Croon—he never claimed personally to be the author of the schemes on which he gave Financial Consultations—"a friend of mine is interested in sending a cargo of wines and spirits to America. Naturally, the expenses are somewhat heavy. He has to charter a ship, engage a crew, purchase the cargo, and arrange to dispose of it on the other side. While he would prefer to find the whole of the money—and, of course, reap all the reward—he is unfortunately left short of about two thousand pounds."

"I see," said the Saint.

He saw much more than Mr Croon told him, but he did not say so.

"This two thousand pounds," said Mr Croon, "represents about one-fifth of the cost of the trip, and in order to complete his arrangements my friend is prepared to offer a quarter of his profits to anyone who will go into partnership with him. As he expects to make at least ten thousand pounds, you will see that there are not many speculations which offer such a liberal return."

If there was one role which Simon Templar could play better than any other, it was that of the kind of man whom financial consultants of every size and species dream that they may meet one day before they die. Mr Croon's heart warmed towards him as Simon laid on the touches of his self-created character with a master's brush.

"A very charming man," thought the Saint as he paused on the pavement outside the building which housed Mr Croon's offices.

Since at various stages of the interview Mr Croon's effusive bonhomie had fairly bubbled with invitations to lunch with Mr Croon, dine with Mr Croon, shoot with Mr Croon, watch Mr Croon's horses win at Goodwood with Mr Croon, and spend weekends with Mr Croon at Mr Croon's house on the river, the character which Simon Templar had been playing might have thought that the line of the Saint's lips was unduly cynical, but Simon was only thinking of his own mission in life.

He stood there with his walking-stick swinging gently in his fingers, gazing at the very commonplace street scene with thoughtful blue eyes, and became aware that a young man with the physique of a pugilist was standing at his shoulder. Simon waited.

"Have you been to see Croon?" demanded the young man suddenly.

Simon looked round with a slight smile.

"Why ask?" he murmured. "You were outside Croon's room when I came out, and you followed me down the stairs."

"I just wondered."

The young man had a pleasantly ugly face with crinkly grey eyes that would have liked to be friendly, but he was very plainly nervous.

"Are you interested in bootlegging?" asked the Saint, and the young man stared at him grimly.

"Listen. I don't know if you're trying to be funny, but I'm not. I'm probably going to be arrested this afternoon. In the last month I've lost about five thousand pounds in Croon's schemes—and the money wasn't mine to lose. You can think what you like. I went up there to bash his face in before they get me, and I'm going back now for that same reason. But I saw you come out, and you didn't look like a crook. I thought I'd give you a word of warning. You can take it or leave it. Goodbye."

He turned off abruptly into the building, but Simon reached out and caught him by the elbow.

"Why not come and have some lunch first?" he suggested. "And let Croon have his. It'll be so much more fun punching him in the stomach when it's full of food."

He waved away the young man's objections and excuses without listening to them, hailed a taxi, and bundled him in. It was the kind of opportunity that the Saint lived for, and he would have had his way if he was compelled to kidnap his guest for the occasion. They lunched at a quiet restaurant in Soho, and in the persuasive warmth of half a litre of Chianti and the Saint's irresistible personality the young man told him what he knew of Mr Melford Croon.

"I suppose I was a complete idiot—that's all. I met Croon through a man I used to see in the place where I always had lunch. It didn't occur to me that it was all a put-up job, and I thought Croon was all right. I was fed to the teeth with sitting about in an office copying figures from one book to another, and Croon's stunts looked like a way out. I put three thousand quid into his Universal Albion Film Company: it was only on paper, and the way Croon talked about it made me think I'd never really be called on for the money. They were going to rent the World Features studio at Teddington—the place is still on the market. When the Universal Albion went smash I had to find the money, and the only way I could get it was to borrow it out of the firm. Croon put the idea into my head, but—oh, hell! It's easy enough to see how things have happened after the damage is done."

He had borrowed another two thousand pounds—without the cashier's knowledge—in the hope of retrieving the first loss. It had gone into a cargo of liquor destined for the thirsty States. Six weeks later Mr Croon broke the news to him that the coastal patrols had captured the ship.

"And that's what'll happen to any other fool who puts money into Croon's bootlegging," said the young man bitterly. "He'll be told that the ship's sunk, or captured, or caught fire, or grown wings and flown away. He'll never see his money back. My God—to think of that slimy swab trying to be a bootlegger! Why, he told me once that the very sight of a ship made him feel sick, and he wouldn't cross the Channel for a thousand pounds."

"What are you going to do about it?" asked the Saint, and the young man shrugged.

"Go back and try to make him wish he'd never been born—as I told you. They're having an audit today at the office, and they can't help finding out what I've done. I stayed away—said I was ill. That's all there is to do."

Simon took out his cheque-book and wrote a cheque for five thousand pounds.

"Whom shall I make it payable to?" he inquired, and his guest's eyes widened.

"My name's Peter Quentin. But I don't want any of your damned—"

"My dear chap, I shouldn't dream of offering you charity." Simon blotted the pink slip and scaled it across the table. "This little chat has been worth every penny of it. Besides, you don't want to go to penal servitude at your age. It isn't healthy. Now be a good fellow and dash back to your office—square things up as well as you can—"

The young man was staring at the name which was scribbled in the bottom right-hand corner of the paper.

"Is that name Simon Templar?"

The Saint nodded.

"You see, I shall get it all back," he said.

He went home with two definite conclusions as the result of his day's work and expenses: first, that Mr Melford Croon was in every way as undesirable a citizen as he had thought, and second, that Mr Melford Croon's contribution to the funds of righteousness was long overdue. Mr Croon's account was, in fact, exactly five thousand pounds overdrawn, and that state of affairs could not be allowed to continue.

Nevertheless, it took the Saint twenty-four hours of intensive thought to devise a poetic retribution, and when the solution came to him it was so simple that he had to laugh.

Mr Croon went down to his house on the river for the weekend. He invariably spent his weekends there in the summer, driving out of London on the Friday evening and refreshing himself from his labours with three happy days of rural peace.

Mr Croon had an unexpected appetite for simple beauty and the works of nature: he was rarely so contented as when he was lying out in a deckchair and spotless white flannels, directing his gardener's efforts at the flower-beds, or sipping an iced whisky-and-soda on his balcony while he watched supple young athletes propelling punts up and down the stream.

This weekend was intended to be no exception to his usual custom. He arrived at Marlow in time for dinner, and prepared for an early night in anticipation of the tireless revels of a mixed company of his friends who were due to join him the next day. It was scarcely eleven o'clock when he dismissed his servant and mixed himself a final drink before going to bed.

He heard the front door bell ring, and rose from his armchair grudgingly. He had no idea who could be calling on him at that hour, and when he opened the door and found that there was no one visible outside he was even more annoyed.

He returned to the sitting room, and gulped down the remainder of his nightcap without noticing the bitter tang that had not been there when he poured it out. The taste came into his mouth after the liquid had been swallowed, and he grimaced. He started to walk towards the door, and the room spun round. He felt himself falling helplessly before he could cry out.

When he woke up, his first impression was that he had been buried alive. He was lying on a hard, narrow surface, with one shoulder squeezed up against a wall on his left, and the ceiling seemed to be only a few inches above his head. Then his sight cleared a little, and he made out that he was in a bunk in a tiny unventilated compartment lighted by a single circular window. He struggled up on one elbow, and groaned. His head was one reeling whirligig of aches, and he felt horribly sick.

Painfully he forced his mind back to his last period of consciousness. He remembered pouring out that last whisky-and-soda—the ring at the front door—the bitter taste in the glass . . . Then nothing but an infinity of empty blackness . . . How long had he been unconscious? A day? Two days? A week? He had no means of telling.

With an agonizing effort he dragged himself off the bunk and staggered across the floor. It reared and swayed sickeningly under him, so that he could hardly keep his balance. His stomach was somersaulting nauseatingly inside him. Somehow he got over to the one round window: the pane was frosted over, but outside he could hear the splash of water and the shriek of wind. The explanation dawned on him dully—he was in a ship!

Mr Croon's knees gave way under him, and he sank moaning to the floor. A spasm of sickness left him gasping in a clammy sweat. The air was stiflingly close, and there was a smell of oil in it which made it almost unbreathable. Stupidly, unbelievingly, he felt the floor vibrating to the distant rhythm of the engines. A ship! He'd been drugged—kidnapped—shanghaied! Even while he tried to convince himself that it could not be true, the floor heaved up again with the awful deliberateness of a seventh wave, and Mr Croon heaved up with it . . .

He never knew how he managed to crawl to the door between the paroxysms of torment that racked him with every movement of the vessel. After what seemed like hours he reached it, and found strength to try the handle. The door failed to budge. It was locked. He was a prisoner—and he was going to die. If he could have opened the door he would have crawled up to the deck and thrown himself into the sea. It would have been better than dying of that dreadful nausea that racked his whole body and made his head swim as if it were being spun round on the axle of a dynamo.

He rolled on the floor and sobbed with helpless misery. In another hour of that weather he'd be dead. If he could have found a weapon he would have killed himself. He had never been able to stand the slightest movement of the water—and now he was a prisoner in a ship that must have been riding one of the worst storms in the history of navigation. The hopelessness of his position made him scream suddenly—scream like a trapped hare—before the ship slumped suckingly down into the trough of another seventh wave and left his stomach on the crest of it.

Minutes later—it seemed like centuries—a key turned in the locked door, and a man came in. Through the bilious yellow mists that swirled over his eyes, Mr Croon saw that he was tall and wiry, with a salt-tanned face and far-sighted, twinkling blue eyes. His double-breasted jacket carried lines of dingy gold braid, and he balanced himself easily against the rolling of the vessel.

"Why, Mr Croon—what's the matter?"

"I'm sick," sobbed Croon, and proceeded to prove it.

The officer picked him up and laid him on the bunk.

"Bless you, sir, this isn't anything to speak of. Just a bit of a blow—and quite a gentle one for the Atlantic."

Croon gasped feebly.

"Did you say the Atlantic?"

"Yes, sir. The Atlantic is the ocean we are on now, sir, and it'll be the same ocean all the way to Boston."

"I can't go to Boston," said Croon pathetically. I'm going to die."

The officer pulled out a pipe and stuffed it with black tobacco. A cloud of rank smoke added itself to the smell of oil that was contributing to Croon's wretchedness.

"Lord, sir, you're not going to die!" said the officer cheerfully. "People who aren't used to it often get like this for the first two or three days. Though I must say, sir, you've taken a long time to wake up. I've never known a man be so long sleeping it off. That must have been a very good farewell party you had, sir."

"Damn you!" groaned the sick man weakly. I wasn't drunk—I was drugged!"

The officer's mouth fell open.

"Drugged, Mr Croon?"

"Yes, drugged!" The ship rolled on its beam ends, and Croon gave himself up for a full minute to his anguish. "Oh, don't argue about it! Take me home!"

"Well, sir, I'm afraid that's—"

"Fetch me the captain!"

"I am the captain, sir. Captain Bourne. You seem to have forgotten, sir. This is the *Christabel Jane*, eighteen hours out of Liverpool with a cargo of spirits for the United States. We don't usually take passengers, sir, but seeing that you were a friend of the owner, and you wanted to make the trip, why, of course we found you a berth."

Croon buried his face in his hands.

He had no more questions to ask. The main details of the conspiracy were plain enough. One of his victims had turned on him for revenge—or perhaps several of them had banded together for the purpose. He had been threatened often before. And somehow his terror of the sea had become known. It was poetic justice—to shanghai him on board a bootlegging ship and force him to take the journey of which he had cheated their investments.

"How much will you take to turn back?" he asked, and Captain Bourne shook his head.

"You still don't seem to understand, sir. There's ten thousand pounds' worth of spirits on board—at least, they'll be worth ten thousand pounds if we get them across safely—and I'd lose my job if I—"

"Damn your job!" said Melford Croon.

With trembling fingers he pulled out a cheque-book and fountain-pen. He scrawled a cheque for fifteen thousand pounds and held it out.

"Here you are. I'll buy your cargo. Give the owner his money and keep the change. Keep the cargo. I'll buy your whole damned ship. But take me back. D'you understand? Take me back—"

The ship lurched under him again, and he choked. When the convulsion was over the captain had gone.

Presently a white-coated steward entered with a cup of steaming beef-tea. Croon looked at it and shuddered.

"Take it away," he wailed.

"The captain sent me with it, sir," explained the steward. "You must try to drink it, sir. It's the best thing in the world for the way you're feeling. Really, sir, you'll feel quite different after you've had it."

Croon put out a white, flabby hand. He managed to take a gulp of the hot soup, then another. It had a slightly bitter taste which seemed familiar. The cabin swam round him again, more dizzily than before, and his eyes closed in merciful drowsiness.

He opened them in his own bedroom. His servant was drawing back the curtains, and the sun was streaming in at the windows.

The memory of his nightmare made him feel sick again, and he clenched his teeth and swallowed desperately. But the floor underneath was quite steady. And then he remembered something else, and struggled up in the bed with an effort which threatened to overpower him with renewed nausea.

"Give me my cheque-book," he rasped. "Quick—out of my coat pocket—"

He opened it frantically and stared at a blank counterfoil with his face growing haggard.

"What's today?" he asked.

"This is Saturday, sir," answered the surprised valet.

"What time?"

"Eleven o'clock, sir. You said I wasn't to call you—"

But Mr Melford Croon was clawing for the telephone at his bedside. In a few seconds he was through to his bank in London. They told him that his cheque had been cashed at ten.

Mr Croon lay back on the pillows and tried to think out how it could have been done.

He even went so far as to tell his incredible story to Scotland Yard, though he was not by nature inclined to attract the attention of the police. A methodical search was made in Lloyd's Register, but no mention of a ship called the *Christabel Jane* could be found.

Which was not surprising, for *Christabel Jane* was the name temporarily bestowed by Simon Templar on a dilapidated Thames tug which had wallowed very convincingly for a few hours in the gigantic tank at the World Features studio at Teddington for the filming of storm scenes at sea, which would undoubtedly have been a great asset to Mr Croon's Universal Albion Film Company if the negotiations for the lease had been successful.

THE OWNERS' HANDICAP

"The art of crime," said Simon Templar, carefully mayonnaising a section of *fruite à la gelée*, "is to be versatile. Repetition breeds contempt—and promotion for flat-footed oafs from Scotland Yard. I assure you, Pat, I have never felt the slightest urge to be the means of helping any detective on his upward climb. Therefore we soak bucket-shops one week and bootleggers the next, and poor old Chief Inspector Teal never knows where he is."

Patricia Holm fingered the stem of her wineglass with a far-away smile. Perhaps the smile was a trifle wistful. Perhaps it wasn't. You never knew. But she had been the Saint's partner in outlawry long enough to know what any such oratorical opening as that portended, and she smiled.

"It dawns upon me," said the Saint, "that our talents have not yet been applied to the crooked angles of the Sport of Kings."

"I don't know," said Patricia mildly. "After picking thc winner of the Derby with a pin, and the winner of the Oaks with a pack of cards—"

Simon waved away the argument.

"You may think," he remarked, "that we came here to celebrate. But we didn't. Not exactly. We came here to feast our eyes on the celebrations of a brace of lads of the village who always tap the champagne here when they've brought off a coup. Let me introduce you. They're sitting at the corner table behind me on your right."

The girl glanced casually across the restaurant in the direction indicated. She located the two men at once—there were three magnums on the table in front of them, and their appearance was definitely hilarious.

Simon finished his plate and ordered strawberries and cream.

"The fat one with the face like an egg and the diamond tie-pin is Mr Joseph Mackintyre. He wasn't always Mackintyre, but what the hell? He's a very successful bookmaker, and, believe it or not, Pat, I've got an account with him."

"I suppose he doesn't know who you are?"

"That's where you're wrong. He does know—and the idea simply tickles him to death. It's the funniest thing he has to talk about. He lets me run an account, pays me when I win, and gets a cheque on the nail when I lose. And all the time he's splitting his sides, telling all his friends about it, and watching everything I do with an eagle eye—just waiting to catch me trying to put something across him."

"Who's the thin one?"

"That's Vincent Lesbon. Origin believed to be Levantine. He owns the horses, and the way those horses run is nobody's business. Lesbon wins with 'em when he feels like it, and Mackintyre fields against 'em so generously that the starting price usually goes out to the hundred-to-eight mark. It's an old racket, but they work it well."

Patricia nodded. She was still waiting for the sequel that was bound to come—the reckless light in the Saint's eyes presaged it like a red sky at morning. But he annihilated his strawberries with innocent deliberation before he leaned back in his chair and grinned at her.

"Let's go racing tomorrow," he said. "I want to buy a horse."

They went down to Kempton Park, and arrived when the runners for the second race were going up. The race was a selling plate, with the aid of his faithful pin, Simon selected an outsider that finished third, but the favourite won easily by two lengths. They went round to the ring after the numbers were posted, and the Saint had to bid up to four hundred guineas before he became the proud owner of Hill Billy.

As the circle of buyers and bystanders broke up, Simon felt a hand on his arm. He looked round, and saw a small thickset man in check breeches and a bowler hat who had the unmistakable air of an ex-jockey.

"Excuse me, sir, have you arranged with a trainer to take care of your horse? My name's Mart Farrell. If I could do anything for you—"

Simon gazed thoughtfully at his new acquisition, which was being held by an expectant groom.

"Why, yes," he murmured. "I suppose I can't put the thing in my pocket and take it home. Let's go and have a drink."

They strolled over to the bar. Simon knew Farrell's name as that of one of the straightest trainers on the Turf, and he was glad that one of his problems had been solved so easily.

"Think we'll win some more races?" he murmured, as the drinks were set up.

"Hill Billy's a good horse," said the trainer judiciously. "I used to have him in my stable when he was a two-year-old. I think he'll beat most things in his class if the handicaps give him a run. By the way, sir, I don't know your name."

It occurred to the Saint that his baptismal title was perhaps too notorious for him to be able to hide the nucleus of his racing stud under a bushel, and for once he had no desire to attract undue publicity.

"Hill Billy belongs to the lady," he said. "Miss Patricia Holm. I'm just helping her to watch it."

As far as Simon Templar was concerned, Hill Billy's career had only one object, and that was to run in a race in which one of the Mackintyre-Lesbon studs was also a competitor. The suitability of the fixture was rather more important and more difficult to be sure of, but his luck was in. Early the next week he learned that Hill Billy was favourably handicapped in the Owners' Plate at Gatwick on the following Saturday, and it so happened that his most serious opponent was a horse named Rickaway, owned by Mr Vincent Lesbon.

Simon drove down to Epsom early the next morning and saw Hill Billy at exercise. Afterwards he had a talk with Farrell.

"Hill Billy could win the first race at Windsor next week if the going's good," said the trainer. "I'd like to save him for it—it'd be a nice win for you. He's got the beating of most of the other entries."

"Couldn't he win the Owners' Handicap on Saturday?" asked the Saint, and Farrell pursed his lips.

"It depends on what they decide to do with Rickaway, sir. I don't like betting on a race when Mr Lesbon has a runner—if I may say so between ourselves. Lesbon had a filly in my stable last year, and I had to tell him I couldn't keep it. The jockey went up before the stewards after the way it ran one day at Newmarket, and that sort of thing doesn't do a trainer's reputation any good. Rickaway's been running down the course on his last three outings, but the way I work out the Owners' Handicap is that he could win if he wanted to."

Simon nodded.

"Miss Holm rather wants to run at Gatwick, though," he said. "She's got an aunt or something from the North coming down for the weekend, and naturally she's keen to show off her new toy."

Farrell shrugged cheerfully.

"Oh, well, sir, I suppose the ladies have got to have their way. I'll run Hill Billy at Gatwick if Miss Holm tells me to, but I couldn't advise her to have much of a bet. I'm afraid Rickaway might do well if he's a trier."

Simon went back to London jubilantly.

"It's a match between Hill Billy and Rickaway," he said. "In other words, Pat, between Saintliness and sin. Don't you think the angels might do a job for us?"

One angel did a job for them, anyway. It was Mr Vincent Lesbon's first experience of any such exquisite interference with his racing activities, and it may be mentioned that he was a very susceptible man.

This happened on the Gatwick Friday. The Mackintyre-Lesbon combination was putting in no smart work that day, and Mr Lesbon had whiled away the afternoon at a betting club in Long Acre, where he would sometimes beguile the time with innocuous half-crown punting between sessions at the snooker table. He stayed there until after the result of the last race was through on the tape, and then took a taxi to his flat in Maida Vale to dress for an evening's diversion.

Feminine visitors of the synthetic blonde variety were never rare at his apartment, but they usually came by invitation, and when they were not invited the call generally foreboded unpleasant news. The girl who stood on Mr Lesbon's doorstep this evening, with the air of having waited there for a long time, was an exception. Mr Lesbon's sensitive conscience cleared when he saw her face.

"May I . . . may I speak to you for a minute?"

Mr Lesbon hesitated fractionally. Then he smiled—which did not make him more beautiful.

"Yes, of course. Come in."

He fitted his key in the lock, and led the way through to his sitting room. Shedding his hat and gloves, he inspected the girl more closely. She was tall and straight as a sapling, with an easy grace of carriage that was not lost on him. Her face was one of the loveliest he had ever seen, and his practised eye told him that the cornfield gold of her hair owed nothing to artifice.

"What is it, my dear?"

"It's . . . oh, I don't know how to begin! I've got no right to come and see you, Mr Lesbon, but . . . there wasn't any other way."

"Won't you sit down?"

One of Mr Lesbon's few illusions was that women loved him for himself. He was a devotee of the more glutinous productions of the cinema, and prided himself on his polished technique.

He offered her a cigarette, and sat on the arm of her chair.

"Tell me what's the trouble, and I'll see what we can do about it."

"Well . . . you see . . . it's my brother . . . I'm afraid he's rather young and . . . well, silly. He's been backing horses. He's lost a lot of money, ever so much more than he can pay. You must know how easy it is. Putting on more and more to try and make up for his losses, and still losing . . . Well, he works in a bank, and his bookmaker's threatened to write to the manager if he doesn't pay up. Of course, Derek would lose his job at once . . ."

Mr Lesbon sighed.

"Dear me!" he said.

"Oh, I'm not trying to ask for money! Don't think that. I shouldn't be such a fool. But . . . well, Derek's made a friend of a man who's a trainer. His name's Farrell—I've met him, and I think he's quite straight. He's tried to make Derek give up betting, but it wasn't any good. However, he's got a horse in his stable called Hill Billy—I don't know anything about horses, but apparently Farrell said Hill Billy would be a certainty tomorrow if your horse didn't win. He advised Derek to do something about it—clear his losses and give it up for good." The girl twisted her handkerchief nervously. "He said—please don't think I'm being rude, Mr Lesbon, but I'm just trying to be honest—he said you didn't always want to win . . . and . . . and . . . perhaps if I came and saw you . . ."

She looked up at Rickaway's owner with liquid eyes, her lower lip trembling a little. Mr Lesbon's breath came a shade faster.

"I know Farrell," he said, as quietly as he could, "I had a horse in his stable last year, and he asked me to take it away—just because I didn't always want to win with it. He's changed his principles rather suddenly."

"I . . . I'm sure he'd never have done it if it wasn't for Derek, Mr Lesbon. He's really fond of the boy. Derek's awfully nice. He's a bit wild, but . . . Well, you see, I'm four years older than he is, and I simply have to look after him. I'd do anything for him."

Lesbon cleared his throat.

"Yes, yes, my dear. Naturally." He patted her hand. "I see your predicament. So you want me to lose the race. Well, if Farrell's so fond of Derek, why doesn't he scratch Hill Billy and let the boy win on Rickaway?"

"Because . . . oh, I suppose I can't help telling you. He said no one ever knew what your horses were going to do, and perhaps you mightn't be wanting to win with Rickaway tomorrow."

Lesbon rose and poured himself out a glass of whisky.

"My dear, what a thing it is to have a reputation!" He gestured picturesquely. "But I suppose we can't all be paragons of virtue . . . But still, that's quite a lot for you to ask me to do. Interfering with horses is a serious offence—a very serious offence. You can be warned off for it. You can be branded, metaphorically. Your whole career"—Mr Lesbon repeated his gesture—"can be ruined!"

The girl bit her lip.

"Did you know that?" demanded Lesbon.

"I . . . I suppose I must have realized it. But when you're only thinking about someone you love . . ."

"Yes, I understand." Lesbon drained his glass. "You would do anything to save your brother. Isn't that what you said?"

He sat on the arm of the chair again, searching her face. There was no misreading the significance of his gaze.

The girl avoided his eyes.

"How much do you think you could do, my dear?" he whispered.

"No!" Suddenly she looked at him again, her lovely face pale and tragic. "You couldn't want that . . . you couldn't be so . . ."

"Couldn't I?" The man laughed. "My dear, you're too innocent!" He went back to the decanter. "Well, I respect your innocence. I respect it enormously. We won't say any more about—unpleasant things like that. I will be philanthropical. Rickaway will lose. And there are no strings to it. I give way to a charming and courageous lady."

She sprang up.

"Mr Lesbon! Do you mean that . . . will you really . . ."

"My dear, I will," pronounced Mr Lesbon thickly. "I will present your courage with the reward that it deserves. Of course," he added, "if you feel very grateful—after Rickaway has lost—and if you would like to come to a little supper party . . . I should be delighted. I should feel honoured. Now, if you weren't doing anything after the races on Saturday . . ."

The girl looked up into his face.

"I should love to come," she said huskily. "I think you're the kindest man I've ever known. I'll be on the course tomorrow, and if you still think you'd like to see me again . . ."

"My dear, nothing in the world could please me more!" Lesbon put a hand on her shoulder and pressed her towards the door. "Now you run along home and forget all about it. I'm only too happy to be able to help such a charming lady."

Patricia Holm walked round the block in which Mr Lesbon's flat was situated, and found Simon Templar waiting patiently at the wheel of his car. She stepped in beside him, and they whirled down into the line of traffic that was crawling towards Marble Arch.

"How d'you like Vincent?" asked the Saint, and Patricia shivered.

"If I'd known what he was like at close quarters, I'd never have gone," she said. "He's got hot, slimy hands, and the way he looks at you . . . But I think I did the job well."

Simon smiled a little, and flicked the car through a gap between two taxis that gave him half an inch to spare on either wing.

"So that for once we can give the pin a rest," he said.

Saturday morning dawned clear and fine, which was very nearly a record for the season. What was more, it stayed fine, and Mart Farrell was optimistic.

"The going's just right for Hill Billy," he said. "If he's ever going to beat Rickaway he'll have to do it today. Perhaps your aunt might have five shillings on him after all, Miss Holm."

Patricia's eyebrows lifted vaguely.

"My . . . er . . ."

"Miss Holm's aunt got up this morning with a bilious attack," said the Saint glibly. "It's all very annoying, after we've put on this race for her benefit, but since Hill Billy's here he'd better have the run."

The Owners' Handicap stood fourth on the card. They lunched on the course, and afterwards the Saint made an excuse to leave Patricia in the Silver Ring and went into Tattersall's with Farrell. Mr Lesbon favoured the more expensive enclosure, and the Saint was not inclined to give him the chance to acquire any premature doubts.

The runners for the three-thirty were being put in the frame, and Farrell went off to give his blessing to a charge of his that was booked to go to the post. Simon strolled down to the rails and faced the expansive smile of Mr Mackintyre.

"You having anything on this one, Mr Templar?" asked the bookie juicily.

"I don't think so," said the Saint. "But there's a fast one coming to you in the next race. Look out!"

As he wandered away, he heard Mr Mackintyre chortling over the unparalleled humour of the situation in the ear of his next-door neighbour.

Simon watched the finish of the three-thirty, and went to find Farrell.

"I've got a first-class jockey to ride Hill Billy," the trainer told him. "He came to my place this morning and tried him out, and he thinks we've a good chance. Lesbon is putting Penterham up—he's a funny rider. Does a lot of Lesbon's work, so it doesn't tell us anything."

"We'll soon see what happens," said the Saint calmly.

He stayed to see Hill Billy saddled, and then went back to where the opening odds were being shouted. With his hands in his pockets, he sauntered leisurely up and down the line of bawling bookmakers, listening to the fluctuation of the prices. Hill Billy opened favourite at two to one, with Rickaway a close second at threes—in spite of its owner's dubious reputation. Another horse named Tilbury, which had originally been quoted at eight to one, suddenly came in demand at nine to two. Simon overheard snatches of the gossip that was flashing along the line, and smiled to himself. The Mackintyre-Lesbon combination was expert at drawing that particular brand of red herring across the trail, and the Saint could guess at the source of the rumour. Hill Billy weakened to five to two, while Tilbury pressed close behind it from fours to threes. Rickaway faded out to five to one.

"There are always mugs who'll go for a horse just because other people are backing it," Mr Mackintyre muttered to his clerk, and then he saw the Saint coming up. "Well, Mr Templar, what's this fast one you promised me?"

"Hill Billy's the name," said the Saint, "and I guess it's good for a hundred."

"Two hundred and fifty pounds to one hundred for Mr. Templar," said Mackintyre lusciously, and watched his clerk entering up the bet.

When he looked up the Saint had gone.

Tilbury dropped back to seven to two, and Hill Billy stayed solid at two and a half. Just before the "off" Mr Mackintyre shouted "Six to one, Rickaway," and had the satisfaction of seeing the odds go down before the recorder closed his notebook.

He mopped his brow, and found Mr Lesbon beside him.

"I wired off five hundred pounds to ten different offices," said Lesbon. "A little more of this and I'll be moving into Park Lane. When that girl came to see me I nearly fainted. What does that man Templar take us for?"

"I don't know," said Mr Mackintyre phlegmatically.

A general bellow from the crowd announced the "off," and Mr Mackintyre mounted his stool and watched the race through his field-glasses.

"Tilbury's jumped off in front, Hill Billy's third, and Rickaway's going well on the outside . . . Rickaway's moving up, and Hill Billy's on a tight rein . . . Hill Billy's gone up to second. The rest of the field's packed behind, but they don't look like springing any surprises . . . Tilbury's finished. He's falling back. Hill Billy leads, Mandrake running second, Rickaway half a length behind with plenty in hand . . . Penterham's using the whip, and Rickaway's picking up. He's level with Mandrake—no, he's got it by a short head. Hill Billy's a length in front, and they're putting everything in for the finish."

The roar of the crowd grew louder as the field entered the last furlong. Mackintyre raised his voice.

"Mandrake's out of it, and Rickaway's coming up. Hill Billy's flat out with Rickaway's nose at his saddle . . . Hill Billy's making a race of it. It's neck-and-neck now. Penterham left it a bit late. Rickaway's gaining slowly . . ."

The yelling of the crowd rose to a final crescendo, and suddenly died away. Mr Mackintyre dropped his glasses and stepped down from his perch.

"Well," he said comfortably, "that's three thousand pounds."

The two men shook hands gravely and turned to find Simon Templar drifting towards them with a thin cigar in his mouth.

"Too bad about Hill Billy, Mr Templar," remarked Mackintyre succulently. "Rickaway only did it by a neck, though I won't say he mightn't have done better if he'd started his sprint a bit sooner."

Simon Templar removed the cigar.

"Oh, I don't know," he said. "As a matter of fact, I rather changed my mind about Hill Billy's chance just before the "off." I was over at the telegraph office, and I didn't think I'd be able to reach you in time, so I wired another bet to your London office. Only a small one—six hundred pounds, if you want to know. I hope Vincent's winnings will stand it." He beamed seraphically at Mr Lesbon, whose face had suddenly gone a sickly grey. "Of course you recognized Miss Holm—she isn't easy to forget, and I saw you noticing her at the Savoy the other night."

There was an awful silence.

"By the way," said the Saint, patting Mr Lesbon affably on the shoulder, "she tells me you've got hot, slimy hands. Apart from that, your technique makes Clark Gable look like something the cat brought in. Just a friendly tip, old dear."

He waved to the two stupefied men and wandered away, and they stood gaping dumbly at his retreating back.

It was Mr Lesbon who spoke first, after a long and pregnant interval.

"Of course you won't settle, Joe," he said half-heartedly.

"Won't I?" snarled Mr Mackintyre. "And let him have me up before Tattersall's Committee for welshing? I've got to settle, you fool!"

Mr Mackintyre choked.

Then he cleared his throat. He had a great deal more to say, and he wanted to say it distinctly.

THE TOUGH EGG

Chief Inspector Teal caught Larry the Stick at Newcastle as he was trying to board an outward-bound Swedish timber-ship. He did not find the five thousand pounds' worth of bonds and jewellery which Larry took from the Temple Lane Safe Deposit, but it may truthfully be reported that no one was more surprised about that than Larry himself.

They broke open the battered leather suitcase to which Larry was clinging as affectionately as if it contained the keys of the Bank of England, and found in it a cardboard box which was packed to bursting-point with what must have been one of the finest collections of small pebbles and old newspapers to which any burglar had ever attached himself, and Larry stared at it with glazed and incredulous eyes.

"Is one of you busies saving up for a rainy day?" he demanded, when he could speak, and Mr Teal was not amused.

"No one's been to that bag except when you saw us open it," he said shortly. "Come on, Larry—let's hear where you hid the stuff."

"I didn't hide it," said Larry flatly. He was prepared to say more, but suddenly he shut his mouth. He could be an immensely philosophic man when there was nothing left for him to do except to be philosophic, and one of his major problems had certainly been solved for him very providentially. "I hadn't anything to hide, Mr Teal. If you'd only let me explain things I could've saved you busting a perfickly good lock and making me miss my boat."

Mr Teal tilted back his bowler hat with a kind of weary patience.

"Better make it short, Larry," he said. "The night watchman saw you before you coshed him, and he said he'd recognize you again."

"He must've been seeing things," asserted Larry. "Now, if you want to know all about it, Mr Teal, I saw the doctor the other day, and he told me I was run down. 'What you want, Larry, is a nice holiday,' he says—not that I'd let anyone call me by my first name, you understand, but this doc is quite a good-class gentleman. 'What you want is a holiday,' he says. 'Why don't you take a sea voyage?' So, seeing I've got an old aunt in Sweden, I thought I'd pay her a visit. Naturally, I thought, the old lady would like to see some newspapers and read how things were going in the old country—"

"And what did she want the stones for?" inquired Teal politely. "Is she making a rock-garden?"

"Oh, them?" said Larry innocently. "Them was for my uncle. He's a geo . . . geo . . ."

"Geologist is the word you want," said the detective, without smiling. "Now let's go back to London, and you can write all that down and sign it."

They went back to London with a resigned but still chatty cracksman, though the party lacked some of the high spirits which might have accompanied it. The most puzzled member of it was undoubtedly Larry the Stick, and he spent a good deal of time on the journey trying to think how it could have happened.

He knew that the bonds and jewels had been packed in his suitcase when he left London, for he had gone straight back to his lodgings after he left the Temple Lane Safe Deposit and stowed them away in the bag that was already half-filled in anticipation of an early departure. He had dozed in his chair for a few hours, and caught the 7:25 from King's Cross—the bag had never been out of his sight. Except . . . once during the morning he had succumbed to a not unreasonable thirst, and spent half an hour in the restaurant car in earnest collaboration with a bottle of Worthington. But there was no sign of his bag having been tampered with when he came back, and he had seen no familiar face on the train.

It was one of the most mystifying things that had ever happened to him, and the fact that the police case against him had been considerably weakened by his bereavement was a somewhat dubious compensation.

Chief Inspector Teal reached London with a theory of his own. He expounded it to the Assistant Commissioner without enthusiasm.

"I'm afraid there's no doubt that Larry's telling the truth," he said. "He's no more idea what happened to the swag than I have. Nobody double-crossed him, because he always works alone, and he hasn't any enemies that I know of. There's just one man who might have done it—you know who I mean."

The Assistant Commissioner sniffed. He had an irritating and eloquent sniff.

"It would be very tiresome if anything happened to the Saint," he remarked pointedly. "The CID would have a job to find another stock excuse that would sound quite as convincing."

When Mr Teal had cooled off in his own room, he had to admit that there was an element of truth in the Assistant Commissioner's acidulated comment. It did not mellow his tolerance of the most unpopular Police Chief of his day; he had had similar thoughts himself, without feeling as if he had discovered the elixir of life.

The trouble was that the Saint refused to conform to any of the traditions which make the capture of the average criminal a mere matter of routine. There was nothing stereotyped about his methods which made it easy to include him in the list of suspects for any particular felony. He was little more than a name in criminal circles; he had no jealous associates to give him away, he confided his plans to no one, he never boasted of his successes in anyone's hearing—he did nothing which gave the police a chance to catch him red-handed. His name and address were known to every constable in the force, but for all any of them could prove in a court of law he was an unassailably respectable citizen who had long since left a rather doubtful past behind him, an amiable young man about town blessed with plentiful private means, who had the misfortune to be seen in geographically close proximity to various lawless events for which the police could find no suitable scapegoat. And no one protested their ignorance of everything to do with him more vigorously than his alleged or prospective victims. It made things very difficult for Mr Teal, who was a clever detective but a third-rate magician.

The taciturnity of Max Kemmler was a more recent thorn in Mr Teal's side.

Max Kemmler was a Dane by birth and an American by naturalization. The phase of his career in which the United States Federal Authorities were interested started in St Louis, when he drifted into Egan's Rats and carved the first notches in his gun. Prudently, he left St Louis during an election cleanup and reappeared in Philadelphia as a strong-arm man in a newsstand racket. That lasted him six months, and he left in a hurry; the tabs caught up with him in New York, where he went over big for a couple of years as typewriter expert in an East Side liquor mob. He shot up the wrong speaker one night after a celebration, and was lucky to be able to make a passage to Cherbourg on a French liner that sailed at dawn the next morning. How he got past the passport barriers into England was something of a mystery. He was down on the deportation list, but Scotland Yard was holding up in the hope of an extradition warrant.

He was a thick-shouldered man of middle height, with a taste for camel-hair coats and very light grey Homburgs. Those who had been able to keep on the right side of him in the States called him a good guy—certainly he could put forth a rugged geniality, when it suited him, which had its appeal for lesser lights who reckoned it a privilege to be slapped on the back by the notorious Max Kemmler. His cigars were uniformly expensive, and the large diamond set in the corner of his black onyx signet ring conveyed an impression of great substance—he had been paying for it at the rate of two dollars eighty-five cents a month until the laborious working-out of the instalment system bored him, and he changed his address.

Max knew from the time he landed that his days in England were numbered, but it was not in his nature to pass up any profitable enterprise on that account. In a very short space of time he had set up a club in a quiet street off the Edgware Road, of which the police had yet to learn. The club boasted a *boule* table, as well as a half-dozen games of *chemin-de-fer*, which were always going: everything was as straight as a die, for Max Kemmler knew that gambling does not need to be crooked to show a long dividend for the bank. The *chemin-de-fer* players paid ten per cent of their winnings to the management, and the smallest chips were priced at half a sovereign. Max did the steering himself and paid his croupiers generously, but he was the only one who made enough out of it to live at the Savoy and put three figures of real money away in his wallet every week in addition.

He had dinner one night with his chief croupier before going north to open the club, and it happened that there was a zealous young detective-sergeant from Vine Street at the next table. It was a small and inexpensive chop-house in Soho, and the detective was not there on business; neither did Max Kemmler know him, for the gambling club was in a different division.

Halfway through the meal Max remembered an enigmatic telephone call that had been put through to his room while he was breakfasting, and asked the croupier about it.

"You ever heard of a guy called Saint?" he queried, and the croupier's jaw fell open.

"Good God! You haven't heard from him?"

Max Kemmler was surprised, to say the least of it.

"Yeah—he did ring me up," he replied guardedly. "What's the matter with you? Is he the wheels in this city?"

The croupier acknowledged, in his own idiom, that Simon Templar was The Wheels. He was a tall hard-faced man, with iron-grey hair, bushy grey eyebrows and moustache, and the curried complexion of a rather decayed retired major, and he knew much more about the Saint than a law-abiding member of the community should have known. He gave Max Kemmler all the information he wanted, but Max was not greatly impressed.

"What you mean is he's a kind of hijacker, is he? Hard-boiled, huh? I didn't know you'd got any racket like that over here. And he figures I ought to pay him for 'protection.' That's funny!" Max Kemmler was grimly amused. "Well, I'd like to see him try it."

"He's tried a lot of things like that and got away with them, Mr Kemmler," said the croupier awkwardly.

Max turned down one corner of his mouth.

"Yeah? So have I. I guess I'm pretty tough myself, what I mean."

He had a reminder of the conversation the next morning, when a plump and sleepy-looking man called and introduced himself as Chief Inspector Teal.

"I hear you've had a warning from the Saint, Kemmler—one of our men heard you talking about it last night."

Max had done some thinking overnight. He was not expecting to be interviewed by Mr Teal, but he had his own ideas on the subject that the detective raised.

"What of it?"

"We want to get the Saint, Kemmler. You might be able to help us. Why not tell me some more about it?"

Max Kemmler grinned.

"Sure. Then you know just why the Saint's interested in me, and I can take the rap with him. That dick at the next table ought to have listened some more—then he could have told you I was warned about that one. No, thanks, Teal! The Saint and me are just buddies together, and he rang me up to ask me to a party. I'm not saying he mightn't get fresh some time, but I can look after that. He might kind of meet with an accident."

It was not the first time that Teal had been met with a similar lack of enthusiasm, and he knew the meaning of the word 'no' when it was pushed up to him in a certain way. He departed heavily, and Simon Templar, who was sipping a cocktail within view of the vestibule, watched him go.

"You might think Claud Eustace really wanted to arrest me," he remarked, as the detective's broad back passed through the doors.

His companion, a young man with the air of a gentlemanly prize-fighter, smiled sympathetically. His position was privileged, for it was not many weeks since the Saint's cheerful disregard for the ordinances of the Law had lifted him out of a singularly embarrassing situation with a slackness that savoured of sorcery. After all, when you have been youthfully and foolishly guilty of embezzling a large sum of money from your employers in order to try and recoup the losses of an equally youthful and foolish speculation, and a cheque for the missing amount is slipped into your hands by a perfect stranger, you are naturally inclined to see that stranger's indiscretions in an unusual light.

"I wish I had your life," said the young man—his name was Peter Quentin, and he was still very young.

"Brother," said the Saint good-humouredly, "if you had my life you'd have to have my death, which will probably be a sticky one without wreaths. Max Kemmler is a tough egg all right, and you never know."

Peter Quentin stretched out his legs with a wry grimace.

"I don't know that it isn't worth it. Here am I, an A1 proposition to any insurance company, simply wasting everything I've got with no prospect of ever doing anything else. You saved me from getting pushed in clink, but of course there was no hope of my keeping my job. They were very nice and friendly when I confessed and paid in your cheque, but they gave me the air all the same. You can't help seeing their point of view. Once I'd done a thing like that I was a risk to the Company, and next time they mightn't have been so lucky. The result is that I'm one of the great unemployed, and no dole either. If I ever manage to get another job, I shall have to consider myself well off if I'm allowed to sit at an office desk for two hundred and seventy days out of the year, while I get fat and pasty and dream about the pension that'll be no use to me when I'm sixty."

"Instead of which you want to go on a bread-and-water diet for a ten-years' sentence," said the Saint. "I'm a bad example to you, Peter. You ought to meet a girl who'll pull all that out of your head."

He really meant what he said. If he refused even to consider his own advice, it was because the perilous charms of the life that he had long ago chosen for his own had woven a spell about him that nothing could break. They were his meat and drink, the wine that made unromantic days worth living, his salute to buccaneers who had had better worlds to conquer. He knew no other life.

Max Kemmler was less poetic about it. He was in the game for what he could get, and he wanted to get it quickly. Teal's visit to him that morning had brought home to him another danger that that accidentally eavesdropping plainclothes man in the restaurant had thrown across his path. Whatever else the police knew or did not know, they now had the soundest possible reason to believe that Max Kemmler's holiday in England had turned towards profitable business, for nothing else could provide a satisfactory reason for the Saint's interest. His croupier had warned him of that, and Max was taking the warning to heart. The pickings had been good while they lasted, but the time had come for him to be moving.

There was big play at the club that night. Max Kemmler inspired it, putting forth all the bonhomie that he could call upon to encourage his patrons to lose their shirts and like it. He ordered in half a gross of champagne, and invited the guests to help themselves. He had never worked so hard in his life before, but he saw the results of it when the club closed down at four in the morning and the weary staff counted over the takings. The *boule* table had had a skinner, and money had changed hands so fast in the *chemin-de-fer* parties that the management's ten per cent commission had broken all previous records. Max Kemmler found himself with a comfortingly large wad of crumpled notes to put away. He slapped his croupiers boisterously on the back and opened the last bottle of champagne for them.

"Same time again tomorrow, boys," he said when he took his leave. "If there's any more jack to come out of this racket, we'll have it."

As a matter of fact, he had no intention of reappearing on the morrow, or on any subsequent day. The croupiers were due to collect their week's salary the following evening, but that consideration did not influence him. His holiday venture had been even more remunerative than he had hoped and he was going while the going was good.

Back at the Savoy he added the wad of notes from his pocket to an even larger wad which came from a sealed envelope, which he kept in the hotel manager's safe, and slept with his booty under his pillow.

During his stay in London he had made the acquaintance of a passport specialist. His passage was booked back to Montreal on the *Empress of Britain*, which sailed the next afternoon, and a brand-new Canadian passport established his identity as Max Harford, grain dealer, of Calgary.

He was finishing a sketchy breakfast in his dressing-gown the next morning, when his chief croupier called. Kemmler had a mind to send back a message that he was out, but thought better of it. The croupier would never have come to his hotel unless there was something urgent to tell him, and Max recalled what he had been told about the Saint with a twinge of vague uneasiness.

"What's the trouble, major?" he asked curtly, when the man was shown in.

The other glanced around at the display of strapped and bulging luggage.

"Are you going away, Mr Kemmler?"

"Just changing my address, that's all," said Kemmler bluffly. "This place is a little too near the high spots—there's always half a dozen bulls snooping around looking for con-men and I don't like it. It ain't healthy. I'm moving over to a quiet little joint in Bloomsbury, where I don't have to see so many policemen."

"I think you're wise." The croupier sat on the bed and brushed his hat nervously. "Mr Kemmler . . . I thought I ought to come and see you at once. Something has happened."

Kemmler looked at his watch.

"Something's always happening in this busy world," he said with a hearty obtuseness which did not quite carry conviction. "Let's hear about it."

"Well, Mr Kemmler . . . I don't quite know how to tell you. It was after we closed down this morning . . . I was on my way home . . ."

He broke off with a start as the telephone bell jangled insistently through the room. Kemmler grinned at him emptily, and picked up the receiver.

"Is that you, Kemmler?" said a somnolent voice, in which a thin thread of excitement was perceptible. "Listen—I'm going to give you a shock, but whatever I say you must not give the slightest indication of what I'm talking about. Don't jump, and don't say anything except 'Yes' or 'No.'"

"Yeah?"

"This is Chief Inspector Teal speaking. Have you got a man with you now?"

"Uh-huh."

"I thought so. That's Simon Templar—the Saint. I just saw him go into the hotel. Never mind if you think you know him. That's his favourite trick. We heard he was planning to hold you up, and we want to get him red-handed. Now what about that idea I mentioned yesterday?"

Kemmler looked round inconspicuously. It was difficult to keep the incredulity out of his eyes. The appearance of his most trusted croupier failed to correspond with the description he had heard of the Saint in any respect except that of height and build. Then he saw that the Anglo-Indian complexion could be a simple concoction of grease-paint, the hardness of the features a matter of expression, the greyness of the hair and the bushiness of moustache and eyebrows an elementary problem in make-up.

The croupier was strolling round the bed, and Kemmler could scarcely control himself as he saw the man touch the pillow underneath which the envelope of notes still lay.

"Well?"

Kemmler fought out a battle with himself of which nothing showed on his face. The Saint's right hand was resting in a side pocket of his coat—there was nothing in that ordinary fact to disturb most people, but to Max Kemmler it had a particular and deadly significance. And his own gun was under the pillow with the money—he had been hoodwinked like the veriest greenhorn.

"What about it?" he demanded as calmly as he could.

"We want to get him," said the detective. "If he's in your room already you can't do a thing. Why not be sensible? You're sailing on the *Empress of Britain* today, and that suits us. We'll turn a blind eye on your new passport. We won't even ask why the Saint wants to rob you. All we ask is for you to help us get that man."

Max Kemmler swallowed. That knowledge of his secret plans was only the second blow that had come to him. He was a tough guy in any circumstances, but he knew when the dice were loaded against him. He was in a cleft stick. The fact that he had promised himself the pleasure of giving the Saint an unwholesome surprise if they ever met didn't enter into it.

"What shall I do?" he asked.

"Let him get on with it. Let him stick you up. Don't fight or anything. I'll have a squad of men outside your door in thirty seconds."

"Okay," said Max Kemmler expressionlessly. "I'll see to it."

He put down the receiver and looked into the muzzle of Simon Templar's automatic. With the detective's warning still ringing in his ears, he let his mouth fall open in well-simulated astonishment and wrath.

"What the hell—"

"Spare my virginal ears," said the Saint gently. "It's been swell helping you to rake in the berries, Max, but this is where the game ends. Stick your hands right up and feel your chest expand!"

He turned over the pillow and put Kemmler's gun in a spare pocket. The envelope of notes went into another. Max Kemmler watched the disappearance of his wealth with a livid face of fury that he could hardly control. If he had not received that telephone call he would have leapt at the Saint and chanced it.

Simon smiled at him benevolently.

"I'm afraid we'll have to see that you don't raise an alarm," he said. "Would you mind turning round?"

Max Kemmler turned round reluctantly. He was not prepared for the next thing that happened to him, and it is doubtful whether even Chief Inspector Teal could have induced him to submit meekly to it if he had. Fortunately he was given no option. A reversed gun-butt struck him vimfully and scientifically on the occiput, and he collapsed in a limp heap.

When he woke up a pageboy was shaking him by the shoulder and his head was splitting with the worst headache that he had ever experienced.

"Is your luggage ready to go, Mr Kemmler?"

Kemmler glared at the boy for a few seconds in silence. Then recollection returned to him, and he staggered up with a hoarse profanity.

He dashed to the door and flung it open. The corridor was deserted.

"Where's that guy who was here a minute ago? Where are the dicks?" he shouted, and the bell-hop gaped at him uncomprehendingly.

"I don't know, sir."

Max Kemmler flung him aside and grabbed the telephone. In a few seconds he was through to Scotland Yard—and Chief Inspector Teal.

"Say, you, what the hell's the idea? What is it, huh? The grand double-cross? Where are those dicks who were going to be waiting for the Saint outside my door? What've you done with 'em? You bit paluka—"

"I don't understand you, Kemmler," said Mr Teal coldly. "Will you tell me exactly what's happened?"

"The Saint's been here. You know it. You rang me up and told me. You told me to let him stick me up—give him everything he wanted—you wouldn't let me put up a fight—you said you'd be waiting for him outside the door and catch him red-handed—"

Kemmler babbled on for a while longer, and then gradually his tale petered out incoherently as he realized just how easily he had been hoodwinked. When the detective came to interview him, Kemmler apologized and said he must have been drunk, which nobody believed.

But it seemed as if the police didn't know anything about his passage on the *Empress of Britain* after all. It was Max Kemmler's only consolation.

THE BAD BARON

"In these days of strenuous competition," said the Saint, "it's an extraordinarily comforting thing to know you're at the top of your profession—unchallenged, undismayed, and wholly beautiful."

His audience listened to him with a very fair simulation of reverence—Patricia Holm because she had heard similar modest statements so often before that she was beginning to believe them, Peter Quentin because he was the very latest recruit to the cause of Saintly lawlessness and the game was still new and exciting.

They had met together at the Piccadilly Hotel for a cocktail, and the fact that Simon Templar's remark was not strictly true did nothing to spoil the prospect of an innocent evening's amusement.

For the Saint certainly had a rival, and of recent days a combination of that rival's boundless energy and Simon Templar's cautious self-effacement had placed another name in the position in the headlines which had once been regularly booked for the Saint. Newspapers screamed his exploits from their bills, music-hall comedians gagged about him, detectives tore their hair and endured the scathing criticisms of the Press and their superiors with as much fortitude as they could call on, and owners of valuable jewellery hurriedly deposited their valuables in safes and found a new interest in patent burglar alarms.

For jewels were the speciality of the man who was known as "The Fox"—there was very little else known about him. He burst upon the public in a racket of sensational banner lines when he held up Lady Palfrey's charity ball at Grosvenor House single-handed, and got clear away with nearly ten thousand pounds' worth of display pieces. The clamour aroused by that exploit had scarcely passed its peak when he raided Sir Barnaby Gerrald's house in Berkeley Square and took a four-thousand-pound pearl necklace from a wall safe in the library while the Gerralds were entertaining a distinguished company to dinner in the next room. He opened and ransacked a Bond Street jeweller's strong-room the very next night at a cost to the insurance underwriters of over twelve thousand pounds. Within a week he was the topic of every conversation: Geneva Conferences were relegated to obscure corners of the news sheets, and even Wimbledon took second place.

All three coups showed traces of careful preliminary spade-work. It was obvious that the Fox had mapped out every move in advance, and that the headlines were merely proclaiming the results of a scheme of operations that had been maturing perhaps for years. It was equally obvious to surmise that the crimes which had already been committed were not the beginning and the end of the campaign. News editors (who rarely possess valuable jewels) seized on the Fox as a Heaven-sent gift in a flat season, and the Fox worked for them with a sense of news value that was something like the answer to their blasphemous prayers. He entered Mrs Wilbur G. Tully's suite at the Dorchester and removed her jewel-case with everything that it contained while she was in the bathroom and her maid had been decoyed away on a false errand. Mrs Tully sobbingly told the reporters that there was only one thing which never could be replaced—a diamond-and-amethyst pendant valued at a mere two hundred pounds, a legacy from her mother, for which she was prepared to offer a reward of twice its value. It was returned to her through the post the next morning, with a typewritten expression of the Fox's sincere apologies. The news editors bought cigars and wallowed in their Hour. They hadn't had anything as good as that since the Saint appeared to go out of business, and they made the most of it.

It was even suggested that the Fox might be the once notorious Saint in a new guise, and Simon Templar received a visit from Chief Inspector Teal.

"For once I'm not guilty, Claud," said the Saint, with considerable sadness, and the detective knew him well enough to believe him.

Simon had his private opinions about the Fox. The incident of Mrs Tully's ancestral pendant did not appeal to him; he bore no actual ill-will towards Mrs Tully, but the very prompt return of the article struck him as being a very ostentatious gesture to the gallery of a kind in which he had never indulged. Perhaps he was prejudiced. There is very little room for friendly rivalry in the paths of crime, and the Saint had his own human egotisms.

The fame of the Fox was brought home to him that evening through another line.

"There's a man who's asking for trouble," said Peter Quentin.

He pointed to a copy of *The Evening News* as it lay open on the table between the glasses. Simon leaned sideways and scanned it lazily.

THE MAN WHO IS NOT AFRAID OF BURGLARS
Three times attacked—three times the winner

NO QUARTER!

BARON VON DORTVENN is one visitor to London who is not likely to spend any sleepless nights on account of the wave of crime with which the police are trying in vain to cope.

He has come to England to look after the bracelet of Charlemagne, which he is lending to the International Jewellery Exhibition which opens on Monday.

The famous bracelet is a massive circle of gold four inches wide and thickly encrusted with rubies. It weighs eight pounds, and is virtually priceless.

At present it is locked in the drawer of an ordinary desk at the house in Campden Hill which the Baron has rented for a short season. He takes it with him wherever he goes. It has been in the care of his family for five centuries, and the Baron regards it as a mascot.

Baron von Dortvenn scorns the precautions which would be taken by most people who found themselves in charge of such a priceless heirloom.

"Every criminal is a coward," the Baron told an Evening News representative yesterday. "I have been attacked three times in the course of my travels with the bracelet—"

"Sounds like a job for our friend the Fox," remarked Peter Quentin carelessly, and was amazed at the look Simon Templar gave him. It leapt from the Saint's eyes liked blued steel.

"Think so?" drawled the Saint.

He skimmed down the rest of the half-column, which was mainly concerned with the Baron's boasts of what he would do to anyone who attempted to steal his heirloom. Halfway down there was an inset photograph of a typical Junker with a double chin, close-cropped hair, monocle, and waxed moustaches. Underneath it there was a cut line saying "Baron von Dortvenn" in case any reader should mistake it for a portrait of Mr Jack Buchanan's new leading lady.

"A nasty-looking piece of work," said the Saint thoughtfully.

Patricia Holm finished her Bronx rather quickly. She knew all the signs—and only that afternoon the Saint had hinted that he might behave himself for a week.

"I'm starving," she said.

They went down to the grill-room, and the subject might have been forgotten during the Saint's profound study of the menu and wine list, for Simon had a very delicate discrimination in the luxuries of life. Let us say that the subject *might* have been forgotten—the opportunity to forget it simply did not arise.

"To get the best out of caviar, you should eat it like they do in Rumania—in half-pound portions, with a soup-ladle," said the Saint, when the cloud of bustling waiters had dispersed.

And then he relaxed in his chair. Relaxed completely, and lighted a cigarette with infinite deliberation.

"Don't look round," he said. "The gent has got to pass our table. Just put it on record that I said I was blowed."

The other two gazed at him vaguely and waited. A superb *chef de restaurant* came past, ushering a mixed pair of guests to a table on the other side of the room. One of them was a blonde girl, smartly dressed and rather good-looking in a statuesque way. The other was unmistakably the Baron von Dortvenn.

Simon could hardly keep his eyes off them. He barely trifled with his food, sipped his wine with no more interest than if it had been water, and lighted one cigarette from another with monotonous regularity. When the orchestra changed over to a dance rhythm, he pleaded that he was suffering from corns and left it to Peter Quentin to take Patricia on the floor.

The Baron was apparently not so afflicted. He danced several times with his companion, and danced very badly. It was after a particularly elephantine waltz that Simon saw the girl, quite openly, dab her eyes with her handkerchief as she left the floor.

He leaned back even more lazily, with his eyes half closed and a cigarette merely smouldering in the corner of his mouth, and continued to watch. The couple were admirably placed for his observations—the girl was facing him, and he saw the Baron in profile. And it became very plain to him that a jolly *soirée* was definitely not being had by all.

The girl and the Baron were arguing—not loudly, but very vehemently—and the Baron was getting red in the face. He was clearly working himself into a vicious rage, and wrath did not make him look any more savoury. The girl was trying to be dignified, but she was breaking down. Suddenly with a flash of spirit, she said something that obviously struck home. The Baron's eyes contracted, and his big hands fastened on the girl's wrists. Simon could see the knuckles whitening under the skin in the savage brutality of the grip, and the girl winced. The Baron released her with a callous fling of his arm that spilled a fork off the table, and without another word the girl gathered up her wrap and walked away.

She came towards the Saint on her way to the door. He saw that her eyes were faintly rimmed with red, but he liked the steady set of her mouth. Her steps were a little uncertain; as she reached his table she swayed and brushed against it, slopping over a few drops from a newly-filled wine-glass.

"I'm awfully sorry," she said in a low voice.

The Saint snapped a match between his fingers, and held her eyes.

"I saw what happened—let me get you a taxi."

He stood up and came round the table while she started to protest. He led her up the stairs and through the lobby to the street.

"Really—it's awfully nice of you to bother—"

"To tell you the truth," murmured the Saint, "I have met people with a better taste in barons."

The commissionaire hailed a taxi at the Saint's nod, and the girl gave an address in St John's Wood. Simon allowed her to thank him again, and coolly followed her in before the commissionaire closed the door. The taxi pulled out from the kerb before she could speak.

"Don't worry," said the Saint. "I was just feeling like a breath of fresh air, and my intentions are fairly honourable. I should probably have been obliged to smite your Baron on the nose if you hadn't left him when you did. Here—have a cigarette. It'll make you feel better."

The girl took a smoke from his case. They were held up a few yards farther on, at the end of Piccadilly, and suddenly the door of the taxi was flung open and a breathless man in a double-breasted dinner-jacket appeared in the aperture.

"Pardon, madame—I did not sink I should catch you. It is yours, isn't it?"

He held up a small drop earring, and as he turned his head Simon recognized him as a solitary diner from a table adjoining his own.

"Oh!" The girl sat up, biting her lip. "Thank you—thank you so much—"

"Il n'y a pas de quoi, madame," said the man happily. "I see it fall and I run after you, but always you're too quick. Now it's all right. I am content. Madame, you permit me to say you a brave woman? I also saw everysing. Zat Baron—"

All at once the girl hid her face in her hands.

"I don't know how to thank you," she said chokingly. "You're all so sweet . . . Oh, my God! If only I could kill him! He deserves to be killed. He deserves to lose his beastly bracelet. I'd steal it myself—"

"Ah, but then you would be in prison, madame—"

"Oh, it'd be easy enough. It's on the ground floor—you'd only have to break open the desk. He doesn't believe in burglar-alarms. He's so sure of himself. But I'd show him. I'd make him pay!"

She turned away to the corner and sobbed hysterically.

Simon glanced at the little Frenchman.

"Elle se trouvera mieux chez elle," he said, and the other nodded sympathetically and closed the door.

The taxi drew away in a wedge of traffic and turned up Regent Street. Simon sat back in his corner and let the girl have her cry. It was the best possible thing for her, and he could have said nothing helpful.

They had a practically clear run through to St John's Wood, and the girl recovered a little as they neared their destination. She wiped her eyes and took out a microscopic powder-puff, with the unalterable vanity of women.

"You must think I'm a fool," she said, as the taxi slowed up. "Perhaps I am. But no one else can understand."

"I don't mind," said the Saint.

The cab stopped, and he leaned across her to open the door. Her face was within two inches of his, and the Saint required all adventures to be complete. In his philosophy, knight-errantry had its own time-honoured rewards.

His lips touched hers unexpectedly, and then in a flash, with a soft laugh, he was out of the taxi. She walked past him and went up the steps of the house without looking back.

Simon rode back jubilantly to the Piccadilly, and found his lady and Peter Quentin patiently ordering more coffee. The Baron had already left.

"I saw you leaving with the blonde Venus," said Peter enviously. "How on earth did you work it?"

"Is this a new romance?" smiled Patricia.

"You want to be careful of these barons," said Peter. "Next thing you know, you'll have a couple of his pals clicking their heels at you and inviting you to meet him in Hyde Park at dawn."

The Saint calmly annexed Peter Quentin's liqueur and tilted his chair backwards. Over the rim of his glass he exchanged bows with the chivalrous Frenchman at the adjoining table, who was paying his bill and preparing to leave, and then he surveyed the other two with a lazily reckless glint in his eye that could have only one meaning.

"Let's go home," he said.

They sauntered in silence down Piccadilly to the block where the Saint's flat was situated, and there the Saint doffed his hat with a flourish, and kissed Patricia's hand.

"Lady, be good. Peter and I have a date to watch the moon rising over the Warrington waterworks."

In the same silence two immaculately dressed young men sauntered on to the garage where the Saint kept his car. Nothing was said until one of them was at the wheel, with the other beside him, and the great silver Hirondel was humming smoothly past Hyde Park Corner. Then the fair-haired one spoke.

"Campden Hill, I suppose?"

"You said it," murmured the Saint. "Baron von Dortvenn has asked for it once too often."

He drove slowly past the house for which Baron von Dortvenn had exchanged the *schloss* that was doubtless his more natural background. It was a gaunt Victorian edifice, standing apart from the adjacent houses in what for London was an unusually large garden surrounded by a six-foot brick wall topped by iron spikes. As far as the Saint could see, it was in darkness, but he was not really concerned to know whether the Baron had come home or whether he had passed on to seek a more amenable candidate for his favours in one of the few night clubs that the police had not yet closed down. Simon Templar was out for justice, and he could not find his opportunity too soon.

Twenty yards beyond the house he disengaged the gear lever and swung himself out onto the running-board while the car was coasting to a standstill. It was then only half-past-eleven, but the road was temporarily deserted.

"Turn the bus round, Peter, and pretend to be tinkering with the engine. Hop back into it at the first sounds of any excitement, and be on your toes for a quick getaway. I know it's bad technique to plunge into a burglary without getting the lie of the land first, but I shall sleep like a child tonight if I have the bracelet of Charlemagne under my mattress."

"You aren't going in alone," said Peter Quentin firmly.

He had the door on his side of the car open, but the Saint caught his shoulder.

"I am, old lad. I'm not making a fully-fledged felon of you sooner than I can help—and if we were both inside there'd be no one to cover the retreat if the Baron's as hot as he tells the world."

His tone forbade argument. There was a quietly metallic timbre in it that would have told any listener that this was the Saint's own private picnic. And the Saint smiled. He punched Peter Quentin gently in the biceps, and was gone.

The big iron gates that gave entrance to the garden were locked—he discovered that at the first touch. He went on a few yards and hooked his fingers over the top of the wall. One quick springy heave, and he was on top of the wall, clambering gingerly over the spikes. As he did so he glanced towards the house, and saw a wisp of black shadow detach itself from the neighbourhood of a ground-floor window and flit soundlessly across a strip of lawn into the cover of a clump of laurels.

The Saint dropped inside the garden on his toes, and stood there, swiftly knotting a handkerchief over the lower part of his face. The set of his lips was a trifle grim. Someone else was also on the job that night—he had only just arrived in time.

He slipped along the side of a hedge towards the spot where the black shadow had disappeared, but he had underrated the first intruder's power of silent movement. There was a sudden scuff of shoes on the turf behind him, and the Saint swerved and ducked like lightning. Something whizzed past his head and struck his shoulder a numbing blow: he shot out an arm and grabbed hold of a coat, jerking his assailant towards him. His left hand felt for the man's throat.

It was all over very quickly, without any noise. Simon lowered the unconscious man to the ground, and flashed the dimmed beam of a tiny pocket torch on his face. A black mask covered it—Simon whipped it off and saw the sallow face of the Frenchman who had followed him with the unfortunate girl's earring.

The Saint snapped off his flashlight and straightened up with his mouth pursed in a noiseless whistle that widened into a smile. Verily, he was having a night out . . .

He glided across the lawn to the nearest window, feeling around for the catch with a thin knife-blade. In three seconds it gave way, and he slid up the sash and climbed nimbly over the sill. His feet actually landed on the baronial desk. The top drawer was locked: he squeezed a fine steel claw in above the lock and levered adroitly. The drawer burst open with a crash, and the beam of his torch probed its interior. Almost the first thing he saw was a heavy circlet of dull yellow, which caught the light from a hundred crimson facets studded over its surface. Simon picked it up and shoved it into his pocket. Its great weight dragged his coat all over on one side.

And at that moment all the lights in the room went on.

The Saint whirled round.

He looked into the single black eye of an automatic held in the hand of Baron von Dortvenn himself. On either side of the Baron was a heavily-built, hard-faced man.

"So you're the Fox?" said the Baron genially.

Simon thanked heaven for the handkerchief that covered his face. The two hard-faced men were advancing towards him, and one of them jingled a pair of handcuffs.

"On the contrary," said the Saint, "I'm the Bishop of Bootle and Upper Tooting."

He held out his wrists resignedly. For a moment the man with the handcuffs was between him and the Baron's automatic, and the Saint took his chance. His left whizzed round in a terrific hook that smacked cleanly to its mark on the side of the man's jaw, and Simon leapt onto the desk. He went through the window in a flying dive, somersaulted over his hands, and was on his feet again in an instant.

He sprinted across the lawn and went over the wall like a cat. A whistle screamed into the night behind him, and he saw Peter Quentin tumble into the car as he jumped down to the pavement. Simon stepped onto the running-board as the Hirondel streaked past, and fell over the side into the seat beside the driver.

"Give her the gun," he ordered briefly, "and dodge as you've never dodged before. I think they'll be after us."

"What happened?" asked Peter Quentin, and the Saint unfastened the handkerchief from his face and grinned.

"It looks like they were waiting for someone," he said.

It took twenty minutes of brilliant driving to satisfy the Saint that they were safe from any possible pursuit. On the way Simon took the heavy jewelled armlet from his pocket and gazed at it lovingly under one of the dash-board lamps.

"That's one thing the Fox didn't put over," he said cryptically.

* * *

He was breakfasting off bacon and eggs the next morning at eleven o'clock when Peter Quentin walked in. Peter carried a morning paper, which he tossed into the Saint's lap.

"There's something for your 'Oh, yeah?' album," he said grimly.

Simon poured out a cup of coffee.

"What is it—some more intelligent utterances by Cabinet Ministers?"

"You'd better read it," said Peter. "It looks as if several people made mistakes last night."

Simon Templar picked up the paper and started at the double-column splash.

> *THE FOX CAPTURED*
> *CID WAKES UP*
> *BRILLIANT COUP IN KENSINGTON*
>
> *ONE OF THE CLEVEREST STRATEGEMS in the history of criminal detection achieved its object at eleven-thirty last night with the arrest of Jean-Baptiste Arvaille, alleged to be the famous jewel thief known as "The Fox."*
>
> *Arvaille will be charged at the police court this morning with a series of audacious robberies totalling over fifty thousand pounds.*
>
> *It will be told how Inspector Henderson, of Scotland Yard, assisted by a woman member of the Special Branch, posed as "Baron von Dortvenn" and baited the trap with a mythical "bracelet of Charlemagne" which he was stated to have brought to England for the International Jewellery Exhibition.*
>
> *The plot owes much of its success to the cooperation of the Press, which gave the fullest possible publicity to the "Baron's" arrival.*
>
> *It was stated in this newspaper yesterday that the "bracelet of Charlemagne" was a circle of solid gold thickly encrusted with rubies.*
>
> *In actual fact it is made of lead, thinly plated with gold, and the stones in it are worthless imitations. Workmen sworn to secrecy created it specially for Inspector Henderson's use.*

Simon Templar read through the whole detailed story. After which he was speechless for some time.

And then he smiled.

"Oh, well," he said, "it isn't everyone who can say he's kissed a woman policeman."

THE BRASS

"Have another drink," said Sir Ambrose Grange.

He was a man with a lot to say, but that was his theme song. He had used it so many times during the course of that evening that Simon Templar had begun to wonder whether Sir Ambrose imagined he had invented a new and extraordinarily subtle philosophy, and was patiently plugging it at intervals until his audience grasped the point. It bobbed up along the line of his conversation like vitamins in a food reformer's menu. Tapping resources which seemed inexhaustible, he delved into the kit-bag of memory for reminiscences and into his trouser pockets for the price of beer, and the Saint obliged him by absorbing both with equal courtesy.

"Yes, sir," resumed Sir Ambrose, when their glasses had been refilled. "Business is business. That is my motto, and it always will be. If you happen to know that something is valuable, and the other fellow doesn't, you have every right to buy it from him at his price without disclosing your knowledge. He gets what he thinks is a fair price, you get your profit, and you're both satisfied. Isn't that what goes on every day on the Stock Exchange? If you receive inside information that certain shares are going to rise, you buy as many as you can.

You probably never meet the man who sells them to you, but that doesn't alter the fact of what you're doing. You're deliberately taking advantage of your knowledge to purchase something for a fraction of its value, and it never occurs to you that you ought to tell the seller that if he held on to his shares for another week he could make all the profit for himself."

"Quite," murmured the Saint politely.

"And so," said Sir Ambrose, patting the Saint's knee impressively with his flabby hand, "when I heard that the path of the new by-pass road cut straight through the middle of that old widow's property, what did I do? Did I go to her and say, madam, in another week or two you'll be able to put your own price on this house, and any bank or building society would be glad to lend you enough to pay off this instalment of the mortgage? Why, if I'd done anything like that I should have been a fool, sir—a sentimental old fool. Of course I didn't. It was the old geezer's own fault if she was too stupid and doddering to know what was going on around her. I simply foreclosed at once, and in three weeks I'd sold her house for fifteen times as much as I gave her for it. That's business." Sir Ambrose chortled wheezily over the recollection. "By Gad, you should have seen the old trout's face when she heard about it. And was she rude? By Gad, if words could break bones I should be wheeling myself about in an invalid chair still. But that kind of thing doesn't worry me! . . . Have another drink."

"Have one with me," suggested the Saint half-heartedly, but Sir Ambrose waved the invitation aside.

"No, sir. I never allow a young man to pay for my drinks. Have a good time with me. The same again?"

Simon nodded, and lighted a cigarette while Sir Ambrose toddled over to the bar. He was a pompous and rather tubby little man, with a waxed moustache that matched his silver-grey spats, and a well-wined complexion that matched the carnation in his button-hole, and the Saint did not like him. In fact, running over a lengthy list of gentlemen of whom he had gravely disapproved, Simon Templar found it difficult to name anyone whom he had felt less inclined to take into his bosom with vows of eternal brotherhood.

He disliked Sir Ambrose no less heartily because he had known him less than a couple of hours. With an idle evening to spend by himself, the Saint had sailed out into the West End to pass it as entertainingly as he could. He had no plans whatever, but his faith in the beneficence of the gods was sublime. Thus he had gone in search of adventure before, and he had rarely been disappointed. To him, the teeming thousands of assorted souls who jostled through the sky-sign area on a Saturday night were so many oysters who might be opened by a man with the clairvoyant eye and delicate touch which the Saint claimed for his genius. It was a business of drifting where the whim guided him, following an impulse and hoping that it might lead to an interest, taking a chance and not caring if it failed.

In just that spirit of careless optimism he had wandered into a small hotel in a quiet street behind the Strand and discovered an almost deserted bar where he could imbibe a glass of ale while seeking inspiration for his next move. And it was there that a casual remark about the weather had floated him into the acquaintance of Sir Ambrose Grange. It was only a matter of minutes after that before Sir Ambrose, having presented his card, pulled out the opening chord of his theme song and said, "Have a drink?"

Simon had a drink. Even before the state of the weather arose as an introduction, he had felt a professional curiosity to know whether anybody could be quite as unsavoury a bore as Sir Ambrose looked. And he had not been disappointed. Within five minutes Sir Ambrose had him sitting in a corner listening to the details of an ingenious trick he had invented as a boy at school for swindling his contemporaries out of their weekly ration of toffee. Within ten minutes Sir Ambrose was leading on to a description of the smart deals on a larger scale which had built up his comfortable fortune. He seemed to have had several drinks on his own before he started intoning his chorus to the Saint. The effects of them had been to make him loquacious and confidential, but they had not added to his charm. And the more cordially Simon learned to detest him, the more intently Simon listened—for it had dawned on the Saint that perhaps his evening was being well spent.

Sir Ambrose returned with steps that could have been steadier, and slopped over some of the beer as he deposited their glasses on the table. He sat down again and leaned back with a sigh of large-waisted well-being.

"Yes, sir," he resumed tirelessly. "Sentiment is no good. My uncle was sentimental, and what did it do for him?"

Not having known Sir Ambrose's uncle, Simon found the question unanswerable.

"It made him a pest to his heirs," said Sir Ambrose, solving the riddle. "That's what it did. Not that he left much for us to inherit—a beggarly ten thousand odd was all that he managed to keep out of the hands of the parasites who traded on his soft heart. But what did he do with it?"

Once again the Saint was nonplussed. Sir Ambrose, however, did not really require assistance.

"Look at this," he said.

He dragged a small brass image out of his pocket and set it up on the table between the glasses. Simon glanced at it, and recognized it at once. It was one of those pyramidal figures of a seated Buddha, miniatures of the gigantic statue at Kamakura, which find their place in every tourists' curio shop from Karachi to Yokohama.

"That, sir," said the sentimentalist's nephew, "was my uncle's. He bought it in Shanghai when he was a young man, and he called it his mascot. He used to burn a joss-stick in front of it every day—said the ju-ju wouldn't work without it. And then, when he died, what do you think we found in his will?"

Simon was getting accustomed to Sir Ambrose's interrogative style, but the Saint was not very easily silenced.

"A thousand quid to buy joss-sticks," he hazarded.

Sir Ambrose shook his head rather impatiently, till both his chins wobbled.

"No, sir. Something much worse than that. We found that not a penny of his money could be touched until this ridiculous thing had been sold for two thousand pounds. He said that only a man who was prepared to pay a sum like that for it would appreciate it properly and give it the attention he wanted. Personally, I think that anyone who paid a sum like that for it could be put in a lunatic asylum without a certificate. But there it is in the will, and the lawyers say we can't upset it. I've been carrying the damned thing about with me half the week, showing it to all the antique shops in London, and the best offer I've had is fifteen shillings."

"But surely," said the Saint, "you could get a friend of yours to buy it, and give him the two thousand back with a spot of interest as soon as the executors unbuttoned?"

"If anything like that could have been done, sir, I'd have done it. But the old fool thought of that himself, and he left strict instructions that the executors were to be satisfied beyond all possible doubt that the sale was a genuine one. And he made his bank the executors, damn him! If you've ever tried to put anything over on a bank you'll know what a hope we've got of doing anything like that. No—the best thing we can ever hope to do is to find some genuine stranger and sell it to him while he's drunk."

Simon picked up the image and examined it closely. It was unexpectedly heavy, and he guessed that the brass casting must have been filled with lead. On the base was a line of Chinese characters cut into the metal and filled with red.

"Funny language," observed Sir Ambrose, leaning over to point to the characters. "I've often wanted to meet a Chink who could tell me what they write on things like this. Look at that thing there like a tadpole with wings. I'll bet that's a particularly dirty swearword—it's twice the size of the other words. Have a drink."

The Saint looked at his watch.

"I'm afraid I'll have to be getting home," he observed.

"Come and see me one evening," said Sir Ambrose. "You've got my address on my card, and I like young company. Come along one night next week, and I'll invite some girls."

Simon reached his flat in time to see Peter Quentin and Patricia Holm climbing out of a taxi. They were in evening dress, and the Saint surveyed them rudely.

"Well," he said, "have you mugs finished pretending to be numbers one and two of the Upper Ten?"

"He's jealous," said Patricia, on Peter Quentin's arm. "His own tails have been in pawn so long that the moth's done them in."

A misguided friend had presented the Saint with tickets for the Opera. Simon Templar, in one of his fits of perversity, had stated in no uncertain terms that it was too hot to put on a starched shirt and listen to perspiring tenors dying in C flat for four hours, and Peter Quentin had volunteered to be Patricia's escort.

"We thought of some bacon and eggs," Peter said, "and we wondered if you'd like to treat us."

"I thought you might treat me," murmured the Saint, "as an inducement for me to be seen out with a girl whose clothes have all slipped down below her waist, and a pie-faced tough disguised as a waiter, it's the least you can offer."

Back in the taxi, they asked him how he had spent the evening.

"I've been drinking beer with one of the most septic specimens in London," said the Saint thoughtfully. "And if I can't make him wish he hadn't told me so much about himself I won't have another bath for six years."

The problem of securing an adequate contribution towards his Old Age Pension from Sir Ambrose Grange occupied the Saint's mind considerably for the next twenty-four hours. Sir Ambrose had gratuitously introduced himself as such a perfect example of the type of man whom the Saint prayed to meet that Simon felt that his reputation was at stake. Unless something suitably unpleasant happened to Sir Ambrose in a very short space of time, the Saint would sink down to somewhere near zero in his own estimation of himself—a possibility that was altogether too dreadful to contemplate.

He devoted most of the Sabbath to revolving various schemes in his mind, all of which were far less holy than the day, but he had not finally decided on any of them when the solution literally fell into his arms by a coincidence that seemed too good to be true.

This happened on the Monday afternoon.

He sallied out of his flat into Piccadilly in the hope of finding a paper with the winner of the Eclipse Stakes, and as he stepped on to the pavement a middle-aged man in horn-rimmed spectacles and a Panama who was hurrying past suddenly staggered in his direction, and would have fallen if the Saint had not caught him. Several passers-by turned and watched curiously, and Simon Templar, whose ideas of grandstanding heroism were not of that type, was tempted to deposit the middle-aged gent tenderly on the pavement and let him do his dying gladiator act alone. The man in the Panama was no human hairpin, and his legs seemed to have turned to rubber.

Then Simon saw that the man's eyes were open. He grinned at the Saint crookedly.

"Sorry, stranger," he said, in the broadest Yankee. "I'll be okay in a minute. Been trying to do too much after my operation, I guess—the doc told me I'd crack up if I didn't take it easy . . . Gosh, look at the rubbernecks waitin' to see me die! Say, do you live in there? Is there a foyer I can sit down in? I don't wanna be stared at like I was the Nelson Monument."

Simon helped the man inside and sat him on a settee beside the lift. The Yank tipped off his Panama and wiped his forehead with a bandanna handkerchief.

"Just four days outa the hospital and tearin' about like a fool for two of 'em. And missed my lunch today. That's what's done it. Say, is there a public telephone here? I promised to meet my wife an hour ago, and she must think I made myself a street accident."

"I'm afraid there isn't," said the Saint. "This is just a block of flats."

"Well, I guess I'll just be bawled out. Gosh, but that poor kid'll be worried stiff!"

Simon looked up at the clock. He was in no great hurry.

"You can phone from my flat if you like," he said. "It's on the first floor."

"Say, that's real white of you!"

The Saint helped him into the elevator, and they shot upwards. Settled in an arm-chair beside the telephone, the American made a reassuring call to the Savoy Hotel number. Simon thought it was excessively sloppy, but it was not his business.

"Well, that's that," said his guest, when the gush was over. "I guess I owe you something for your kindness. Have a cigar?"

Simon accepted a weed. It was a large fat one, with a lovely picture on the band.

"Think of me cracking up like that in your arms!" prattled the American, whose vocal chords at least seemed unimpaired. "Gosh, you musta thought I was something out of a flower-bed. I didn't know they could take that much outa you along with your appendix. And all this fuss just to find a damn brass Buddha! Gosh, it makes you wonder what nut started this collecting game."

The Saint, with a match halfway to his cigar, stared at him till the flame scorched his fingers.

"Brass Buddha?" he said faintly. "Who wants a brass Buddha?"

"Louis Froussard wants one, if that means anything to you, stranger. Say, but here am I in your apartment, and you don't even know my name. Allow me." The American dug out his wallet, extracted a card, and handed it over. "James G. Amberson, at your service. Any time you want one of Napoleon's skulls, or the original pyjamas the Queen of Sheba gave to King Solomon—I'm the man to go and find 'em. Yes, sir. That's my job—huntin' for missing links for museums and millionaires who feel they gotta collect something so's they can give the reporters something to write about. That's me."

"And you want a brass Buddha?" said the Saint, almost caressingly.

James G. Amberson (according to his card, the "G" stood for Gardiner, which the Saint thought was very modest—it might have been Gabriel.) flapped a raw-boned hand deprecatingly.

"Aw, you ain't gonna offer me the thing your auntie brought home last time she went on a world cruise, are you?" he pleaded. "That's what I been getting every place I've tried. Everyone in London's got a brass Buddha, but none of 'em is the right one. This one's a special one—you wouldn't know it to look at it, but it is. Some Chink emperor back in about two million BC had three of 'em made for his three daughters, who were no better than they shouldha been, accordin' to history—you don't wanna know all that hooey, do you? I guess I'm a bit fuddled over it myself. But anyhow, Lou Froussard has got two of 'em, and he wants the third. I gotta find it. Sounds like I'd taken on a long job, don't it?"

Simon drew on his cigar a little less impetuously.

"How will you know this particular one when you find it?" he asked.

"Say, that's easy. It's gotta little Chinese dedication carved in the base and filled with red paint. I don't know any language except plain

English, but this daughter's name comes in the dedication, and I got a Chink to show me what it looked like . . . Gosh, is that cigar corked or something?"

"No—it's a swell cigar. Would you mind showing me what this name looks like?"

The American's eyes opened rather blankly, but he took out a pencil and sketched a character on the back of an envelope.

"There she is, stranger. Say, you're looking at me like I was a mummy come to life. What's the matter?"

The Saint filled his lungs. For him, the day had suddenly bloomed out into a rich surpassing beauty that only those who have shared his delight in damaging the careers of pompous old sinners with bushy grey face-hair can understand. The radiance of his own inspiration dazzled him.

"Nothing's the matter," he said seraphically. "Nothing on earth could be the matter on a day like this. How many millions will your Mr Froussard give for that Buddha?"

"Well, millions is a large word," said Amberson cautiously, looking at the Saint in not unreasonable perplexity. "But I guess I could pay fifteen thousand iron men for it."

"You find the iron men, and I'll find your Buddha," said the Saint.

The American grinned, and stood up.

"I don't know whether you've got an ace in the hole or whether you're just pulling my leg," he remarked, "but if you can find that Buddha the fifteen grand are waitin' for you. Say, but I'm real grateful to you for helpin' me out like this. Come to the Savoy and have lunch tomorrow—and you can bring the Buddha with you if you've found it."

"Thanks," said the Saint. "I'll do both."

He showed Amberson to the door, and came straight back to grab the telephone. Sir Ambrose Grange was out, he was informed, but he was expected back about six. Simon bought his evening paper, found that the favourite had won—he never backed favourites—and was at the telephone again when the hour struck.

"I'm taking you at your word and coming round to see you, Sir Ambrose."

"Delighted, my dear sir," said the knight, somewhat plaintively. "But if you'd told me I could have got hold of some girls—"

"Never mind the girls," said Simon.

He arrived at the lodgings in Seymour Street where Sir Ambrose maintained his modest bachelor *pied-à-terre* half an hour later, and plunged into his business without preliminaries.

"I've come to buy your Buddha," he said. "Two thousand was what your uncle wanted, wasn't it?"

Sir Ambrose goggled at him for some seconds, and then he laughed feebly.

"Ho, ho, ho! I bought that one, didn't I, by Gad! Getting a bit slow on the uptake, what? Never mind, sir—have a drink."

"I'm not being comic," said the Saint. "I want your Buddha and I'll give you two thousand for it. I backed sixteen losers last week, and if I don't get a good mascot I shall be in the bankruptcy court."

After several minutes he was able to convince Sir Ambrose that his lunacy, if inexplicable, was backed up by a ready cheque-book. He wrote the figures with a flourish, and Sir Ambrose found himself fumbling for a piece of paper and a stamp to make out the receipt.

Simon read the document through—it was typical.

> *Received from Mr Simon Templar, by cheque, the sum of Two Thousand Pounds, being payment for a brass Buddha which he knows is only worth fifteen shillings.*
>
> *Ambrose Grange.*

"Just to prove I knew what I was doing? I expected that."

Sir Ambrose looked at him suspiciously.

"I wish I knew what you wanted that thing for," he said. "Even my uncle only wanted us to get a thousand for it, but I thought I'd double it for luck. Two thousand couldn't be much more impossible than one." He heaved with chin-flivvering mirth. "Well, my dear sir, if you can make a profit on two thousand, I shan't complain. Ho, ho, ho, ho, ho! Have a drink."

"Sometimes," said the Saint quite affably, "I wonder why there's no law classifying men like you as vermin and authorizing you to be sprayed with weed-killer on sight."

He routed out Peter Quentin before going home that night, and uttered the same philosophy to him—ever more affably. The brass Buddha sat on a table beside his bed when he turned in, and he blew it a kiss before he switched out the light and sank into the dreamless sleep of a contented corsair.

* * *

He paraded at the Savoy at twelve-thirty the next day.

At two o'clock Patricia Holm found him in the grill-room.

Simon beckoned the waiter who had just poured out his coffee, and asked for another cup.

"Well," he said, "where's Peter?"

"His girlfriend stopped in a shop window to look at some stockings, so I came on." Her eyebrows were faintly questioning. "I thought you were lunching with that American."

Simon dropped two lumps of sugar into his cup and stirred it lugubriously.

"Pat," he said, "you may put this down in your notes for our textbook on Crime—the perfect confidence trick, Version Two. Let me tell you about it."

She lighted a cigarette slowly, staring at him.

"The Mug," said the Saint deliberately, "meets an Unpleasant Man. The Unpleasant Man purposely makes himself out to be so sharp that no normally healthy Mug could resist the temptation to do him down if the opportunity arose, and he may credit himself with a title just to remove all suspicion. The Unpleasant Man has something to sell—it might be a brass Buddha, valued at fifteen shillings, for which he's got to realize some fantastic sum like two thousand quid under the terms of an eccentric will. The Mug admits that the problem is difficult, and passes out into the night."

Simon annexed Patricia's cigarette, and inhaled from it.

"Shortly afterwards," he said, "the Mug meets the Nice American who is looking for a very special brass Buddha valued at fifteen thousand bucks. The Nice American gives away certain information which allows the Mug to perceive, beyond all possible doubt, that this rare and special Buddha is the very one for which the Unpleasant Man was trying to get what he thought was the fantastic price of two thousand quid. The Mug, therefore, with the whole works taken right down into his stomach—hook, line, and sinker—dashes round to the Unpleasant Man and gives him his two thousand quid. And he endorses a receipt saying he knows it's only worth fifteen bob, so that the Unpleasant Man can prove himself innocent of deception. Then the Mug goes to meet the Nice American and collect his profit . . . And, Pat, I regret to say that he pays for his own lunch."

The Saint gazed sadly at the folded bill which a waiter had just placed on the table.

Patricia was wide-eyed.

"Simon! Did you—"

"I did. I paid two thousand quid of our hard-won boodle to the perambulating sausage—"

He broke off, with his own jaw sinking.

James G. Amberson was flying across the room, with his Panama hat waving in his hand and his spectacles gleaming. He flung himself into a chair at the Saint's table.

"Say, did you think I was dead? My watch musta stopped while I was huntin' round junk stores in Limehouse—I saw a clock outa the taxi window as I was comin' back, and had a heart attack. Gosh, I'm sorry!"

"That's all right," murmured the Saint. "Pat, you haven't met Mr Amberson. This is our Nice American. James G.—Miss Patricia Holm."

"Say, I'm real pleased to meet you, Miss Holm. Guess Mr Templar told you how I fainted in his arms yesterday." Amberson reached over and wrung the girl's hand heartily. "Well, Mr Templar, if you've had lunch you can have a liqueur." He waved to a waiter. "And, say, did you find me that Buddha?"

Simon bent down and hauled a small parcel out from under the table.

"This is it."

Amberson gaped at the package for a second, and then he grabbed it and tore it open. He gaped again at the contents—then at the Saint.

"Well, I'm a son of a—excuse me, Miss Holm, but—"

"Is that right?" asked the Saint.

"I'll say it is!" Amberson was fondling the image as if it were his own long-lost child. "What did I promise you? Fifteen thousand berries?"

He pulled out his wallet and spilled American bills on to the table.

"Fifteen grand it is, Mr Templar. And I guess I'm grateful. Mind if I leave you now? I gotta get on the transatlantic phone to Lou Froussard and tell him, and then I gotta rush this little precious into a safe deposit. Say, let me ring you up and invite you to a real dinner next week."

He shook hands again, violently, with Patricia and the Saint, caught up his Panama, and vomited out of the room again like a human whirligig.

In the vestibule a podgy and pompous little man with bushy moustachios was waiting for him. He seized James G. Amberson by the arm.

"Did you get it, Jim?"

"You bet I did!" Amberson exhibited his purchase. His excessively American speech had disappeared. "And now d'you mind telling me why we've bought it? I'm just packing up for our getaway when you rush me round here to spend fifteen thousand dollars—"

"I'll tell you how it was, Jim," said the other rapidly. "I'm sitting on top of a bus, and there's a man and girl in front of me. The first thing I heard was 'Twenty thousand pounds' worth of black pearls in a brass Buddha.' I just had to listen. This chap seemed to be a solicitor's clerk, and he was telling his girl about an old miser who shoved these pearls into a brass Buddha after his wife died, and nobody found the letter where he said what he'd done till long after he was buried. 'And we've got to try and trace the thing,' says this young chap. 'It was sold to a junk dealer with a lot of other stuff, and heaven knows where it may be now.' 'How d'you know you've got it when you find it?' says the girl. 'Easy,' says this chap. 'It's got a mark on it like this.' He drew it on his paper, and I nearly broke my neck getting a look. Come on, now—let's get home and open it."

* * *

"I hope Ambrose and James G. are having lots of fun looking for your black pearls, Peter," drawled the Saint piously, as he stood at the counter of Thomas Cook and watched American bills translating themselves into English bank-notes with a fluency that was all the heart could desire.

THE PERFECT CRIME

"The defendants," said Mr Justice Goldie, with evident distaste, "have been unable to prove that the agreement between the plaintiff and the late Alfred Green constituted a money-lending transaction within the limits of the Act, and I am therefore obliged to give judgement for the plaintiff. I will consider the question of costs tomorrow."

The Saint tapped Peter Quentin on the shoulder as the court rose, and they slipped out ahead of the scanty assembly of spectators, bored reporters, dawdling solicitors, and traditionally learned counsel. Simon Templar had sat in that stuffy little room for two hours, bruising his marrow-bones on an astonishingly hard wooden bench and yearning for a cigarette, but there were times when he could endure many discomforts in a good cause.

Outside, he caught Peter's arm again.

"Mind if I take another look at our plaintiff?" he said. "Just over here—stand in front of me. I want to see what a snurge like that really looks like."

They stood in a gloomy corner near the door of the court, and Simon sheltered behind Peter Quentin's hefty frame and watched James Deever come out with his solicitor.

It is possible that Mr Deever's mother loved him. Perhaps, holding him on her knee, she saw in his childish face the fulfilment of all those precious hopes and shy incommunicable dreams which (if we can believe the *Little Mothers' Weekly*, are the joy and comfort of the prospective parent. History does not tell us that. But we do know that since her death, thirty years ago, no other bosom had ever opened to him with anything like that sublime mingling of pride and affection.

He was a long, cadaverous man with a face like a vulture and shaggy white eyebrows over closely-set greenish eyes. His thin nose swooped low down over a thin gash of a mouth, and his chin was pointed and protruding. In no respect whatsoever was it the kind of countenance to which young children take an instinctive shine. Grown men and women, who knew him, liked him even less.

His home and business address were in Manchester, but the City Corporation had never been heard to boast about it. Simon Templar watched him walk slowly past, discussing some point in the case he had just won with the air of a parson conferring with a church-warden after matins, and the reeking hypocrisy of the performance filled him with an almost irresistible desire to catch Mr Deever's frock-coated stern with the toe of his shoe and start him on one sudden magnificent flight to the foot of the stairs. The Manchester City Corporation, Simon considered, could probably have kept their ends up without Mr Deever's name on the roll of ratepayers. But the Saint restrained himself, and went on peaceably with Peter Quentin five minutes afterwards.

"Let us drink beer," said the Saint.

They entered a convenient tavern, lighting cigarettes as they went, and found a secluded corner in the saloon bar. The court had sat on late, and the hour had struck at which it is lawful for Englishmen to consume the refreshment which can only be bought at any time of the day in nasty uncivilized foreign countries.

And for a few minutes there was silence . . .

"It's wonderful what you can do with the full sanction of the Law," Peter Quentin said presently, in a rather sourly reflective tone, and the Saint smiled at him wryly. He knew that Peter was not thinking about the more obvious inanities of the Defence of the Realm Act.

"I rather wanted to get a good close-up of James, and watch him in action," he said. "I guess all the stories are true."

There were several stories about James Deever, but none of them ever found their way into print—for libel actions mean heavy damages, and Mr Deever sailed very comfortably within the Law. His business was plainly and publicly that of a moneylender and as a moneylender he was duly and legally registered according to the Act which has done so much to bring the profession of usury within certain humane restrictions. And as a plain and registered moneylender Mr Deever retained his offices in Manchester, superintending every detail of his business in person, trusting nobody, sending out beautifully-worded circulars in which he proclaimed his readiness to lend anybody any sum from ten pounds to fifty thousand pounds on note of hand alone, and growing many times richer than the Saint thought anyone but himself had any right to be. Nevertheless, Mr Deever's business would probably have escaped the Saint's attentions if those few facts had covered the whole general principle of it.

They didn't. Mr Deever, who, in spite of the tenor of his artistically-printed circulars, was not in the money-lending business on account of any urge to go down to mythology as the little fairy godmother of Manchester, had devised half a dozen ingenious and strictly legal methods of evading the limitations placed on him by the Act. The prospective borrower who came to him, full of faith and hope, for the loan of ten to fifty thousand pounds was frequently obliged—not, one must admit, on his note of hand alone, but eventually on the basis of some very sound security. And if the loan were promptly repaid, there the matter ended—at the statutory rate of interest for such transactions. It was only when the borrower found himself in further difficulties that Mr Deever's ingenious schemes came into operation. It was then that the victim found himself straying little by little into a maze of complicated mortgages, discounted cheques, "nominal" promissory notes, mysterious "conversions," and technically-worded transfers—straying into that labyrinth so gradually at first that it all seemed quite harmless, slipping deeper into it over an easy path of documents and signatures, floundering about in it at last, and losing his bearings more and more hopelessly in his struggles to climb back—finally awakening to the haggard realization that by some incomprehensible jugglery of papers and figures he owed Mr Deever five or six times as much money as Mr Deever had given him in cash, and having it proved to him over his own signature that there was no question of the statutory rate of interest having been exceeded at any time.

Exactly thus had it been proved to the widow of a certain victim in the case that they had listened to that afternoon, and there were other similar cases that had come to the Saint's receptive knowledge.

"There were days," remarked the Saint, rather wistfully, "when some lads of the village and I would have carved Brother Deever into small pieces and baited lobster-pots with him from the North Foreland to the Lizard."

"And what now?" queried Peter Quentin.

"Now," said the Saint, regretfully, we can only call on him for a large involuntary contribution to our Pension Fund for Deserving Outlaws."

Peter lowered the first quarter of his second pint.

"It'll have to be something pretty smart to catch that bird," he said. "If you asked me, I should say you couldn't take any story to him that wouldn't have to pass under a microscope."

"For which reason," murmured Simon Templar, with the utmost gravity, "I shall go to him with a story that is absolutely true. I shall approach him with a hook and line that the cleverest detective on earth couldn't criticize. You're right, Peter—there probably isn't a swindle in the encyclopedia that would get a yard past Brother James. It's a good thing we aren't criminals, Pete—we might get our fingers burned. No, laddie. Full of righteousness and the stuff that passes for beer in this country, we shall draw nigh to Brother James with our haloes fairly glistening. It was just for a man like him that I was saving up my Perfect Crime."

If the Saint's halo was not actually visibly luminous when he called at Mr Deever's offices the next morning, he at least looked remarkably harmless. A white flower ("for purity," said the Saint) started in his button-hole and flowed in all directions over his coat lapel, a monocle was screwed into his right eye, his hat sat precariously on the back of his head, and his face was relaxed into an expression of such amiable aristocratic idiocy that Mr Deever's chief clerk—a man hardly less sour-visaged than Mr Deever himself—was even more obsequious than usual.

Simon said he wanted a hundred pounds, and would cheerfully give a jolly old note of hand for it if some Johnnie would explain to him what a jolly old note of hand was. The clerk explained, oleaginously, that a jolly old note of hand was a somewhat peculiar sort of thing that sounded nice in advertisements, but wasn't really used with important clients. Had Mr . . . er . . . Smith?—had Mr Smith any other kind of security?

"I've got some jolly old premium bonds," said the Saint, and the clerk nodded his head in a perfect sea of oil.

"If you can wait a moment, sir, perhaps Mr Deever will see you himself."

The Saint had no doubt that Mr Deever would see him. He waited around patiently for a few minutes, and was ushered into Mr Deever's private sanctum.

"You see, I lost a bally packet at Derby yesterday—every blinkin' horse fell down dead when I backed it. I work a system, but of course you can't back a winner every day. I know I'll get it back, though—the chappie who sold me the system said it never let him down."

Mr Deever's eyes gleamed. If there was anything that satisfied every one of his requirements for a successful loan, it was an asinine young man with a monocle who believed in racing systems.

"I believe you mentioned some security, Mr . . . er . . . Smith. Naturally we should be happy to lend you a hundred pounds without any formalities, but—"

"Oh, I've got these jolly old bonds. I don't want to sell 'em, because they're having a draw this month. If you hold the lucky number you get a fat bonus. Sort of lottery business, but quite gilt-edged an' all that sort of thing."

He produced a large envelope, and passed it across Mr Deever's desk. Deever extracted a bunch of expensively watermarked papers artistically engraved with green and gold lettering which proclaimed them to be Latvian 1929 Premium Loan (British Series) Bearer Bonds, value twenty-five pounds each.

The financier crunched them between his fingers, squinted at the ornate characters suspiciously through a magnifying glass, and looked again at the Saint.

"Of course, Mr Smith, we don't keep large sums of money on the premises. But if you'd like to leave these bonds with me until, say, two o'clock this afternoon, I'm sure we shall be able to make a satisfactory arrangement."

"Keep 'em by every manner of means, old bean," said the Saint airily. "So long as I get the jolly old quidlets in time to take 'em down to the three-thirty today, you're welcome."

Conveniently enough, this happened to be the first day of the Manchester September meeting. Simon Templar paraded again at two o'clock, collected his hundred pounds, and rejoined Peter Quentin at their hotel.

"I have a hundred pounds of Brother James's money," he announced. "Let's go and spread it around on the most frantic outsiders we can find."

They went to the races, and it so happened that the Saint's luck was in. He had doubled Mr Deever's hundred pounds when the result of the last race went up on the board—but Mr Deever would not have been seriously troubled if he had lost the lot. Five hundred pounds' worth of Latvian Bearer Bonds had been deposited as security for the advance, and in spite of the artistic engraving on them there was no doubt that they were genuine. The interval between Simon Templar's visit to Mr Deever in the morning and the time when the money was actually paid over to him had been devoted to an expert scrutiny of the bonds, coupled with inquiries at Mr Deever's brokers, which had definitely established their authenticity—and the Saint knew it.

"I wonder," Simon Templar was saying as they drove back into the town, "if there's any place here where you could buy a false beard. With all this money in our pockets, why should you wait for Nature to take her course?"

Nevertheless, it was not with the air of a man who has collected a hundred pounds over a couple of well-chosen winners that the Saint came to Mr Deever the next day. It was Saturday, but that meant nothing to Mr Deever. He was a man who kept only the barest minimum of holidays and much good business might be done with temporarily embarrassed members of the racing fraternity on the second day of the meeting.

It appeared very likely on this occasion.

"I don't know how the horse managed to lose," said the Saint mournfully.

"Dear me!" said Mr Deever unctuously. "Dear me! Did it lose?"

The Saint nodded.

"I don't understand it at all. The chappie who sold me this system said it had never had more than three losers in succession. And the stakes go up so frightfully fast. You see, you have to put on more money each time, so that when you win you get back your losses as well. But it simply must win today—"

"How much do you need to put on today, Mr Smith?"

"About eight hundred pounds. But what with buzzing around an' having a few drinks and what not, don't you know—if you could make it an even thou—"

Mr Deever rubbed his hands over each other with a face of abysmal gloom.

"A thousand pounds is quite a lot of money, Mr . . . er . . . Smith, but of course if you can offer some security—purely as a business formality, you understand—"

"Oh, I've got lots of those jolly old Latvian Bonds," said the Saint. "I think I bought about two hundred of 'em. Got to try and pick up a bonus somehow, what?"

Mr Deever nodded like a mandarin.

"Of course, Mr Smith. Of course. And it just happens that one of our advances was repaid today, so I may be able to find a thousand pounds for you in our safe." He pressed a bell on his desk, and a clerk appeared. "Mr Goldberg, will you see if we can oblige this gentleman with a thousand pounds?"

The clerk disappeared again, and came back in a few moments with a sheaf of bank-notes. Simon Templar produced another large envelope, and Mr Deever drew from it an even thicker wad of bonds. He counted them over and examined them carefully one by one, then he took a printed form from a drawer, and unscrewed the cap of a Woolworth fountain-pen.

"Now if you will just complete our usual agreement, Mr Smith—"

Through the glass partition that divided Mr Deever's sanctum from the outer office there suddenly arose the expostulations of an extraordinarily loud voice. Raised in a particularly raucous north-country accent, it made itself heard so clearly that there was no chance of missing anything it said.

"I tell you, I'd know thaat maan anywhere. I'd know 'im in a daark room if I was blind-fooalded. It was Simon Templar, I tell you. I saw 'im coom in, an' I says to myself, 'Thaat's Saaint, thaat is.' I 'aad wife an' loogage with me, so I taakes 'em into 'otel an' cooms straaight baack. I'm going to see thaat Saaint if I waait here two years—"

The buttery voice of Mr Goldberg could be heard protesting. Then the north-country voice drowned it again.

"Then if you won't let me in, I'll go straaight out an' fetch policeman. Thaat's what I'll do."

There was an eruption without, as of someone departing violently into the street, and the Saint looked at Mr Deever. Simon's hand was outstretched to grasp the pile of bank-notes—then he saw Deever's right hand come out of a drawer, and a nickel-plated revolver with it.

"Just a moment, Mr . . . er . . . Smith," Deever said slowly. "I think you're in too much of a hurry."

He touched the bell on his desk again. Mr Goldberg reappeared, mopping his swarthy brow. There was a glitter in Deever's greenish eyes which told Simon that the revolver was not there merely for the purposes of intimidation. The Saint sat quite still.

"Look in this gentleman's pockets, Mr Goldberg. Perhaps he has some evidence of identity on him."

The clerk came over and began a search. The monocle had vanished from the Saint's right eye, and the expression on his face was anything but vacuous.

"You filthy miser!" he blazed. "I'll see that you're sorry for this. No one has insulted me like this for years—"

Coolly Deever leaned over the desk and smacked Simon over the mouth. The blow cut the Saint's lip.

"A crook should be careful of his tongue," Deever said.

"There's a letter here, Mr Deever," said the clerk, laying it on the blotter. "It's addressed to Simon Templar. And I found this as well."

"'This' was another large envelope, the exact replica of the one in which Simon had handed over his Latvian Bonds. Deever opened it, and found that it contained a similar set of bonds, and when he had counted them he found that they were equal in number to those which he had accepted for security.

"I see, Mr . . . er . . . Smith." The close-set eyes gloated. "So I've been considered worthy of the attentions of the famous Saint. And a very pretty swindle too. First you borrow money on some genuine bonds, then you come back and try to borrow more money on some more genuine bonds—but when I'm not looking you exchange them for forgeries. Very neat, Mr Templar. It's a pity that man outside recognized you. Mr Goldberg, I think you might telephone for the police."

"You'll be sorry for this," said the Saint more calmly, with his eyes on Deever's revolver.

A police inspector arrived in a few minutes. He inspected the two envelopes, and nodded.

"That's an old trick, Mr Deever," he said. "It's lucky that you were warned. Come along, you—put your hands out."

Simon looked down at the handcuffs.

"You don't need those," he said.

"I've heard about you," said the inspector grimly, "and I think we do. Come on, now, and no nonsense."

For the first time in his life Simon felt the cold embrace of steel on his wrists. A constable put his hat on for him, and he was marched out into the street. A small crowd had collected outside, and already the rumour of his identity was passing from mouth to mouth.

The local inspector did not spare him. Simon Templar was a celebrity, a capture that every officer in England had once dreamed of making, even if of late it had been found impossible to link his name with any proven crimes, and once arrested he was an exhibit to be proud of. The police station was not far away, and the Saint was compelled to walk to it, with his manacled wrists chained to the burly constable on his left and the inspector striding on his right.

He was charged with attempting to obtain money under false pretences, and when it was all written down they asked him if he had anything to say.

"Only that my right sock is wearing a bit thin at the heel," answered the Saint. "D'you think someone could beetle along to my hotel and dig out a new pair?"

He was locked in a cell to be brought before the magistrate on the following Monday. It was Simon Templar's third experience of that, but he enjoyed it no more than the first time.

During Sunday he had one consolation. He was able to divert himself with thoughts of what he could do with about ten thousand pounds.

* * *

Monday morning brought a visitor to Manchester in the portly shape of Chief Inspector Claud Eustace Teal, who automatically came north at the news of the sensational arrest which had been the front-page splash of every newspaper in the kingdom. But the expert witness who came with him caused a much greater sensation. He examined the contents of the two envelopes, and scratched his head.

"Is this a joke?" he demanded. "Every one of these bonds is perfectly genuine. There isn't a forgery among them."

The local inspector's eyes popped halfway out of his head.

"Are you sure?" he blurted.

"Of course I'm sure," snapped the disgusted expert. "Any fool can see that with half an eye. Did I have to give up a perfectly good day's golf to tell you that?"

Chief Inspector Teal was not interested in the expert's golf. He sat on a bench and held his head in his hands. He was not quite certain how it had been worked, but he knew there was something very wrong somewhere.

Presently he looked up.

"And Deever struck him in the office—that isn't denied?"

"No, sir," admitted the local inspector. "Mr Deever said—"

"And you marched Templar through the streets in broad daylight, handcuffed to a constable?"

"Yes, sir. Knowing what I did about him—"

"I'd better see the Saint," said Teal. "If I'm not mistaken, someone's going to be sorry they knew so much."

He was shown into Simon's cell, and the Saint rose languidly to greet him.

"Hullo, Claud," he murmured. "I'm glad you've arrived. A gang of these local half-wits in funny hats—"

"Never mind that," said Teal bluntly. "Tell me what you're getting out of this."

Simon pondered.

"I shouldn't accept anything less than ten thousand pounds," he said finally.

The light in Chief Inspector Teal's understanding strengthened slowly. He turned to the local inspector, who had accompanied him.

"By the way," he said, "I suppose you never found that man from Huddersfield, or whoever it was that blew the gaff?"

"No, sir. We've made inquiries at all the hotels, but he seems to have disappeared. I've got a sort of description of him—a fairly tall broad-shouldered man with a beard—"

"I see," said Teal, very sleepily.

Simon dipped into the local inspector's pocket and calmly borrowed a packet of cigarettes. He lighted one.

"If it's any help to you," he said, "the report of everything that happened in Deever's office is perfectly true. I went to him for some money, and then I went to him for some more. Every time I offered excellent security. I behaved myself like a law-abiding citizen—"

"Why did you call yourself Smith?"

"Why shouldn't I? It's a grand old English name. And I always understood that you could call yourself anything you liked so long as you didn't do it with intent to defraud. Go and tell Deever to prove the fraud. I just had to have some cash to go to the races. I had those Latvian bonds with me, and I thought that if I gave my real name I'd be making all sorts of silly difficulties. That's all there was to it. But did anyone make an honest attempt to find out if there was a fraud?"

"I see," said Teal again—and he really did see.

"They did not," said the Saint in a pained voice. "What happened? I was assaulted. I was abused. I was handcuffed and marched through the streets like a common burglar, followed by shop girls and guttersnipes, snapped by press photographers. I was shoved in a cell for forty-eight hours, and I wasn't even allowed to send for a clean pair of socks. A bunch of flat-footed nincompoops told me when to get up, when to eat, when to take exercise, and when to go to bed again—just as if

I'd already been convicted. Deever's story has been published in every paper in the United Kingdom. And d'you know what that means?"

Teal did not answer. And the Saint's forefinger tapped him just where his stomach began to bulge, tapped him debonairly in the rhythm of the Saint's seraphic accents, in a gesture that Teal knew only too well.

"It means that there's one of the swellest legal actions on earth waiting for me to win it—an action for damages for wrongful imprisonment, defamation of character, libel, slander, assault, battery, and the Lord alone knows what not. I wouldn't take a penny less than ten thousand pounds. I may even want more. And do you think James Deever won't come across?"

Chief Inspector Teal had no reply. He knew Deever would pay.

THE APPALLING POLITICIAN

INTRODUCTION

It is not too easy at first sight to visualize a character so active and extraverted as Simon Templar in the somewhat abstract and dreamy setting of a story of pure detection. All the same, it is equally difficult to conceive a life so busily concerned with every possible variation on the theme of Crime which had never contained any such problems. As a matter of fact, the Saint has so far had two of them, of which this was the first. (The second, which I called "The Noble Sportsman," can be found in the book *Boodle*, also known as *The Saint Intervenes.*)

I only have one other explanation to add to this story.

It has been suggested to me on more than one occasion that the broadcast speech of the Politician, with which the story opens, is an excessively farcical exaggeration. Solely in self-defence, I take this opportunity to plead Not Guilty. I wrote the quotation down practically verbatim, altering only the occasion and the sport referred to. I only regret that I cannot substantiate this defence with the name of the actual speechmaker. One reason, of course, which prevents me from doing so is that this speech was really grafted on to the Politician in the story, and should not be taken to mean that there is any other similarity whatever between the Speechmaker and the Appalling Politician of this piece. I used it simply because, as an artist, I felt that such a deathless gem of statesmanlike oratory should not be allowed to perish from the earth.

And the other reason is that, for all I know, before this book is out of print, the gentleman who made the speech might easily be Prime Minister of Great Britain. And how could he frighten Hitler and Mussolini if they could dig a speech like that out of his past?

—Leslie Charteris (1939)

"Badminton," boomed the frog-like voice of Sir Joseph Whipplethwaite, speaking from the annual dinner of the British Badminton Society, "is an excellent means of acquiring and retaining that fitness of body which is so necessary to all of us in these strenuous times. We politicians have to keep fit, the same as everyone else. And many of us—as I do myself—retain that fitness by playing badminton. Badminton," he boomed, "is a game which pre-eminently requires physical fitness—a thing which we politicians also require. I myself could scarcely be expected to carry out my work at the Ministry of International Trade if I were not physically fit. And badminton is the game by which I keep myself fit to carry out my duties as a politician. Of course I shall never play as well as you people do, but we politicians can only try to do our best in the intervals between our other duties. Badminton," boomed the frog-like voice tirelessly, "is a game which makes you fit and keeps you fit, and we politicians—"

Simon Templar groaned aloud, and hurled himself at the radio somewhat hysterically. At odd times during the past year he had accidentally switched on to Sir Joseph Whipplethwaite speaking at the annual dinners of the North British Lacrosse League, the British Bowling Association, the Southern Chess Congress, the International Ice Skating Association, the Royal Toxophilite Society, and the British Squash Racquets Association; and he could have recited Sir Joseph Whipplethwaite's speech from memory, with all its infinite variations. In the mellow oak-beamed country pub, where he had gone to spend a restful weekend, the reminder of that appalling politician was more than he could bear.

"It's positively incredible," he said, returning limply to his beer. "Pat, I'll swear that if you put that into a story as an illustration of the depths of imbecility that can be reached by a man who's considered fit to govern this purblind country, you'd simply raise a shriek of derisive laughter. And yet you've heard it with your own ears—half a dozen times. You've heard him playing every game under the sun in his after-dinner speeches, and mixing it fifty-fifty with his god-like status as a politician. And that . . . that . . . that blathering oaf is a member of His Majesty's Cabinet and one of the men on whom the British Empire's fate depends. O God, O Ottawa!"

Words failed him, and he buried his face wrathfully in his tankard.

But he was not destined to forget Sir Joseph Whipplethwaite that weekend or ever again, for early on the Monday morning a portly man with a round red face and an unrepentant bowler hat walked into the hotel, and Simon recognized him with some astonishment.

"Claud Eustace himself, by the Great White Spat of Professor Clarence Skinner!" he cried. "What brings my little ray of sunshine here?"

Chief Inspector Claud Eustace Teal looked at him suspiciously.

"I might ask the same question."

"I'm recuperating," said the Saint blandly, "from many months of honest toil. There are times when I have to get away from London just to forget what petrol fumes and soot smell like. Come and have a drink."

Teal handed his bag to the boots and chewed on his gum continuously.

"What I'm wanting just now is some breakfast—I've been on the go since five o'clock this morning without anything to eat."

"That suits me just as well," murmured the Saint, taking the detective's arm and steering him towards the dining room. "I see you're staying. Has some sinister local newsagent been selling newspapers after eight o'clock?"

They sat down in the deserted room, and Teal ordered himself a large plate of porridge. Then his sleepily cherubic blue eyes gazed at the Saint again, not so suspiciously as before, but rather regretfully.

"There are times when I wish you were an honest man, Saint," he said, and Simon raised his eyebrows a fraction.

"There's something on your mind, Claud," he said. "May I know it?"

Mr Teal pondered while his porridge was set before him, and dug a spoon into it thoughtfully.

"Have you heard of Sir Joseph Whipplethwaite?"

Simon stared at him, and then he covered his eyes.

"Have I not!" he articulated tremulously. He flung out a hand. "'Badminton,'" he boomed, "'is a game that has made we politicians what we are. Without badminton, we politicians—'"

"I see you have heard of him. Did you know he lived near here?"

Simon shook his head. He knew that Sir Joseph Whipplethwaite had acquired the recently-created portfolio of the Minister of International Trade, and had gathered from broadcast utterances that Sir Joseph considered Whipplethwaite an ideal man for the job, but he had not felt moved to investigate the matter further. His energetic life was far too full to allow him time to trace the career of every pinhead who exercised his jaw in the Houses of Parliament at the long-suffering taxpayer's expense.

"His house is only about a mile away—a big modern place with four or five acres of garden. And whatever you like to think about him yourself, the fact remains that he has fairly important work to do. Things go through his office that it's sometimes important to keep absolutely secret until the proper time comes to publish them."

Simon Templar had never been called slow.

"Good Lord, Teal—is this a stolen treaty business?"

The detective nodded slowly.

"That sounds a little sensational, but it's about the truth of it. The draft of our commercial agreement with the Argentine is going before the House tomorrow, and Whipplethwaite brought it down here on Saturday night late to work on it—he has the pleasure of introducing it for the Government. I don't know much about it myself, except that it's to do with tariffs, and some people could make a lot of money out of knowing the text of it in advance."

"And it's been stolen?"

"On Sunday afternoon."

Simon reached thoughtfully for his cigarette case.

"Teal, why are you telling me this?"

"I don't really know," said the detective, looking at him soberly.

"When you walked in and found me here, I suppose you thought I was the man."

"No—I didn't think that. A thing like that is hardly in your line, is it?"

"It isn't. So why bring me in?"

"I don't really know," repeated the detective stubbornly, watching his empty porridge plate being replaced by one of bacon and eggs. "In fact, if you wanted to lose me my job you could go right out and sell the story to a newspaper. They'd pay you well for it."

The Saint tilted back his chair and blew a succession of smoke-rings towards the ceiling. Those very clear and challenging blue eyes rested almost lazily on the detective's somnolent pink half-moon of a face.

"I get you, Claud," he said seriously, "and for once the greatest criminal brain of this generation shall be at the disposal of the Law. Shoot me the whole works."

"I can do more than that," said Teal, with a certain relief. "I'll show you the scene presently. Whipplethwaite's gone to London for a conference with the Prime Minister."

The detective finished his breakfast, and refused a cigarette. After a few minutes they set out to walk to Whipplethwaite's house, where Teal had already spent several hours of fruitless searching for clues after a special police car had brought him down from London. Teal, having given his outline of the barest facts, had become taciturn, and Simon made no attempt to force the pace. He appreciated the compliment of the detective's confidence—although perhaps it was only one of many occasions on which those two epic antagonists had been silent in a momentary recognition of the impossible friendship that might have been just as epic if their destinies had lain in different paths. Those were the brief interludes when a truce was possible between them, and the hint of a sigh in Teal's silent ruminations might have been taken to indicate that he wished the truce could have been extended indefinitely.

In the same silence they turned in between the somewhat pompous concrete gate-pillars that gave entrance to the grounds of Sir Joseph Whipplethwaite's country seat. From there, a gravelled carriage drive led them in a semicircular curve through a rough, densely-grown plantation and brought them rather suddenly into sight of the house, which was invisible from the road. A uniformed local constable was patrolling in front of the door: he saluted as he saw Teal, and looked at the Saint inquiringly. Teal, however, was uncommunicative. He stood aside for the Saint to pass, and ushered him personally through the front door—a performance which, from the village constable's point of view, was sufficient introduction to one who could scarcely have been less than an Assistant Commissioner.

The house was not only modern, as Teal had described it—it was almost prophetic. From the outside, it looked at first glance like the result of some close in-breeding between an aquarium, a wedding cake, and a super cinema. It was large, white and square, with enormous areas of window and erratic balconies which looked as if they had been transferred bodily from the facade of an Atlantic liner. Inside, it was remarkably light and airy, with a certain ascetic barrenness of furnishing that made it seem too studiously sanitary to be comfortable, like a hospital ward. Teal led the way down a long wide white hall, and opened a door at the end. Simon found himself in a room that needed no introduction as Sir Joseph's study. Every wall had long book-shelves let into its depth in the modern style, and there was a glass-topped desk with a steel-framed chair behind it; the upper reaches of the walls were plastered with an assortment of racquets, bats, skis, skates, and illuminated addresses that looked oddly incongruous.

"Is this architecture Joseph's idea?" asked the Saint.

"I think it's his wife's," said Teal. "She's very progressive."

It certainly looked like a place in which any self-respecting mystery should have died of exhaustion looking for a suitable place to happen. The safe in which the treaty had reposed was the one touch about it that showed any trace of fantasy, for it was sunk in flush with the wall and covered by a mirror, which, when it was opened, proved to be the door of the safe itself, and the keyhole was concealed in a decorative scroll of white metal worked into the frame of the glass which slid aside in cunningly-fashioned grooves to disclose it. Teal demonstrated its working, and the Saint was interested.

"The burglars don't seem to have damaged it much," he remarked, and Teal gave him a glance that seemed curiously lethargic.

"They haven't damaged it at all," he said. "If you go over it with a magnifying glass you won't find a trace of its having been tampered with."

"How many keys?"

"Two. Whipplethwaite wears one on his watch-chain, and the other is at his bank in London."

For the first time that day two thin hair-lines of puzzlement cut vertically down between the Saint's level brows. They were the only outward signs of a wild idea, an intuition too ludicrous even to hint at, that flickered through his mind at the tone of the detective's voice.

"Whipplethwaite went to church on Sunday morning," said Teal, with an expressionless face, "and worked over the treaty when he came back. He took it up to lunch with him, and then he locked it up in the safe and went upstairs to his room to rest. He was rather taken up with the importance of secrecy, and he had demanded two guards from the local police. One of them was at the front door, where we came in. The other was outside here."

Teal walked towards the tall windows which filled nearly the whole of one wall of the room. Right in the centre of these windows, on the stone-flagged terrace outside, the back of a seated man loomed against the light like a statuette in a glass case. Simon had noticed him as soon as they entered the room: he appeared to be painting a scene of the landscape, and as they went through the windows and came out behind him Simon observed that the canvas on his easel was covered with brightly-coloured daubs of paint in various abstruse geometrical shapes. He looked up at the sound of their footsteps, gave the Saint a casual nod, and bowed politely to the detective.

"Well, sir," he said, with a trace of mockery, "how are the investigations going?"

"We're doing the best we can," said Teal vaguely, and turned to Simon. "This is Mr Spencer Vallance, who was painting exactly where you see him now when the robbery took place. Down there"—he pointed to a grass tennis-court which was cut bodily, like a great step, out of the fairly steep slope below them—"those same four people you see were playing. They're the finalists of the South of England Junior Championships, and they're staying here as Whipplethwaite's guests for a week. The other constable on guard was supposed to be patrolling the back of the house—we're at the back here, now—and at the time when the burglary was committed he was about three-quarters of the way down this slope, with his back to the house, watching the game. In fact, the scene you see is almost exactly the same as it was at half-past-three yesterday afternoon."

Simon nodded, and glanced again at Mr Vallance, who had resumed his interrupted task of painting a neat blue border round a green isosceles triangle on a short brown stalk that was presumably intended to represent a poplar in the foreground. The Art of Mr Spencer Vallance was so perfectly appropriate to his background that it gave one a sense of shock. One felt that such a preposterous aptness outraged one's canons of that human inconsistency which we have come to accept as normal. It was like seeing a commissionaire in Arab costume outside a restaurant called "The Oasis," and discovering that he really was a genuine Arab. Vallance's picture was exactly like the house behind it: scientific, hygienic, and quite inhuman. Simon spent a few seconds trying to coordinate the masses of colour on the canvas with the scene before his eyes, which was particularly human and charming. To left and right of him strips of untouched plantation which were probably continuations of the spinney through which they had approached the house flanked the grounds right down beyond the tennis-court to the banks of a stream; while beyond the stream the land rose again up a long curve of hill crowned with a dark sprawl of woods.

There are two poplars there, Mr Vallance," Simon ventured to point out, when he had got his bearings on the picture, and the artist turned to him with an exasperated glare.

"My dear sir, what people like you want isn't an artist—it's a photographer. There are millions of blades of grass on that lawn, and you'd like me to draw every one of them. What I paint," said Spencer Vallance magnificently, "is the Impression of Poplar. The Soul of all Poplars is expressed in this picture, if you had the eyes to see it."

Mr Vallance himself was the very antithesis of his art, being a small straggly man with straggly hair and a thin straggly beard. His clothes hung about him shapelessly, but his scrawny frame was obviously capable of so much superb indignation under criticism that Simon thought it best to accept the rebuke in all humility. And then Chief Inspector Teal took the Saint's arm and urged him firmly down the slope away from temptation.

"I'd better tell you what happened from our point of view," said the detective. "At twenty minutes to four the constable who was out here turned round and started to walk back towards the house. He had then been watching the tennis for about a quarter of an hour, and you might remember that all this time both the back and the front of the house had been covered, and nothing smaller than a field-mouse could have come through the plantation at the sides without making a noise that would certainly have attracted attention. The constable noticed that Vallance was not at his easel, and the windows of Whipplethwaite's study behind were open—he couldn't remember if they had been open before. Of course he thought nothing of that—I don't think I mentioned that Vallance is also staying here as a guest. Then, just as the constable reached the top of the slope, Vallance came staggering out of the study, holding his head and bellowing that he'd been sandbagged. He was working at his painting, it appeared, when he was hit on the head from behind and stunned, and he remembered nothing more until he woke up on the floor of the study. The constable found a sandbag lying on the terrace just behind Vallance's stool. He went into the study and found the safe wide open. The theory, of course, would be that the robber dragged Vallance inside so that his body would not attract attention if the constable looked round."

Teal's voice was as detached and expressionless as if he had been making his statement in court, but once again that uncanny premonition flashed through the Saint's mind, rising ridiculously from that odd-sounding subjunctive in the detective's last sentence. Simon lighted a cigarette.

"I gather that Vallance is Lady Whipplethwaite's guest," he said presently, and Teal was only slightly surprised.

"That is correct. How did you know?"

"His art fits in too perfectly with the house—and you said she was very progressive. I suppose he's been investigated?"

"This is Lady Whipplethwaite's statement," he said, taking out a note-book. "I'll read it to you."

"'I first met Mr Vallance in Brisbane fifteen years ago. He fell in love with me and wanted to marry me, but I refused him. For five years after that he continued to pester me, although I did my best to get rid of him. When I became engaged to Sir Joseph he was insanely jealous. There was never anything between us that could have given him the slightest grounds for imagining that he had a claim on me. For a few years after I was married he continued to write and implore me to leave Sir Joseph and run away with him, but I did not answer his letters. Six months ago he wrote to me again in London, apologizing humbly for the past and begging me to forgive him and meet him again, as he said he was completely cured of his absurd infatuation. I met him with my husband's consent, and he told me that he had been studying art in Paris and was getting quite a name among the Moderns. I liked his pictures, and when he begged me to let him paint me a picture of our house to give me I asked him down to stay, although Sir Joseph was very much against it. Sir Joseph has never liked him. They have had several heated arguments while he has been staying with us.'"

Teal closed the note-book and put it away.

"As soon as the theft was discovered," he said, "Sir Joseph wanted me to arrest Vallance at once, and I had a job to make him see that we couldn't possibly do that without any evidence."

They had reached a rustic seat at the end of the tennis-court. Teal rested his weight on it gingerly, and produced a fresh packet of chewing-gum.

"Our problem," he said, gazing intently at the tennis-players, "is to find out how the man who opened the safe got in here—and got out again."

Simon nodded quietly.

"The tennis-players would hardly make any difference," he remarked. "They'd be so intent on their game that they wouldn't notice anything else."

"And yet," said Teal, "the man who did it had to pass the constable in front or the constable at the back—and either of them should have seen him."

"It sounds impossible," said the Saint, and the man beside him put a slip of gum in his mouth and masticated stolidly.

"It does," he said, without moving a muscle, and at that moment the fantastic idea that had been creeping round the Saint's mind sprang into incredulous life.

"Good God! Teal—you don't mean—"

"I don't mean anything," said Teal in the same toneless voice. "I can't possibly tell you any more than I've told you already. If I mentioned that Whipplethwaite was badly hit in the Doncaster Steel Company's crash three months ago—that a Cabinet Minister's salary may be a large one, but you need a lot more than that to keep up the style that the Whipplethwaites like to live in—I should only be mentioning things that have nothing to do with the case. If I said the man who could open that safe without damaging it in any way would be a miracle worker, I'd only be theorizing."

Simon's cigarette had gone out, but he did not notice it.

"And I suppose," he said, in a slightly strained voice, "just taking an entirely mythical case—I suppose that if the details of that treaty got about, the Powers would know that there'd been a leakage? I mean, if there were only one man through whom the leakage could have occurred, he'd have to cover himself by staging some set of circumstances that would account for it without hurting his reputation?"

"I suppose so," agreed Teal formally. "Unfortunately there's no Third Degree in this country, and when you get into high places you have to walk very carefully. Sometimes we're set almost impossible tasks. My orders are to avoid a scandal at any cost."

The Saint sat quietly, taking in the full significance of that astounding revelation that was so much more momentous for having been made without any direct statement. And, as he looked up at the house in a kind of breathlessness, he visualized the scene. There was no space for secret passages in such an edifice as that, but for reasons known only to the architect a sun balcony on the first floor, built over the study, was linked with the ground by two flying buttresses on either side of it that angled down on either side of the study windows like gigantic staircases of three-foot steps. He could see the podgy figure of Sir Joseph Whipplethwaite creeping out with exaggerated caution, like a rhinoceros walking on tiptoe, and surveying the scene below. He saw the man clambering down the steps of the flying buttress, one by one, hampered by the sandbag clutched in one hand . . . saw him creeping up behind the unconscious artist . . . striking that single clumsy blow. With a scapegoat whom he disliked so heartily ready to be accused, why should he think he ran any risk?

"I know what you think of our abilities at the Yard," Teal was saying, in the same passionless way. "But we do get ideas sometimes. What you don't make allowances for is the fact that in our position we can't act on nothing more substantial than a brilliant idea, like detectives do in stories." He was chewing monotonously, with his cherubic blue eyes fixed expressionlessly on the flying white ball on the court. "I think that if the treaty could somehow be recovered and put back where it was taken from, the guilty man would have to confess. An adventurer in a story, I suppose, might kidnap the suspected person and force him to say where it was hidden, but we can't do that. If anything like that happened in real life, and the kidnapper was caught, he'd be for it. By the way, Whipplethwaite will be driving back from London this evening. He has a green Rolls-Royce, number XZ9919 . . . I expect you've had enough of this, haven't you?"

The detective stood up, and for the first time in a long while he looked at the Saint again. Simon had rarely seen those baby blue eyes so utterly sleepy and impassive.

"Yes—it's about time for my morning tankard of ale," he murmured easily.

They strolled slowly back to the house.

"That's Joseph's room—the one with the balcony—is it?" he asked idly, and Teal nodded.

"Yes. That's where he was lying down."

"Does he suffer from indigestion?"

The detective flashed a glance at him.

"I don't know. Why?"

"I should like to know," said the Saint.

Back in the house, he asked to be shown the dining room. On the sideboard he discovered a round cardboard box carefully labelled—after the supererogatory habit of chemists—"The Pills." Underneath was the inscription:

Two to be taken with water after each meal, as required.

He examined the tablets, and smiled gently to himself.

"Now could I see the bathroom?"

A very mystified Mr Teal rang for the butler, and they were shown upstairs. The bathroom was one of those magnificent halls of coloured marble and chromium plate which the most modern people find necessary for the preservation of their personal cleanliness, but Simon was interested only in the cupboard over the washbasin. It contained an imposing array of bottles, which Simon surveyed with some awe. Sir Joseph was apparently something of a hypochondriac.

Simon read the labels one by one, and nodded.

"Is he short-sighted?"

"He wears glasses," said the detective.

"Splendid," murmured Simon, and went back to the hotel to supervise the refuelling of his car without relieving Teal's curiosity.

At six o'clock that evening a very frightened man, who had undergone one of the slickest feats of abduction with violence that he could ever have imagined, and who had been very efficiently gagged, bound, blindfolded, and carried across country by the masked bandit who was responsible, sat with his back to a tree where he had been roughly propped up in a deep glade of the New Forest and watched the movements of his captor with goggling eyes. The Saint had kindled a small, crisp fire of dry twigs, and he was feeding more wood to it and blowing into it with the dexterity of long experience, nursing it up into a solid cone of fierce red heat. Down there in the hollow where they were, the branches of the encircling trees filtered away the lingering twilight until it was almost as dark as midnight, but the glow of the fire showed up the Saint's masked face in macabre shadings of red and black as he worked over it, like the face of a pantomime devil illuminated on a darkened stage. The Saint's voice, however, was far from devilish—it was almost affectionate.

"You don't seem to realize, brother," he said, "that stealing secret treaties is quite a serious business, even when they're the daft sort of treaties that We Politicians amuse ourselves with. And it's very wrong of you to think that you can shift the blame for your crimes on to that unfortunate ass whom you dislike so much. So you're going to tell me just where you put that treaty, and then there'll be no more nonsense about it."

The prisoner's eyes looked as if they might pop out of his head at any moment, and strangled grunts came through the gag as he struggled with the ropes that bound his arms to his sides, but the Saint was unmoved. The fire had been heaped up to his complete satisfaction.

"Our friend Mr Teal," continued the Saint, in the same oracular vein, as he began to unlace the captive's shoes, "has been heard to complain about there being no Third Degree in this country. Now that's obviously ridiculous, because you can see for yourself that there is a Third Degree, and I'm it. Our first experiment is the perfect cure for those who suffer from cold feet. I'll show it to you now—unless you'd rather talk voluntarily?"

The prisoner shook his head vigorously, and emitted further strangled grunts which the Saint rightly interpreted as a refusal. Simon sighed, and hauled the man up close to the fire.

"Very well, brother. There's no compulsion at all. Any statement you like to make will be made of your own free will." He drew one of the man's bared feet closer to his little fire. "If you change your mind," he remarked genially, "you need only make one of those eloquent guggling noises of yours, and I expect I shall understand."

It was only five minutes before the required guggling noise came through the gag, but after the gag had been taken out it was another five minutes before the red-faced prisoner's speech became coherent enough to be useful.

Simon left him there, and met Teal in the hotel at half-past-seven.

"The treaty is pushed under the carpet in Whipplethwaite's study," he said, and the detective's pose of mountainous sleepiness failed him for once in his life.

"As near as that?" he ejaculated. "Good Lord!"

The Saint nodded.

"I don't think you'll have to worry your heads about whether you'll prosecute," he said. "The man's mentally deficient—thought so from the beginning. And my special treatment hasn't improved his balance a lot . . . As a general rule, problems in detection bore me stiff—it's so much more entertaining to commit the crime yourself—but this one had its interesting points. A man who could hate a harmless ass like that enough to try and ruin him in such an elaborate way is a bit of a museum specimen. You know, Claud, I've been thinking about those brilliant ideas you say you policemen get sometimes; it strikes me that the only thing you want—"

"Tell me about it when I come back," said Teal, looking at his watch. "I'd better see Whipplethwaite at once and get it over."

"Give him my love," drawled the Saint, dipping his nose into the pint of beer which the detective had bought for him. "He'll get his satisfaction all right when you arrest Vallance."

The detective stood stock still and stared at him with an owl-like face.

"Arrest who?" he stammered.

"Mr Spencer Vallance—the bloke who put insomnia tablets in Whipplethwaite's dyspepsia companion at lunch-time, nipped up to Whipplethwaite's room for the key, opened the safe, replaced the key, and then staggered out of the study bellowing that he'd been sandbagged. The bloke I've just been having words with," said the Saint.

Teal leaned back rather limply against the bar.

"Good Lord alive, Templar—"

"You meant well, Claud," said the Saint kindly. "And it was quite easy really. The only difficult part was that insomnia-tablet business, but I figured that the culprit might want to make quite sure that Joseph would be sleeping soundly when he buzzed up for the key, and the method was just an idea of mine. Then I saw that Joseph's insomnia dope was white, while his indigestion muck was light grey, and I guessed he must have been short-sighted to fall for the change-over. When I looked up at the house it was quite obvious that if anyone could climb down that flying buttress, someone else could just as easily climb up. That's why I was going to say something about your brilliant police ideas."

He patted the detective consolingly on the back.

"Policemen are swell so long as they plod along in their methodical way and sort out facts—they catch people that way quite often. But directly they get on to a really puzzling case, and for some reason it strikes them that they ought to be Great Detectives just for once—then they fall down with the gooseberries. I've noticed those symptoms of detectivosis in you before, Claud. You ought to keep a tighter hand on yourself."

"How long have you known it wasn't Whipplethwaite?" asked Teal.

"Oh, for months," said the Saint calmly. "But when your elephantine hints conjured up the vision of Joseph creeping stealthily down from the balcony upon his foe, couldn't you see a sort of grisly grotesqueness about it? I could. To stage a crime so that another man would naturally be suspected requires a certain warped efficiency of brain. To think for a moment that Joseph could have produced a scheme like that was the sort of brilliant idea that only a policeman in your condition would get. How on earth could Joseph have worked all that out? He's only a politician."

THE UNPOPULAR LANDLORD

There were periods in Simon Templar's eventful life when that insatiable wanderlust which had many times sent him halfway round the world on fantastic quests that somehow never materialized in quite the way they had been intended to, invaded even his busy life in London. He became bored with looking out on to the same street scene from his windows every day, or he saw some other domicile on the market which appealed to his catholic taste in residences, or else he moved because he thought that too long an interval of stability would weaken his resistance to regular hours and *Times*-reading and other low forms of human activity. At these periods he would change his address with such frequency that his friends despaired of ever establishing contact with him again. It was one of the few aimless things he did, and it never provided any exciting sequels—except on this one historic occasion which the chronicler has to record.

Simon Templar awoke on this particular morning with that familiar feeling of restlessness upon him, and, having nothing else of importance to distract him that day, he sallied forth to interview an estate agent. This interviewing of estate agents is a business that is quite sufficient to discourage any migratory urges which may afflict the average man, but Simon Templar had become inured to it over the course of years. He sought out the offices of Messrs Potham & Spode, obtained the services of Mr Potham, and prepared to be patient.

Mr Potham was a thin, angular man, with grey hair, gold-rimmed spectacles, and a face that receded in progressive stages from his eyebrows to the base of his neck. He was a harmless man enough, kind to his children and faithful to his wife, a man whose income-tax returns were invariably honest to the uttermost farthing, but twenty years of his profession had had their inevitable effect.

"I want," said the Saint distinctly, "an unfurnished non-service flat, facing south or west, with four large rooms, and a good open outlook, at not more than five hundred a year."

Mr Potham rummaged through a large file, and eventually, with an air of triumph, drew forth a sheet.

"Now here," he said, "I think we have the very thing you're looking for. Number one-o-one, Park Lane: one bedroom, one reception room—"

"Making four rooms," murmured the Saint patiently.

Mr Potham peered at him over the rims of his glasses, and sighed. He replaced the sheet carefully, and drew forth another.

"Now this," he said, "seems to suit all your requirements. There are two bed, two reception, kitchen and bath, and the rent is extremely moderate. Our client is actually paying fifteen hundred a year, exclusive of rates, but in order to secure a quick let he is ready to pass on the lease at the very reasonable rent of twelve hundred—"

"I said five hundred," murmured the Saint.

Mr Potham turned back to his file with a hurt expression.

"Now here, Mr Templar," he said "we have number twenty-seven, Cloudesley Street, Berkeley Square—"

"Which faces north," murmured the Saint.

"Does it?" said Mr Potham, in some pain.

"I'm afraid it does," said the Saint ruthlessly. "All the odd numbers in Cloudesley Street do."

Mr Potham put back the sheet with the air of an adoring mother removing her offspring from the vicinity of some stranger who had wantonly smacked it. He searched through his file for some time before he produced his next offering.

"Well, Mr Templar," he said, adjusting his spectacles rather nervously, "I have here a very charming service flat—"

Simon Templar knew from bitter experience that this process could be prolonged almost indefinitely, but that day he had one or two helpful ideas.

"I saw a flat to let as I came along here—just round the corner, in David Square," he said. "It looked like the sort of thing I'm wanting, from the outside."

"David Square?" repeated Mr Potham, frowning. "I don't think I know of anything there."

"It had a Potham and Spode board hung out," said the Saint relentlessly. "Perhaps Spode hung it up one dark night when you weren't looking."

"David Square!" re-echoed Mr Potham, like a forsaken bass in an oratorio. "David Square!" He polished his spectacles agitatedly, burrowed into his file again, and presently looked up over his gold rims. "Would that be number seventeen?"

"I think it would."

Mr Potham extracted the page of particulars and leaned back, gazing at the Saint with a certain tinge of pity.

"There is a flat to let at number seventeen, David Square," he admitted in a hushed voice, as if he were reluctantly discussing a skeleton in his family cupboard. "It is one of Major Bellingford Smart's buildings."

He made this announcement as though he expected the Saint to recoil from it with a cry of horror, and looked disappointed when the cry did not come. But the Saint pricked up his ears. Mr Potham's tone, and the name of Bellingford Smart, touched a dim chord of memory in his mind, and never in his life had one of those chords led the Saint astray. Somewhere, sometime, he knew that he had heard the name of Bellingford Smart before, and it had not been in a complimentary reference.

"What's the matter with that?" he asked coolly. "Is he a leper or something?"

Mr Potham smoothed down the sheet on his blotter with elaborate precision.

"Major Bellingford Smart," he said judiciously, "is not a landlord with whose property we are anxious to deal. We have it on our books, since he sends us particulars, but we don't offer it unless we are specially asked for it."

"But what does he do?" persisted the Saint.

"He is . . . ah . . . somewhat difficult to get on with," replied Mr Potham cautiously.

More than that his discretion would not permit him to say, but the Saint's appetite was far from satisfied. In fact, Simon Templar was so intrigued with the unpopularity of Major Bellingford Smart that he took his leave of Mr Potham rather abruptly, leaving that discreet gentleman gaping in some astonishment at a virginal pad of Orders to View on which he had not been given a chance to inscribe any addresses for the Saint's inspection.

Simon Templar was not actively in search of trouble at that time. His hours of meditation, as a matter of fact, were almost exclusively occupied with the problem of devising for himself an effective means of entering the town house of the Countess of Albury (widow of Albury's Peerless Pickles), whose display of diamonds at a recent public function had impressed him as being a potential contribution to his Old Age Pension that he could not conscientiously pass by. But one of those sudden impulses of his had decided that the time was ripe for knowing more about Major Bellingford Smart, and in such a mood as that, a comparatively straightforward proposition like the Countess of Albury's diamonds had to take second place.

Simon went along to a more modern estate agency than the honourable firm of Potham & Spode, one of those marble-pillared, super-card-index billeting offices where human habitations are shot at you over the counter like sausages in a cafeteria; and there an exquisitely dressed young man with a double-breasted waistcoat and hair even more impossibly patent-leather than the Saint's own, who looked as if he could have been nothing less than the second son of a duke or an ex-motor-salesman, was more communicative than Mr Potham had been. It is also worthy of note that the exquisite young man thought that he was volunteering the information quite spontaneously, as a matter of interest to an old friend of his youth, for the Saint's tact and guile could be positively Machiavellian when he chose.

"It's rather difficult to say exactly what is the matter with Bellingford Smart. He seems to be one of these sneaking swine who get pleasure out of taking advantage of their position in petty ways. As far as his tenants are concerned, he keeps to the letter of his leases and makes himself as nasty as possible within those limits. There are lots of ways a landlord can make life unbearable for you if he wants to, as you probably know. The people he likes to get into his flats are lonely widows and elderly spinsters—they're easy meat for him."

"But I don't see what good that does him," said the Saint puzzledly. "He's only getting himself a bad name—"

"I had one of his late tenants in here the other day—she told me that she'd just paid him five hundred pounds to release her. She couldn't stand it any longer, and she couldn't get out any other way. If he does that often, I suppose it must pay him."

"But he's making it more and more difficult to let his flats, isn't he?"

The exquisite young man shrugged.

"All the estate agencies know him—we refuse to handle his stuff at all, and we aren't the only ones. But there are plenty of prospective tenants who've never heard of him. He advertises his flats and lets them himself whenever he can, and then the tenants don't find out their mistake till it's too late. It must seem amazing to you that anything like that can go on in this neighbourhood, but his petty persecutions are all quite legal, and nobody seems to be able to do anything about it."

"I see," said the Saint softly.

The solution of the mystery, now that he knew it, struck him as being one of the most original, and at the same time one of the meanest and most contemptible, forms of blackmail that he had ever heard of, and the fact that it skulked along under the cover of the Law made it twice as sickening. He had no doubt that it was all true—even the worthiest of estate agents are not in the habit of turning down commissions without the strongest possible grounds, and Major Bellingford Smart's nastiness appeared to be common knowledge in the profession. There were some forms of unpleasantness that filled the Saint with an utter loathing, and the meanness of Major Bellingford Smart was one of them. Simon had an entirely immoral respect for the whole-hearted criminal who gambled his liberty on the success of his enterprises, but a livelihood that was gained principally by bullying and swindling fat-headed old women turned his stomach.

"He has quite a lot of property around here," the exquisite young man was informing him. "He buys up houses and converts them into flats. You'll see what sort of man he is when I tell you that while his conversions are being carried out it's his habit to hire a room in the neighbourhood from which he can overlook the site, and he prowls around there at odd times with a pair of field-glasses to see if he can catch his workmen slacking. Once he saw a couple of men having a cup of tea in the afternoon, and went round and fired them on the spot."

"Isn't there anything he doesn't sink to?" asked the Saint.

"I can't think of it," said the exquisite young man slanderously. "A few months ago he had a porter at seventeen, David Square, who'd stayed with him eleven years—I can't think why. The porter's wife acted as a sort of housekeeper, and their daughter was employed in the Major's own flat as a maid. You can imagine what a man like that must be like to work for, and this daughter soon found she couldn't stick it. She tried to give notice, and Smart told her that if she left him her father and mother would be fired out into the street—the porter was an old man of well over sixty. The girl tried to stay on, but at last she had to run away. The first the porter and his wife knew about it was when Smart sent for them and gave them a month's notice. And at the end of the month they duly were fired out, with Smart still owing them three weeks' wages which they tried for weeks to get out of him until the son of one of the tenants went round and saw Smart and damned well made him pay up under the threat of putting his own solicitors on the job. The porter died shortly afterwards. I expect it all sounds incredible, but it's quite true."

Simon departed with a sheaf of Orders to View which he destroyed as soon as he got outside, and walked round very thoughtfully in the direction of David Square. And the more he thought of it, the more poisonous and utterly septic the personality of Major Bellingford Smart loomed in his consciousness. It occurred to the Saint, with a certain honest regret, that the calls of his own breezy buccaneering had lately taken his thoughts too far from that unlawful justice which had once made his name a terror more salutary than the Law to those who sinned secretly in tortuous ways that the Law could not touch. And it was very pleasant to think that the old life was still open to him . . .

With those thoughts he sauntered up the steps of No. 17, where he was stopped by a uniformed porter who looked more like a prison warder—which, as a matter of fact, he had once been.

"Can you tell me anything about this flat that's to let here?" Simon inquired, and the man's manner changed.

"You'd better see Major Bellingford Smart, sir. Will you step this way?"

Simon was led round to an extraordinarily gloomy and untidy office on the ground floor, where a man who was writing at a desk littered with dust-smothered papers rose and nodded to him.

"You want to see the flat, Mr . . . er . . ."

"Bourne," supplied the Saint. "Captain Bourne."

"Well, Captain Bourne," said the Major dubiously, "I hardly know whether it would be likely to suit you. As a matter of fact—"

"It doesn't have to suit me," said the Saint expansively. "I'm inquiring about it for my mother. She's a widow, you know, and she isn't very strong. Can't go on walking around London all day looking at flats. I have to go back to India myself at the end of the week, and I very much wanted to see the old lady fixed up before I sailed."

"Ah," said the Major, more enthusiastically, "that alters the situation. I was going to say that this flat would be quite ideal for an old lady living alone."

Simon was astounded once again at the proven simplicity of womankind. Major Bellingford Smart's transparent sliminess fairly assaulted him with nausea. He was a man of about forty-five, with black hair, closely-set eyes, and a certain stiff-necked poise to his head that gave him a slightly sinister appearance when he moved. It seemed almost unbelievable that anyone could ever have been taken in by such an obvious excrescence, but the fact remained that many victims had undoubtedly fallen into his net.

"Would you like to see it?" suggested the Major.

Simon registered a mental biographical note that Bellingford Smart's military rank must have been won well out of sight of the firing line. If that Major had ever gone over the top he would certainly have perished from a mysterious bullet in the back—such accidents have happened to unpopular officers before.

The Saint said that he would like to see the flat, and Bellingford Smart personally escorted him up to it. It was not at all a bad flat, with good large rooms overlooking the green oasis of the square, and Simon was unable to find fault with it. This was nice for him, for he would have offered no criticism even if the roof had been leaking and the wainscoting had been perforated with rat-holes till it looked like a colander.

"I believe this is the very thing I've been looking for," he said, and Major Bellingford Smart lathered his hands with invisible soap.

"I'm sure Mrs Bourne would be very comfortable here," he said greasily. "I do everything I can to make my tenants feel thoroughly at home. I'm on the premises myself all day, and if she wanted any help I'd always be delighted to give it. The rent is as moderate as I can make it—only three hundred and fifty per annum, including rates."

Simon nodded.

"That seems quite reasonable," he said. "I'll tell my mother about it and see what she says."

"I'll show her round myself at any time she likes to call," said Bellingford Smart cordially. "I don't want to hurry you in any way," he added, as they were going down in the lift, "but for your own sake I ought to mention that I've already shown another lady the flat today, and I'm expecting to hear her decision in a day or two."

At any other time that hoary old bait would have evoked nothing more serious than one of the Saint's most silent razz-berries, but that morning he felt very polite. His face assumed the correct expression of thinly-veiled alarm which attacks the veteran house-hunter's features when he visualizes his prize being snatched away from under his nose.

"I'll let you know definitely sometime this evening," he said.

The Saint's patience and caution could be infinite when he felt that way, but there were other times when he felt that to pass over the iron while it was hot was a crime that would lay heavily on his conscience, and this was one of them. His sense of the poetry of buccaneering demanded that the retribution which he had devised for Major Bellingford Smart should strike swiftly, and he spent that afternoon on a tour of various shipping offices with no other idea in his mind. The Countess of Albury's diamonds crawled in second by several lengths. It meant taking risks of which in a less indignant mood he would never have been guilty, for Simon Templar had made it a rule in life never to attack without knowing every inch of the ground and the precise density of every tuft of grass behind which he might want to take cover; but the strafing of Major Bellingford Smart was a duty that could not be delayed for that.

Nevertheless, he did take certain elementary precautions, as a result of which three well-dressed and subtly dependable-looking men gathered in the apartment of one of their number and slaked their thirsts with beer which the Saint had provided. This was at six o'clock.

The apartment was rented by Peter Quentin, and the other two were Roger Conway and Monty Hayward, who had been summoned by urgent telephone calls by a man whom they had not seen for many months.

"It seems years since I called out the Old Guard, souls," said the Saint, glancing at Roger and Monty. "But this is one evening when your little Simon has need of you."

"What's it all about?" asked Monty expectantly, and Simon drained his glass and told them as briefly as he could about the leprousness of Major Bellingford Smart.

"But," said the Saint, "I am about to afflict him with much sorrow, and that's where you stiffs come in. We are going to settle down to a stag party. Peter, your janitor saw me come in, and at about a quarter to ten we shall send for him and bribe him to go out and buy us some more beer—which will give him another chance to observe that I'm still here. But as soon as he's brought the beer, which I'm afraid I shall have to leave you toughs to drink, I shall hop nimbly out of the window on to the roofs below, descend smartly to the area at the back, proceed thence to the street, and go about my business, returning in about an hour by the same route. As soon as I'm in, we shall ring for the janitor again and demand further supplies of beer. He will reply that it's past closing time, and there will be some argument in which I shall play a prominent part—thereby establishing the fact that we have been together the whole jolly evening. And so we shall. We shall have been playing bridge steadily all the while, and there will be four markers all filled up with the identical scores to prove it—in addition to your solemn oaths. Do you get me?"

"What is this?" asked Roger Conway. "An alibi?"

"No more and no less, old dear," answered the Saint seraphically. "I spent this afternoon wading through passenger lists, and discovered that there actually is a Captain Bourne sailing on the *Otranto* from Tilbury at seven o'clock tonight, which saved me the trouble and expense of booking a passage in that name myself. So when Major Bellingford Smart tries to put over his story it will indubitably receive the polite ha-ha. You soaks are just here in case the episode comes to the ears of Claud Eustace Teal and he tries to work me into it."

Roger Conway shrugged rather ruefully.

"You're on, of course," he said. "But I wish there was more action in it."

Simon looked at him with a smile, for those two had shared many adventures in the old days, as also more recently had Monty Hayward, and he knew that both men sometimes looked back a trifle wistfully on those days out of the respectable surroundings that had subsequently engulfed them.

"Perhaps we may work together again before we die, Roger," he said.

Monty Hayward had another suggestion.

"What are you going to do to Bellingford Smart? Couldn't we all go after him and tar and feather him, or something?"

"I don't think so," said the Saint carefully. "You see, that would be against the Law, and these days I'm developing quite an agile technique for strafing the ungodly by strictly legal means."

His method in this case was not so unimpeachably legal as it might have been, but the Saint had a superb breadth of vision that was superior to such trivial details. At half-past-six the most unpopular landlord in London received a telephone call.

"Is that Mr Shark?" asked the Saint innocently.

"This is Major Bellingford Smart speaking," admitted the landlord, shaking the receiver at his end, which did not seem to be working very well. In any case, he was rather particular about being given his full appellation. "Who is that?"

"This is Captain Bourne. You remember I saw your flat this morning? . . . Well, I've had urgent orders to get back as quickly as possible, and I've had to change my plans. I'm catching the *Otranto* at midnight."

"Are you really?" said Major Bellingford Smart.

"I've told my mother all about the flat, and she seems to think it would suit her down to the ground. She's decided to take it on my recommendation, so if it's still available—"

"Oh, yes, the flat is still available," said Major Bellingford Smart eagerly. "If Mrs Bourne could call round any time tomorrow—"

"I rather wanted to see her settled before I left," said the Saint. "Naturally my time's rather limited, having to pack up in a rush like this, and I'm afraid I've several engagements to get through. I don't know if you could possibly call round here about half-past-ten—you could bring the lease with you, so that I could go through it—and my mother would sign it tonight."

Major Bellingford Smart had arranged to go to a theatre that evening, but the theatre would still be there the next day. And suitable tenants were becoming considerably harder to find than they had been.

"Certainly I'll come round at half-past-ten, if that'll help you at all, Captain Bourne. What is the address?"

"Number one-o-eight, Belgrave Square," said the Saint, and rang off happily.

Major Bellingford Smart was punctual if he was nothing else. It was exactly half-past-ten when he arrived in Belgrave Square, and Simon Templar himself opened the door to him as he came up the steps.

"I'm afraid we're having a bit of trouble with the lights," remarked the Saint genially. "The hall light's just fizzled out. Can you see your way into the sitting room?"

He had an electric torch in his hand, and with it he lighted Major Bellingford Smart into the nearest room. Bellingford Smart heard him clicking the switch up and down, and cursing under his breath.

"Now this one's gone on strike, Major. I'm awfully sorry. Will you take the torch and make yourself at home while I go and look at the fuses? There's a decanter over in the corner—help yourself."

He bumped into Bellingford Smart in the darkness, recovered his balance, apologized, and thrust his flashlight into the Major's hand. The door closed behind him.

Major Bellingford Smart turned the beam of the torch round the room in search of a chair—and, possibly, the decanter referred to. In another second he was not thinking of either, for in one corner the circle of light splashed over a safe whose door hung drunkenly open, half separated from its hinges; lowering the beam a trifle, he saw an array of gleaming tools spread out on the floor beside it.

He gasped, and instinctively moved over to investigate. Outside in the hall he heard the crash of a brass tray clattering to the floor, and straightened up with a start. Then heavy feet came pounding along the passage, the door burst open, and the lights were switched on. The hall lights outside were also on—nothing seemed to be the matter with them. For a few moments they dazzled him, and then, when he had blinked the glare out of his eyes, he saw that the doorway was filled by a black-trousered butler, with his coat off, and a footman with his tunic half-buttoned. They looked at him, then at the open safe, and then back at him again, and there was no friendliness in their eyes.

"Ho," said the butler at length, appearing to swell visibly. "So that's hit. Caught in the very hact, eh?"

"What the devil do you mean?" spluttered Major Bellingford Smart. "I came here at Captain Bourne's invitation to see Mrs Bourne—"

"Not 'alf you didn't," said the butler austerely. "There ain't no Mrs Bourne 'ere, and never 'as been. This is the Countess of Halbury's 'ouse, and you don't 'ave to tell me what you are." He turned to the footman. "James, you go hout and fetch a copper, quick. I can look hafter this bloke. Just let 'im try something!"

He commenced to roll up his right sleeve, with an anticipatory glint in his eye. He was a very large butler, ever so much larger than Major Bellingford Smart, and he looked as if he would like nothing better than a show of violence. Even the best butlers must yearn sometimes for the simple human pleasure of pushing their fists into a face that offends them.

"You'll be sorry for this," fumed Major Bellingford Smart impotently. If this is the Countess of Halbury's house there must be some mistake—"

"Ho, yes," said the butler pleasantly. "There his a mistake, and you made it."

There followed a brief interval of inhospitable silence, until the footman returned with a constable in tow.

"There 'e is," announced the footman, but the butler quelled him with a glance.

"Hofficer," he said majestically, "we 'ave just caught this person red-'anded in the hact of burgling the 'ouse. 'Er ladyship is at present hout dining with Lady Hexmouth. 'Earing the sound of footsteps, we thought 'er ladyship 'ad returned, halthough James remarked that it was not 'er ladyship's custom to let 'erself in. Then we 'eard a crash as if the card tray in the 'all 'ad been hupset, and we noticed that the lights were hout, so we came along to see what it was."

"I can explain everything, officer," interrupted Major Bellingford Smart. "I was asked to come here to get a Mrs Bourne's signature to the lease of a flat—"

"You was, was you?" said the constable, who had ambitions of making his mark in the CID at some future date. "Well, show me the lease."

Major Bellingford Smart felt in his pocket, and a sudden wild look came into his eyes. The lease which he had brought with him was gone, but there was something else there—something hard and knobbly.

The constable did not miss that change of expression. He came closer to Major Bellingford Smart.

"Come on, now," he ordered roughly. "Out with it—whatever it is. And no monkey business."

Slowly, stupidly, Major Bellingford Smart drew out the hard, knobbly object. It was a very small automatic, and looped loosely round it was a diamond and sapphire pendant—one of the least valuable items in the Countess of Albury's vanished collection. He was still staring at it when the constable grabbed it quickly out of his hand.

"Carrying firearms, eh? And that talk about having a lease in your pocket—just to get a chance to pull it out and shoot me! You've got it coming to you, all right."

He glanced round the room with a professional air, and saw the open window.

"Came in through there," he remarked, with some satisfaction at the admiring silence of his audience of butler and footman. "There'd be a lot of dust outside on that sill, wouldn't there? And look at 'is trousers."

The audience bent its awed eyes on Major Bellingford Smart's nether garments, and the Major also looked down. Clearly marked on each knee was a circular patch of sooty grime which had certainly not been there before the Saint cannoned into him in that very helpful darkness.

***

On the far side of the square, Simon Templar heard the constable's whistle shrilling into the night, and drifted on towards the beer that waited for him.

THE NEW SWINDLE

Mr Alfred Tillson ("Broads" Tillson to the trade) was only one of many men who cherished the hope that one day they might be privileged to meet the Saint again. Usually those ambitions included a dark night, a canal, and a length of lead pipe, with various trimmings and decorations according to the whim of the man concerned. But no bliss so unalloyed as that had ever come the way of any of those men, for canals and lengths of lead pipe did not enter into Simon Templar's own plans for his brilliant future, and on dark nights he walked warily as a matter of habit.

Mr Alfred Tillson, however, enjoyed the distinction of being a man who did achieve his ambition and meet the Saint for a second time; although the encounter did not by any means take place as he would have planned it.

He was a lean grey-haired man with a long, horse-like face and the air of a retired church-warden—an atmosphere which he had created for himself deliberately as an aid to business, and which he had practised for so long that in the end he could not have shaken it off if he tried. It had become just as much a part of his natural make-up as the faintly ecclesiastical style of dress which he affected, and over the course of years it had served him well. For Mr Broads Tillson, as his name conveyed, was acknowledged in the trade to be one of the greatest living card manipulators in the world. To see those long tapering fingers of his ruffling through a pack of cards and dealing out hands in which every pip had been considered and placed individually was an education in itself. He could do anything with a pack of cards except make it talk. He could shuffle it once, apparently without looking at it, and in that shuffle sort it out suit by suit and card by card, stack up any sequence he wanted, and put it all together again, with one careless flick of his hands that was too quick for the eye to follow. If you were in the trade, if you were "regular" and you could induce him to give you a demonstration of his magic, he would invite you to deal but four hands of bridge, write down a list of the cards in every hand, shuffle the pack again as much as you cared to, and give it back to him; whereupon he would take one glance at your list, shuffle the pack once himself, and proceed to deal out the four hands again exactly as you had listed them. And if you were unlucky enough to be playing with him in the way of business, you could order brand-new packs as often as you cared to pay for them, without inconveniencing him in the least. Mr Alfred Tillson had never marked a card in his life, and he could play any card game that had ever been invented with equal success.

On the stage he might have made a very comfortable income for himself but his tastes had never led him that way. Mr Tillson was partial to travel and sea air, and for many years he had voyaged the Atlantic and Pacific ocean routes, paying himself very satisfactory dividends on every trip, and invariably leaving his victims with the consoling thought that they had at least evaded the wiles of sharpers and lost their money to an honest man. He might have retired long ago, if he had not had a weakness for beguiling the times between voyages with dissipations of a highly unclerical kind; and as a matter of fact it was to this weakness of his that he owed his first meeting with the Saint.

He had made a very profitable killing on a certain trip which he took to Madeira, but coming back overland from Lisbon a sylph-like blonde detained him too long in Paris, and he woke up one morning to find that he was a full twenty pounds short of his fare to New York. He set out for London with this pressing need of capital absorbing his mind, and it was merely his bad luck that the elegant young man whom he discovered lounging idly over the rail when the cross-Channel boat left Boulogne should have "been christened Simon Templar."

Simon was not looking for trouble on that trip, but he was never adverse to having his expenses paid, and when Mr Tillson hinted that it was distressingly difficult to find any congenial way of passing the time on cross-Channel journeys, he knew what to expect. They played casino, and Simon won fifteen pounds in the first half-hour.

"A bit slow, don't you think?" observed the benevolent Mr Tillson, as he shuffled the cards at this point and called for another brace of double whiskies. "Shall we double the stakes?"

This was what Simon had been waiting for—and that gift of waiting for the psychological moment was one which he always employed on such occasions. Fifteen pounds was a small fish in his net, but who was he to criticize what a beneficent Providence cast kindly into his lap?

"Certainly, brother," he murmured. "Treble 'em if you like. I'll be with you again in a sec—I've just got to see a man about a small borzoi."

He faded away towards a convenient place, and that was the last Mr Tillson saw of him. It was one of Mr Tillson's saddest experiences, and three years later it was still as fresh in his memory as it had been the day after it happened. "Happy" Fred Jorman, that most versatile of small-time confidence men, whose round face creased up into such innumerable wrinkles of joy when he smiled, heard that Broads Tillson was in London, called on him on that third anniversary, and had to listen to the tale. They had worked together on one coup several years ago, but since then their ways had lain apart.

"That reminds me of a beggar I met this spring," said Happy Fred, not to be outdone in anecdote—and the ecclesiastical-looking Mr Tillson hoped that "beggar" was the word he used. "I met him in the Alexandra—he seemed interested in horses, and he looked so lovely and innocent. When I told him about the special job I'd got for Newmarket that afternoon—"

This was one of Happy Fred's favourite stories, and much telling of it had tended to standardize the wording.

There was a certain prelude of this kind of conversation and general reminiscence before Happy Fred broached the real reason for his call.

"Between ourselves, Broads, things aren't going too well in my business. There's too many stories in the newspapers these days to tell the suckers how it's done. Things have got so bad that one or two of the boys have had to go on the legit just to keep themselves alive."

"The circumstances are somewhat similar with me, Fred," confessed Mr Tillson regretfully. "The Atlantic liners are half empty, and those gentlemen who are travelling don't seem to have the same surplus of lucre for the purposes of—um—recreation as they used to."

Happy Fred nodded.

"Well, that's how it struck me, Broads," he said. "And what with one thing and another, I said to myself, 'Fred,' I said, 'the old tricks are played out, and you'd better admit it. Fred,' I said, 'You've got to keep up with the times or go under. And what's wanted these days,' I said to myself, 'is a New Swindle.'"

Mr Tillson raised his episcopal eyebrows.

"And have you succeeded in devising this—um—novel system of remunerative equivocation?"

"I have invented a new swindle, if that's what you mean," said Happy Fred. "At least, it's new enough for me. And the beauty of it is that you don't have to do anything criminal—anyway, not that anyone's ever going to know about. It's all quite straight and above-board, and whatever happens you can't get pinched for trying it, if you're clever enough about the way you work it."

"Have you made any practical experiments with this new method?" inquired Mr Tillson.

"I haven't," said Happy Fred lugubriously. "And the trouble is that I can't. Here am I carrying this wonderful idea about with me, and I can't use it. That's why I've come to you. What I need, Broads, is a partner who won't double-cross me, who's clever with his hands, and hasn't got any kind of police record. That's why I can't do it myself. The bloke who does this has got to be a respectable bloke that nobody can say anything against. And that's where you come in. I've been worrying about it for weeks, thinking of all the good money there is waiting for me to pick up, and wondering who I could find to come in with me that I could trust. And then just last night somebody told me that you were back, and I said to myself, 'Fred,' I said 'Broads Tillson is the very man you want. He's the man who'll give you a square deal, and won't go and blow your idea about.' So I made up my mind to come and see you and see what you felt about it. I'm willing to give you my idea, Broads, and put up the capital—I've got a bit of money saved up—if you'll count me in fifty-fifty."

"What is this idea?" asked Mr Tillson cautiously.

Happy Fred helped himself to another drink, swallowed half of it, and wiped his mouth on the back of his hand.

"It goes like this," he said, with the unconscious reverence of a poet introducing his latest brain-child to the world. "You go to one of the big jewellers, posing as a rich man who's got a little bit of stuff in Paris, see? That ought to be easy for you. You want to send this girl a lovely big diamond necklace or something, and you choose something out of his stock that you can get for about a thousand quid—that's as much as I can put up. This necklace has got to be sent by post, and so of course it's got to be insured. Now it's made into a parcel, and all this time you've got in your pocket another box about the same size, with pebbles in it to make it about the same weight. This is where the man who does it has got to be clever with his hands, like you are. As soon as the necklace has been packed in its box—"

Mr Tillson sighed.

"There's nothing new about that," he protested. "You haven't got the money to reimburse this jeweller for his necklace, and therefore you desire the sealed packet to be preserved in his safe until you post him the money and request him to send it to you. And when he tires of waiting for his instructions he opens the package and discovers that you have absconded with the necklace and left him the receptacle containing the pebbles. That's a very old one, Fred, don't you think?"

"Haven't got the money nothing!" said Happy Fred scornfully. "Of course you've got the money—I tell you I'm putting up a thousand quid for this job. No jeweller would be taken in with that old trick you're thinking of these days—he'd send for the police as soon as you suggested it. You pay cash for this bit of jewellery you buy, and it's all square and above-board. Now listen to what I've got to say."

Mr Alfred Tillson listened, and was impressed. Happy Fred's variation on an old theme appeared to have many of the qualities that were claimed for it by its proud inventor, and although it did not exactly come within Mr Tillson's self-chosen province, it was true that the recent falling off in transatlantic travel had left him particularly receptive to ideas that opened up new possibilities of income. The new swindle is a thing that every confidence man dreams of creating; it is the brainwave that sweeps through the trade once in a generation, and produces a golden harvest for its pioneers before the officious publicity of the press sends the soaring market slumping back again. Life is like that for *chevaliers d'industrie* like Happy Fred Jorman: the criminological trend of the Sunday newspaper reduces the ranks of the suckers every Sabbath, and the movies they see during the week haven't helped either. But this new swindle looked as if it might enjoy a fair run of success before it went the way of all other brilliant inventions.

Possibly it was because both partners in the new alliance were so pleased with the potentialities of their own brilliance that they temporarily forgot their common ambition to meet Simon Templar again—with a convenient canal and a length of lead pipe thrown in.

Simon himself was not thinking about them, for he had his own views on the kind of acquaintance which he was anxious to renew. Ruth Eden was a very different proposition. The fact that he had been privileged to rescue her in romantic circumstances from the attentions of the unspeakable Mr Julian Lamantia, and that subsequently Mr Lamantia had been one of three men who found themselves unexpectedly poorer for that meeting, included her among the register of people whom Simon Templar would have been pleased to meet again at any time. He had managed to get her a job with another acquaintance of his, who was such an exclusive jeweller that he had an office instead of a shop, and produced his treasures out of a vast safe instead of leaving them about in glass-topped counters, but after that he had heard nothing of her for some while.

She rang him up one day about this time, and he was delighted to hear her voice. From the date of their first meeting she had exhibited commendable symptoms of hero-worship, and Simon Templar had no modesty in his composition.

"Have you forgotten me altogether?" she demanded, and the Saint chuckled into the transmitter.

"To tell you the truth, I've been so busy murdering people that I've hardly had a minute to spare. I thought you must have got married or something. Come and have dinner and see my collection of skulls."

"I'd love to. When?"

"Why not tonight? What time does Alan let you go?"

"Half-past-five."

"I'll call round for you at six—that'll just give you time to put your hat on, darling," said the Saint angelically, and rang off before she could make a suitable reply.

He was engaged in a running commentary on her inevitable feminine manoeuvres in front of a mirror in Alan Emberton's outer office when the glass-panelled door of the inner sanctum opened, and the sound of a voice that seemed vaguely familiar made him break off in the middle of a sentence. In another second, to her intense astonishment, he had vanished under a desk like a rabbit into its burrow, and if she had not turned abruptly back to her mirror while Emberton showed his client out she would have had to burst out laughing.

But Simon was on his feet again when the jeweller came back and he was completely unruffled by his own extraordinary behaviour.

"Hullo, Templar," said Emberton, noticing him with some surprise. "Where did you spring from?"

He was a big man, with a jovial red face, who looked more like a retired butcher than an exclusive jeweller, and he liked the Saint in spite of his sins. He held out his beefy hand.

"I was under the desk," said the Saint unblushingly. "I dropped a penny and I was looking for it. How's life?"

"Not so good as it might be," answered the other frankly. "However, I suppose I can't grumble. I've just sold a thousand-pound diamond bracelet to that fellow I was showing out. Did you see him?"

"No," said the Saint untruthfully.

He had seen Mr Alfred Tillson quite distinctly, and the problem of what Broads Tillson could possibly want with a thousand-pound bracelet bothered him quite a lot in the taxi in which he carried Ruth Eden off to the West End. Broads Tillson, he knew, was often extravagantly generous to his lady friends, but somehow he could not associate thousand-pound diamond bracelets even with that amorous man. Either Mr Tillson had recently made no small click, or else there was more in that purchase than met the eye, and Simon had a constitutional objection to his old acquaintances embarking on enterprises of which he knew nothing.

The girl noticed his silence and challenged him.

"Why did you disappear under that desk, Simon? I feel there's some thrilling secret behind it."

"It was pure instinct," said Saint brazenly, "to avoid being recognized. You see, Alan's latest client is one of the slickest cardsharpers in the world, and I once diddled him out of fifteen quid that he threw out for ground bait."

Her eyes opened wide.

"Are you sure? Gee, why ever didn't you tell Mr Emberton at once?"

"Because I'd like to know what his new trick is first." The blithe cavalier's blue eyes glinted at her mockingly. "Didn't you once tell me you'd love to be an adventurer's partner, Ruth? Well, here's a chance for you. Find out the whole details of the deal, every single fact you can get hold of, without saying anything to Alan. Give your best imitation of an adventuress worming out secrets so that the victim doesn't even know they've been wormed. And come and tell me. I'll promise you I'll see Alan doesn't get swindled, but wouldn't you hate to do anything so dull as just tell him to send for the police?"

She met him the next evening, full of excitement over the triumph of her maiden effort at sleuthing. She could hardly contain her news until he had ordered her a cocktail.

"I can't see the catch in it at all, but perhaps you can. Mr Tillson gave Mr Emberton a cheque for the bracelet yesterday, and he particularly asked Mr Emberton to get a special clearance so that there wouldn't be any difficulty about it. So the cheque must be all right. Mr Tillson is sending it to a friend of his in Paris for a birthday present, he says, and he's having it insured to go over. A valuer came from the insurance company today to have a look at it. Mr Tillson—"

"Call him Broads," suggested the Saint. "He'd take it as a compliment."

"Why 'Broads'?" she asked, wrinkling her forehead.

"'Broads' are cards, in the language. How exactly is this bracelet being sent?"

"By post. Mr Till—Broads is coming in tomorrow to see it off and enclose a letter, and a man from the insurance company is coming down as well—that seems an awful lot of formality, but I suppose they have to be careful. Now what do you think will happen? Will Broads pull out a gun and hold us all up?"

"I doubt it," murmured the Saint mildly. "Broads isn't a violent man. Besides, if there was anything like that in the air he'd have done it yesterday. Let me think."

He leaned back and scowled thoughtfully into space. More than once he had truthfully admitted that the solving of ancient mysteries wasn't in his line, but the imaginative construction of forthcoming ones was another matter. The Saint's immoral mind worked best and most rapidly along those lines.

And then, as he scowled into space, a headline in the evening paper that was being read by a fat gent at an adjoining table percolated into his abstracted vision, and he sat up with a start that made the fat gent turn round and glare at him.

"I've got it!" he cried. "Whoops—and what a beauty!"

She caught at his sleeve.

"Tell me, Simon."

"No, darling. That I can't do—not till afterwards. But you shall hear it, if you like to meet me again on Saturday. What time is this posting party?"

"Eleven o'clock. But listen—I must tell Mr Emberton—"

"You must do nothing of the sort." The Saint shook his head at her sadly. "What do you want to do, Ruth—ruin the only bit of business the poor man's done this week? He's got his money, hasn't he? The rest of the show is purely private."

When she continued to try and question him he returned idiotic answers that made her want to smack him, and she went home, provoked and disappointed, and not entirely consoled by his repeated promise to tell her the whole story after it was all over.

But her sense of excitement returned when Mr Tillson presented himself at the office the next morning. Looking at that rather pathetically horse-faced gentleman in his faintly clerical garb, it was difficult to believe that he could possibly be the man that the Saint had described him. He was punctual to the minute, and the insurance company's representative came in soon afterwards. She showed them into the inner office, and found it easy to stay around herself while the package was being prepared and sealed. She watched the entire proceedings with what she would always believe was well-simulated unconcern, but which actually would have seemed like a hypnotic stare to anyone who had noticed her; and yet when it was all over and the various parties had shaken hands and departed, she could not recall the slightest incident that had deviated from the matter-of-fact formality which should have been expected of the affair. She even began to wonder, with a feeling that her doubt was almost sacrilegious, whether the Saint could have been mistaken . . .

Mr Alfred Tillson was not so reassured. He was perspiring a little when he met Happy Fred Jorman on the street corner.

"Yes, I effected the substitution," he said shortly, in answer to his partner's questions. "I trust I have aroused no suspicion. There was a kind of girl amanuensis in the room all the time, and she stared at me from the minute I arrived until the minute I left. I expected her to make some comment at any moment, but she took her eyes off me for a second when I knocked my hat off the desk. Let's get back to my hotel."

They took a taxi to the hotel in Bloomsbury where Mr Tillson had taken a modest suite—Broads Tillson had luxurious tastes which had never helped him to save money, and he had insisted that this setting was necessary for the character he had to play. Happy Fred Jorman, whose liberty was not in jeopardy, was elated.

"That was just your imagination, Broads," he said as they let themselves in. "She was probably wishing she had a friend who sent her thousand-pound bracelets. It's just the newness of it that's upset you—you'll get used to it after you've done it a few times. I was saying to myself all the time you were practising, 'Fred,' I was saying, 'Broads Tillson rings the changes better than anyone else you've ever met in your life. You've picked the best partner—'"

Mr Tillson poured himself out a whisky-and-soda and sank into a chair. From his breast-pocket he drew a packet with one seal on it—it was the exact replica of the packet that had been posted to Paris, as it had appeared after the first seal had been placed on it in Mr Emberton's office.

"You'll have to fence the article, Fred," said Mr Tillson. "I've never had anything to do with these things."

"I'll fence it all right," said Happy Fred. "We'll get four hundred for it easily. And then what happens? That other little packet I registered at the same time blows off and sets the mailbag on fire in the train, and when they've cleared up the mess they find your bracelet is missing. Then there's just another sensational mailbag robbery for the newspapers, and everybody's wondering how it was done, while we just collect the insurance money. That's four hundred pounds profit for a couple of hours' work, and we can turn that over every week while it lasts." Happy Fred slapped his thigh. "Gosh, Broads, when I think of the money we're going to make out of that idea of mine—"

"You might live to make it," remarked a very pleasant voice behind them, "if you both sat quite still."

The two men did not sit quite still. They would have been superhuman stoics if they had. They spun round as if they had each been hit on the side of the jaw with a black-jack. And they saw the Saint.

The door of Mr Tillson's private bathroom had opened and closed while they were talking without them hearing it, and now it served as a neat white background for the lean and smiling man who was propping himself gracefully up against it. There was an automatic in his hand, and it turned from side to side in a lazy arc that gave each of them an opportunity to blink down its black uncompromising barrel.

"Possibly I intrude," murmured the Saint, very pleasantly, "but that's just too bad."

On the faces of the two men were expressions of mingled astonishment, fear, indignation, horror, and simple wrath, which would have done credit to a pair of dyspeptic cows that had received an electric shock from a clump of succulent grass. And then Mr Tillson's voice returned.

"Good God!" he squeaked. "It's the man I was telling you about—"

"The bloke *I* was telling *you* about!" ejaculated Happy Fred savagely. "The skunk who took thirty pounds of my money in the Alexandra, and then—"

The two men's heads revolved until they looked into each other's eyes and gazed into the souls beyond. And the Saint hitched himself off the door and came towards them.

"A very neat piece of work, if I may say so, Fred," he remarked. "Not so original as it might have been, perhaps, but new enough. It's very kind of you to have worked so hard for me."

"What are you going to do?" asked Mr Tillson weakly.

Simon took the packet out of his hands.

"Relieve you of this encumbrance, brother. It's a very pretty bracelet, but I don't think you could wear it. People might think it was rather odd."

"I'll have the police on to you for this, you—"

Simon raised his eyebrows.

"The police? To tell them that I've stolen your bracelet? But I understood your bracelet was in the post, on its way to your little girl in Paris? Can I be mistaken, Alfred?"

Mr Tillson swallowed painfully, and then Happy Fred jumped up.

"Damn the police!" he snarled. "I'll settle with this bluffer. He wouldn't dare to shoot—"

"Oh, but you're quite wrong about that," said the Saint gently. "I shouldn't have any objection to shooting you if you asked for it. It's quite a long time since I last shot anyone, and I often feel afraid that if I abstain for too long I may get squeamish. Don't tempt me, Fred, because I'm feeling nervous enough already."

But the Saint's blue eyes were as steady as the gun in his hand, and it was Happy Fred's gaze that wavered.

"I shall have to tie you up while I make my getaway," said the Saint amiably, "so would you both mind turning round? You'll be able to undo yourselves quite quickly after I've gone."

"You wouldn't be a party to a low insurance swindle, would you?" protested Happy Fred aggrievedly, as the Saint looped coils of rope deftly round his wrists.

"I wouldn't be a party to any kind of swindle," said the Saint virtuously. "I'm an honest hold-up man, and your insurance policies have nothing to do with me."

He completed the roping of the two men, roughly gagged them with their own handkerchiefs, and retreated leisurely to the door. Neither of them made any attempt to wave him goodbye, which Simon felt was rather rude.

THE FIVE-THOUSAND-POUND KISS

It has been said that Simon Templar was a philanderer, but the criticism was not entirely just. A pretty face, or the turn of a slim ankle, appealed to him no more—and not a bit less—than they do to the next man. Perhaps he was more honest about it.

It is true that sometimes, in a particularly buccaneering mood, as he swung down a broad highway leading to infinite adventure, he would sing one of his own inimitable songs against the pompous dreariness of civilization as he saw it, with a chorus:

But if red blood runs thin with years,
By God! If I must die,
I'll kiss red lips and drink red wine
And let the rest go by,
My son,
And let the rest go by!

But there was a gesture in that, to be taken with or without salt as the audience pleased, and a fat lot the Saint cared. He was moderate in nothing that he said or did. That insurgent vitality which made him an outlaw first and last and in everything rebelled perhaps too fiercely against all moderation; and if at the same time it made him, to those who knew him best, the one glamorous and romantic figure of his day, that was the judgement which he himself would have asked for.

These chronicles are concerned mainly with episodes in which he provided himself with the bare necessities of life by cunning and strategy rather than daring, but even in those times there were occasions when his career hung on the thread of a lightning decision. That happened in the affair of Mrs Dempster-Craven's much-advertised pink diamond, and if the Saint philandered then, he would have told you that he had no regrets.

"The idea that such a woman should have a jewel like that keeps me awake at nights," he complained. "I've seen her twice, and she is a Hag."

This was at dinner one night. Peter Quentin was there, and so was Patricia Holm, who, when all was said and done, was the lady who held the Saint's reckless heart and knew best how to understand all his misdeeds. The subject of the "Star of Mandalay" had cropped up casually in the course of conversation, and it was worth mentioning that neither of Simon Templar's guests bothered to raise any philosophical argument against his somewhat heterodox doctrine about the rights of Hags. But it was left for Peter Quentin to put his foot in it.

Peter read behind the wistfulness of the Saint's words, and said, "Don't be an idiot, Simon. You don't need the money, and you couldn't pinch the Star of Mandalay. The woman's got a private detective following her around wherever she goes—"

"Couldn't I pinch it, Peter?" said the Saint, very softly.

Patricia saw the light in his eyes, and clutched Peter's wrist.

"You ass!" she gasped. "Now you've done it. He'd be fool enough to try—"

"Why 'try'?" asked the Saint, looking round mildly. "That sounds very much like an aspersion on my genius, which I shall naturally have to—"

"I didn't mean it like that," protested the girl frantically. "I mean that after all, when we don't need the money—You said you were thinking of running over to Paris for a week—"

"We can go via Amsterdam, and sell the Star of Mandalay en route," said the Saint calmly. "You lie in your teeth, my sweetheart. You meant that the Star of Mandalay was too much of a problem for me and I'd only get in a mess if I tried for it. Well, as a matter of fact, I've been thinking of having a dart at it for some time."

Peter Quentin drank deeply of the Chambertin to steady his nerves.

"You haven't been thinking anything of the sort," he said. "I'll withdraw everything I said. You were just taking on a dare."

Simon ordered himself a second slice of melon, and leaned back with his most seraphic and exasperating smile.

"Have I," he inquired blandly, "ever told you my celebrated story about a bob-tailed ptarmigan named Alphonse, who lived in sin with a couple of duck-billed platypi in the tundras of Siberia? Alphonse, who suffered from asthma and was a believer in Christian Science . . ."

He completed his narrative at great length, refusing to be interrupted, and they knew that the die was cast. When once Simon Templar had made up his mind it was impossible to argue with him. If he didn't proceed blandly to talk you down with one of his most fatuous and irrelevant anecdotes, he would listen politely to everything you had to say, agree with you thoroughly, and carry on exactly as he had announced his intentions from the beginning; which wasn't helpful. And he had made up his mind, on one of his mad impulses, that the Star of Mandalay was due for a change of ownership. It was not a very large stone, but it was reputed to be flawless, and it was valued at ten thousand pounds. Simon reckoned that it would be worth five thousand pounds to him in Van Roeper's little shop in Amsterdam, and five thousand pounds was a sum of money that he could find a home for at any time.

But he said nothing about that to Mrs Dempster-Craven when he saw her for the third time and spoke to her for the first. He was extremely polite and apologetic. He had good reason to be, for the rakish Hirondel which he was driving had collided with Mrs Dempster-Craven's Rolls-Royce in Hyde Park, and the glossy symmetry of the Rolls-Royce's rear elevation had been considerably impaired.

"I'm terribly sorry," he said. "Your chauffeur pulled up rather suddenly, and my hand-brake cable broke when I tried to stop."

His hand-brake cable had certainly divided itself in the middle, and the frayed ends had been produced for the chauffeur's inspection, but no one was to know that Simon had filed it through before he started out.

"That is not my fault," said Mrs Dempster-Craven coldly. She was going to pay a call on the wife of a minor baronet, and she was pardonably annoyed at the damage to her impressive car. "Bagshaw, will you please find me a taxi?"

"The car'll take you there all right, ma'am," said the chauffeur incautiously.

Mrs Dempster-Craven froze him through her lorgnettes.

"How," she required to know, "can I possibly call on Lady Wiltham in a car that looks as if I had picked it up at a second-hand sale? Kindly call me a taxi immediately, and don't argue."

"Yes, ma'am," said the abashed chauffeur, and departed on his errand.

"I really don't know how to apologize," said the Saint humbly.

"Then don't try," said Mrs Dempster-Craven discouragingly.

The inevitable small crowd had collected, and a policeman was advancing ponderously towards it from the distance. Mrs Dempster-Craven liked to be stared at as she crossed the pavement to Drury Lane Theatre on a first night, but not when she was sitting in a battered car in Hyde Park. But the Saint was not so self-conscious.

"I'm afraid I can't offer you a lift at the moment, but if my other car would be of any use to you for the reception tonight—"

"What reception?" asked Mrs Dempster-Craven haughtily, having overcome the temptation to retort that she had three other Rolls-Royces no less magnificent than the one she was sitting in.

"Prince Marco d'Ombria's," answered the Saint easily. "I heard you say that you were going to call on Lady Wiltham, and I had an idea that I'd heard Marco mention her name. I thought perhaps—"

"I am not going to the reception," said Mrs Dempster-Craven, but it was noticeable that her tone was not quite so freezing. "I have a previous engagement to dine with Lord and Lady Bredon."

Simon chalked up the point without batting an eyelid. He had not engineered that encounter without making inquiries about his victim, and it had not taken him long to learn that Mrs Dempster-Craven's one ambition was to win for herself and her late husband's millions an acknowledged position among the Very Best People. That carelessly-dropped reference to a Prince, even an Italian Prince, by his first name, had gone over like a truck-load of honey. And it was a notable fact that if Mrs Dempster-Craven had pursued her own inquiries into the reference, she would have found that the name of Simon Templar was not only recognized but hailed effusively, for there had once been a spot of bother involving a full million pounds belonging to the Bank of Italy which had made the Saint for ever persona grata at the Legation."

The chauffeur returned with a taxi, and Mrs Dempster-Craven's fifteen stone of flesh were assisted ceremoniously out of the Rolls. Having had a brief interval to consider pros and cons, she deigned to thank the Saint for his share in the operation with a smile that disclosed a superb set of expensive teeth.

"I hope your car isn't seriously damaged," she remarked graciously, and the Saint smiled in his most elegant matter.

"It doesn't matter a bit. I was just buzzing down to Hurlingham for a spot of tennis, but I can easily take a taxi." He took out his wallet and handed her a card. "As soon as you know what the damage'll cost to put right, I do hope you'll send me in the bill."

"I shouldn't dream of doing such a thing," said Mrs Dempster-Craven. "The whole thing was undoubtedly Bagshaw's fault."

With which startling volte-face, and another display of her expensive denture, she ascended regally into the cab, and Simon Templar went triumphantly back to Patricia.

"It went off perfectly, Pat! You could see the whole line sizzling down her throat till she choked on the rod. The damage to the Hirondel will cost about fifteen quid to put right, but we'll charge that up to expenses. And the rest of it's only a matter of time."

The time was even shorter than he expected, for Mrs Dempster-Craven was not prepared to wait any longer than was necessary to see her social ambitions fulfilled, and the highest peak she had attained at that date was a weekend at the house of a younger son of a second viscount.

Three days later Simon's postbag included a scented mauve envelope, and he knew before he opened it that it was the one he had been waiting for.

118 Berkeley Square,
Mayfair W1

My dear Mr Templar,

I'm sure you must have thought me rather abrupt after our accident in Hyde Park on Tuesday, but these little upsets seem so much worse at the time than they really are. Do try and forgive my rudeness.

I am having a little party here on Tuesday next. Lord and Lady Palfrey are coming, and the Hon. Celia Mallard, and lots of other people whom I expect you'll know. I'd take it as a great favour if you could manage to look in, any time after 9:00, just to let me know you weren't offended.

I do hope you got to Hurlingham all right.

Yours sincerely,
Gertrude Dempster-Craven

"Who said my technique had ever failed me?" Simon demanded of Peter Quentin at lunch-time that day.

"I didn't," said Peter, "as I've told you all along. Thank God you won't be going to prison on Thursday, anyway—if it's only a little party she's invited you to I don't suppose you'll even see the Star of Mandalay."

Simon grinned.

"Little party be blowed," he said. "Gertrude has never thrown a little party in her life. When she talks about a 'little' party she means there'll only be two orchestras and not more than a hundred couples. And if she doesn't put on the Star of Mandalay for Lady Palfrey's benefit I am a bob-tailed ptarmigan and my name is Alphonse."

Nevertheless, when he suggested that Peter Quentin should come with him there was not much argument.

"How can you get me in?" Peter demurred. "I wasn't invited, and I don't know any princes."

"You've got an uncle who's a lord or something, haven't you?"

"I've got an uncle who's the Bishop of Johannesburg, but what does Mrs Dempster-Craven care about South African bishops?"

"Call him Lord Johannesburg," said the Saint. "She won't look him up in Debrett's while you're there. I'll say we were dining together and I couldn't shake you off."

At that point it all looked almost tediously straightforward, a commonplace exploit with nothing but the size of the prize to make it memorable. And when Simon arrived in Berkeley Square on the date of his invitation it seemed easier still, for Mrs Dempster-Craven, as he had expected, was proudly sporting the Star of Mandalay on her swelling bosom, set in the centre of a pattern of square-cut sapphires in a platinum pendant that looked more like an illuminated sky-sign than anything else. True, there was a large-footed man in badly fitting dress clothes who trailed her around like a devoted dachshund, but private detectives of any grade the Saint felt competent to deal with. Professionals likewise, given a fair warning—although he was anticipating no professional surveillance that night. But he had not been in the house twenty minutes before he found himself confronting a dark slender girl with merry brown eyes whose face appeared before him like the Nemesis of one of his most innocent flirtations—and even then he did not guess what Fate had in store for him.

At his side he heard the voice of Mrs Dempster-Craven cooing like a contralto dove: "This is Miss Rosamund Armitage—a cousin of the Duke of Trayall." And then, as she saw their eyes fixed on each other, "But have you met before?"

"Yes—we have met," said the Saint, recovering himself easily. "Wasn't it that day when you were just off to Ostend?"

"I think so," said the girl gravely.

A plaintive baronet in search of an introduction accosted Mrs Dempster-Craven from the other side and Simon took the girl in his arms as the second orchestra muted its saxophones for a waltz.

"This is a very happy reunion, Kate," he murmured. "I must congratulate you."

"Why?" she asked suspiciously.

"When we last met—in that famous little argument about the Kellman necklace—you weren't so closely related to the Duke of Trayall."

They made a circuit of the floor—she danced perfectly, as he would have expected—and then she said, bluntly, "What are you doing here, Saint?"

"Treading the light fantastic—drinking free champagne—and watching little monkeys scrambling up the social ladder," he answered airily. "And you?"

"I'm here for exactly the same reason as you are—my Old Age Pension."

"I can't imagine you getting old, Kate."

"Let's sit out somewhere," she said suddenly.

They left the ballroom and went in search of a secluded corner of the conservatory, where there were armchairs and sheltering palm trees providing discreet alcoves for romantic couples. Simon noticed that the girl was quite sure of her way around, and said so.

"Of course I've been here before," she said. "I expect you have, too."

"On the contrary—this is my first visit. I never take two bites at a cherry."

"Not even a ten-thousand-pound one?"

"Not even that."

She produced a packet of cigarettes from her bag and offered him one. Simon smiled, and shook his head.

"There are funny things about your cigarettes that don't make me laugh out loud, Kate," he said cheerfully. "Have one of mine instead."

"Look here," she said. "Let's put our cards on the table. You're after that pendant, and so am I. Everything on our side is planned out, and you've just told me this is your first visit. You can't possibly get in front of us this time. You took the Kellman necklace away under our noses, but you couldn't do it again. Why not retire gracefully?"

He gazed at her thoughtfully for a few seconds, and she touched his hand.

"Won't you do that—and save trouble?"

"You know, Kate," said the Saint, "you're a lovely child. Would you mind very much if I kissed you?"

"I could make it worth a hundred pounds to you—for nothing—if you gave us a clear field."

Simon wrinkled his nose.

"Are there forty-nine of you?" he drawled. "It seems a very small share-out to me."

"I might be able to make it two hundred. They wouldn't agree to any more."

The Saint blew smoke-rings towards the ceiling.

"If you could make it two thousand I don't think you'd be able to buy me off, darling. Being bought off is so dull. So what's the alternative? Am I slugged with another sandbag and locked up in the pantry?"

Suddenly he found that she was gripping his arm, looking straight into his face.

"I'm not thinking about your health, Saint," she said quietly. "I want that pendant. I want it more than I'd expect you to believe. I've never asked any other man a favour in my life. I know that in our racket men don't do women favours—without getting paid for it. But you're supposed to be different, aren't you?"

"This is a new act, Kate," murmured the Saint interestedly. "Do go on—I want to hear what the climax is."

"Do you think this is an act?"

"I don't want to be actually rude, darling, especially after all the dramatic fervour you put into it, but—"

"You've got every right to think so," she said, and he saw that the merriment was gone from her great brown eyes. "I should think the same way if I were in your place. I'll try to keep the dramatic fervour out of it. Can I tell you—that the pendant means the way out of the racket for me? I'm going straight after this." She was twisting her handkerchief, turning away from him now. "I'm going to get married—on the level. Funny, isn't it?"

He glanced at her doubtfully, with that mocking curve still lingering on his lips. For some reason he refrained from asking whether her other husbands had been informed of this plan: he knew nothing about her private life. But even with the best intentions a modern Robin Hood must get that way, and he did not know why he was silent.

And then, quite clearly, he heard the tread of leisurely feet on the other side of the clump of imported vegetation behind which they were concealed. Instinctively they glanced at one another, listening, and heard a man's fat chuckle beyond the palms.

"I guess this new plan makes it a lot easier than the way we were going to work it."

Simon saw the girl half rising from the settee. In a flash he had flung one arm round her, pinning her down, and clapped his other hand over her mouth.

"Maybe it'll save a little trouble, anyway," spoke the second man. There came the scratch of a match, and then: "What are you doing about the girl?"

"I don't know . . . She's a pretty little piece, but she's getting too serious. I'll have to ditch her in Paris."

"She'll be sore."

"Well, she ought to know how to take the breaks. I had to keep her going to get us in here, but it ain't my fault if she wants to make it a permanency."

"What about her share?"

"Aw, I might send her a couple a hundred, just for conscience money. She ain't a bad kid. Too sentimental, that's all."

A short pause, and then the second man again: "Well, that's your business. It's just a quarter after eleven. Guess I better see Watkins and make sure he's ready to fix those lights."

The leisured feet receded again, and Simon released the girl slowly. He saw that she was as white as a sheet, and there were strange tears in her eyes. He lighted a cigarette methodically. It was a tough life for women—always had been. They had to know how to take the breaks.

"Did you hear?" she asked, and he looked at her again.

"I couldn't very well help it. I'm sorry, kid . . . That was your prospective husband, I suppose?"

She nodded.

"Anyway, you'll know it wasn't an act."

There was nothing he could say. She stood up, and he walked beside her back to the ballroom. She left him there, with a smile that never trembled, and the Saint turned and found Peter Quentin beside him.

"Must you keep all the fun to yourself, old boy?" pleaded Peter forlornly. "I've been treading on the toes of the fattest dowager in the world. Who's your girlfriend? She looks a stunner."

"She stunned me once," said the Saint reminiscently. "Or some pals of hers did. She's passing here as Rosamund Armitage, but the police know her best as Kate Allfield, and her nickname is The Mug."

Peter's eyes were following the girl yearningly across the room.

"There ought to be some hideous punishment for bestowing names like that," he declared, and the Saint grinned absent-mindedly.

"I know. In a story-book she'd be Isabelle de la Fontaine, but her parents weren't thinking about her career when they christened her. That's real life in our low profession—and so is the nickname."

"Does that mean there's competition in the field?"

"It means just that." Simon's gaze was sweeping systematically over the other guests, and at that moment he saw the men he was looking for. "You see that dark bird who looks as if he might be a gigolo? Face like a pretty boy, till you see it's just a mask cut in granite . . . That's Philip Carney. And the big fellow beside him—just offering the Dempster-Craven a cigarette? That's George Runce. They're two of the slickest jewel thieves in the business. Mostly they work the Riviera—I don't think they've ever been in England before. Kate was talking in the plural all the time, and I wondered who she meant."

Peter's mouth shaped a silent whistle.

"What's going to happen?"

"I don't know definitely, but I should like to prophesy that at any moment the lights will go out—"

And as he spoke, with a promptness that seemed almost uncanny, the three enormous cut-glass chandeliers which illuminated the ballroom simultaneously flicked out as if a magic wand had conjured them out of existence, and the room was plunged into inky blackness.

The buzz of conversation rose louder, mingled with sporadic laughter. After trying valiantly to carry on for a couple of bars, the orchestra faded out irregularly, and the dancers shuffled to a standstill. Over in one corner, a facetious party started singing, in unison: "Where—was—Moses—when—the lights—went—out?" . . . And then, rising above every other sound, came Mrs Dempster-Craven's hysterical shriek:

"Help!"

There was a momentary silence, broken by a few uncertain titters. And Mrs Dempster-Craven's voice rang wildly through the room again.

"My pendant! My pendant! Put on the lights!"

Then came the sharp vicious smash of a fist against flesh and bone, a coughing grunt, and the thud of a fall. Peter Quentin felt around him, but the Saint had gone. He started across the room, plunging blindly among the crowd that was heaving helplessly in the darkness. Then one or two matches flared up, and the light grew as other matches and lighters were struck to augment the illumination. And just as suddenly as they had gone out, the great chandeliers lighted up again.

Peter Quentin looked at the scene from the front rank of the circle of guests. George Runce was lying on the floor, with blood trickling from a cut in his chin, and a couple of yards from him sat Simon Templar, holding his jaw tenderly. Between them lay Mrs Dempster-Craven's priceless pendant, with the chain broken, and while Peter looked she snatched it up with a sob, and he saw that the Star of Mandalay was missing from its centre.

"My diamond!" she wailed. "It's gone!"

Her private detective came elbowing through from the back of the crowd, pushing Peter aside, and grabbed the Saint's shoulder.

"Come on, you!" he barked. "What happened?"

"There's your man," said the Saint, pointing to the unconscious figure beside him. "As soon as the lights went out, he grabbed the pendant—"

"That's a lie!"

Philip Carney had fallen on his knees beside Runce, and was loosening the man's collar. He turned round and yapped the denial indignantly enough, but Peter saw that his face had gone pale.

"I was standing beside Mr Runce." He pointed to the Saint. "That man snatched the pendant, and Mr Runce tried to stop him getting away."

"Why weren't you here, Watkins?" wailed Mrs Dempster-Craven, shaking the detective wildly by the arm. "Why weren't you watching? I shall never see my diamond again—"

"I'm sorry, madam," said the detective. "I just left the room for one minute to find a glass of water. But I think we've got the man all right." He bent down and hauled the Saint to his feet. "We'd better search this fellow, and one of the footmen can go for the police while we're doing it."

Peter saw that the Saint's face had gone hard as polished teak. In Simon's right hand was the Star of Mandalay, pressed against his jaw as he was holding it. As soon as the lights had gone out he had guessed what was going to happen: he had crossed the floor like a cat, grasped it neatly as Runce tore it out of its setting, and sent the big man flying with one well-directed left. All that he had been prepared for, but there were wheels turning that he had never reckoned with.

He looked the detective in the eyes.

"The less you talk about the police the better," he said quietly. "I was in the conservatory a few minutes ago, and I happened to hear Mr Carney say: "I'd better see Watkins and make sure he's ready to fix those lights." I didn't think anything of it at the time, but this looks like an explanation."

There was an instant's deadly silence, and then Philip Carney laughed.

"That's one of the cleverest tricks I've ever heard of," he remarked. "But it's a bit libellous, isn't it?"

"Not very," said a girl's clear voice.

Again the murmur of talk was stifled as if a blanket had been dropped on it, and in the hush Kate Allfield came into the front of the crowd. George Runce was rising on his elbows, and his jaw dropped as he heard her voice. She gave him one contemptuous glance, and faced Mrs Dempster-Craven with her head erect.

"It's perfectly true," she said. "I was with Mr Templar in the conservatory, and I heard it as well."

Carney's face had gone grey.

"The girl's raving," he said, but his voice was a little shaky. "I haven't been in the conservatory this evening."

"Neither have I," said Runce, wiping the frozen incredulity off his features with an effort. "I'll tell you what it is—"

But he did not tell them what it was, for at that point a fresh authoritative voice interrupted the debate with a curt "Make way, please," and the crowd opened to let through the burly figure of a detective-sergeant in plainclothes. Simon looked round, and saw that he had posted a constable at the door as he came in. The sergeant scanned the faces of the group, and addressed Mrs Dempster-Craven.

"What's the trouble, madam?"

"My pendant—"

She was helped out by a chorus of bystanders whose information, taken in the mass, was somewhat confusing. The sergeant sorted it out phlegmatically, and at the end he shrugged.

"Since these gentlemen are all accusing each other, I take it you don't wish to make any particular charges?"

"I cannot accuse my guests of being thieves," said Mrs Dempster-Craven imperially. "I only want my diamond."

The sergeant nodded. He had spent twelve years in C Division, and had learned that Berkeley Square is a region where even policemen have to be tactful.

"In that case," he said, "I think it would help us if the gentlemen agreed to be searched."

The Saint straightened up.

It had been a good evening, and he had no regrets. The game was worth playing for its own sake, to him: the prizes came welcomely, but they weren't everything. And no one knew better than he that you couldn't win all the time. There were chances that couldn't be reckoned with in advance, and the duplicity of Mr Watkins was one of those. But for that, he would have played his hand faultlessly, out-bluffed and out-manoeuvred the Carney-Runce combination in a fair field, and made as clean a job of it as anything else he had done. But that single unexpected factor had turned the scale just enough to bring the bluff to a show-down, as unexpected factors always would. And yet Peter Quentin saw the Saint was smiling.

"I think that's a good idea," said the Saint.

Between Philip Carney and George Runce flashed one blank glance, but their mouths remained closed.

"Perhaps there's another room we could go to," said the sergeant, almost genially, and Mrs Dempster-Craven inclined her head like a queen dismissing a distasteful odour.

"Watkins will show you to the library."

Simon turned on his heel and led the way towards the door, with Mr Watkins still gripping his arms, but as his path brought him level with Kate Allfield he stopped and smiled down at her.

"I think you're a swell kid," he said.

His voice sounded a trifle strange. And then, before two hundred shocked and startled eyes, including those of Lord and Lady Bredon, the Honourable Celia Mallard, three baronets, and the aspiring Mrs Dempster-Craven herself, he laid his hands gently on her shoulders and kissed her outrageously on the mouth; and in the silence of appalled aristocracy which followed that performance made his stately exit.

"How the devil did you get away with it?" asked Peter Quentin weakly, as they drove away in a taxi an hour later. "I was fairly sweating blood all the time you were being stripped."

The Saint's face showed up in the dull glow as he drew at his cigarette.

"It was in my mouth," he said.

"But they made you open your mouth—"

"It was there when I kissed Kate, anyway," said the Saint, and sang to himself all the rest of the way home.

THE GREEN GOODS MAN

"The secret of contentment," said Simon Templar oratorically, "is to take things as they come. As is the daily office-work of the City hog in his top hat to the moments when he signs his supreme mergers, so are the bread-and-butter exploits of a pirate to his great adventures. After all, one can't always be ploughing through thrilling escapes and captures with guns popping in all directions, but there are always people who'll give you money. You don't even have to look for them. You just put on a monocle and the right expression of half-wittedness, and they come up and tip their purses into your lap."

He offered this pearl of thought for the approval of his usual audience, and it is a regrettable fact that neither of them disputed his philosophy. Patricia Holm knew him too well, and even Peter Quentin had by that time walked in the ways of Saintly lawlessness long enough to know that such pronouncements inevitably heralded another of the bread-and-butter exploits referred to. It wasn't, of course, strictly true that Simon Templar was in need of bread and butter, but he liked jam with it, and a generous world had always provided him abundantly with both.

Benny Lucek came over from New York on a falling market to try his luck in the Old World. He had half a dozen natty suits which fitted him so well that he always looked as if he would have burst open from his wrists to his hips if his blood-pressure had risen two degrees; he had a selection of mauve and pink silk shirts in his wardrobe trunk, pointed and beautifully polished shoes for his feet, a pearl pin for his tie, and no less than three rings for his fingers. His frankly Hebraic features radiated honesty, candour, and good humour, and as a stock-in-trade those gifts alone were worth several figures of solid cash to him in any state of the market. Also he still had a good deal of capital, without which no Green Goods man can even begin to operate.

Benny Lucek was one of the last great exponents of that gentle graft, and although they had been telling him in New York that the game was played out, he had roseate hopes of finding virgin soil for a new crop of successes among the benighted *bourgeoisie* of Europe. So far as he knew, the Green Goods ground had scarcely been touched on the eastern side of the Atlantic, and Benny had come across to look it over. He installed himself in a comfortable suite on the third floor of the Park Lane Hotel, changed his capital into English bank-notes, and sent out his feelers into space.

In the most popular Personal Columns appeared temptingly-worded advertisements of which the one that Simon Templar saw was a fair specimen.

> *ANY LADY or GENTLEMAN in reduced circumstances, who would be interested in an enterprise showing GREAT PROFITS for a NEGLIGIBLE RISK, should write in STRICT CONFIDENCE, giving some personal information, to Box No.—*

Benny Lucek knew everything there was to know about letters. He was a practical graphologist of great astuteness, and a deductive psychologist of vast experience. Given a two-page letter which on the surface conveyed the vaguest particulars about the writer, he could build up in his mind a character study with a complete background filled in that fitted his subject without a wrinkle ninety-nine times out of a hundred; and if the mental picture he formed of a certain Mr Tombs, whose reply to that advertisement was included among several scores of others, was one of the hundredth times, it might not have been entirely Benny's fault. Simon Templar was also a specialist in letters, although his art was creative instead of critical.

Patricia came in one morning and found him performing another creative feat at which he was no less adept.

"What on earth are you doing in those clothes?" she asked, when she had looked at him.

Simon glanced over himself in the mirror. His dark blue suit was neat but unassuming, and had a well-worn air as if it were the only one he possessed and had been cared for with desperate pride. His shoes were old and strenuously polished; his socks dark grey and woollen, carefully darned. He wore a cheap pin-striped poplin shirt, and a stiff white collar without one saving grace of line. His tie was dark blue, like his suit, and rather stringy. Across his waistcoat hung an old-fashioned silver watch-chain. Anything less like the Simon Templar of normal times, who always somehow infused into the suits of Savile Row a flamboyant personality of his own, and whose shirts and socks and ties were the envy of the young men who drank with him in the few clubs which he belonged to, it would have been almost impossible to imagine.

"I am a hard-working clerk in an insurance office, earning three hundred a year with the dim prospect of rising to three hundred and fifty in another fifteen years, age about forty, with an anaemic wife and seven children and a semi-detached house at Streatham." He was fingering his face speculatively, staring at it in the glass. "A little too beautiful for the part at present, I think, but we'll soon put that right."

He set to work on his face with the quick unhesitating touches of which he was such an amazing master. His eyebrows, brushed in towards his nose, turned grey and bushy; his hair also turned grey, and was plastered down to his skull so skilfully that it seemed inevitable that any barber he went to would remark that he was running a little thin on top. Under the movements of his swift fingers, cunning shadows appeared at the sides of his forehead, under his eyes, and around his chin—shadows so faint that even at a yard's range their artificiality could not have been detected, and yet so cleverly placed that they seemed to change the whole shape and expression of his face. And while he worked he talked.

"If you ever read a story-book, Pat, in which anyone disguises himself as someone else so perfectly that the impersonated bloke's own friends and secretaries and servants are taken in, you'll know there's an author who's cheating on you. On the stage it might be done up to a point, but in real life, where everything you put on has got to get by in broad daylight and close-ups, it's impossible. I," said the Saint unblushingly, "am the greatest character actor that never went on the stage, and I know. But when it comes to inventing a new character of your own that mustn't be recognized again—then you can do things."

He turned round suddenly, and she gasped. He was perfect. His shoulders were rounded and stooping; his head was bent slightly forward, as if set in that position by years of poring over ledgers. And he gazed at her with the dumb passionless expression of his part—an under-nourished, under-exercised, middle-aged man without hopes or ambitions, permanently worried, crushed out of pleasure by the wanton taxation which goes to see that the paladins of Whitehall are never deprived of an afternoon's golf, utterly resigned to the sombre purposelessness of his existence, scraping and pinching through fifty weeks of the year in order to let himself be stodgily swindled at the seaside for a fortnight in August, solemnly discussing the antics of politicians as if they really mattered and honestly believing that their cow-like utterances might do something to alleviate his burdens, holding a crumbling country together with his own dour stoicism and the stoicism of millions of his own kind . . .

"Will I do?" he asked.

From Benny Lucek's point of view he could scarcely have done better. Benny's keen eyes absorbed the whole atmosphere of him in one calculating glance that took in every detail from the grey hair that was running a little thin on top down to the strenuously polished shoes.

"Please to meet you, Mr Tombs. Come along and have a cocktail—I expect you could do with one."

He led his guest into the sumptuous lounge, and Mr Tombs sat down gingerly on the edge of a chair. It is impossible to refer to that man of the Saint's creation as anything but "Mr Tombs"—the Simon Templar whom Patricia knew might never have existed inside that stoical stoop-shouldered frame.

"Er . . . a glass of sherry, perhaps," he said.

Benny ordered Amontillado, and knew that the only sherry Mr Tombs had ever tasted before came from the nearest grocer. But he was an expert at putting strangers at their ease, and the Simon Templar who stood invisibly behind Mr Tombs's chair had to admire his technique. He chattered away with a disarming lack of condescension that presently had Mr Tombs leaning back and chuckling with him, and ordering a return round of Amontillados with the feeling that he had at last met a successful man who really understood and appreciated him. They went in to lunch with Benny roaring with infectious laughter over a vintage Stock Exchange story which Mr Tombs had dug out of his memory.

"Smoked salmon, Mr Tombs? Or a spot of caviar? . . . Then we might have *oeufs en cocotte Rossini*—done in cream with *foie gras* and truffles. And roast pigeons with mushrooms and red currant jelly. I like a light meal in the middle of the day—it doesn't make you sleepy all the afternoon. And a bottle of Liebfraumilch off the ice to go with it?"

He ran through menu and wine list with an engaging expertness which somehow made Mr Tombs an equal partner in the exercise of gastronomic virtuosity. And Mr Tombs, whose imagination had rarely soared above roast beef and Yorkshire pudding and a bottle of Australian burgundy, thawed still further and recalled another story that had provoked howls of laughter in Threadneedle Street when he was in his twenties.

Benny did his work so well that the sordid business aspect of their meeting never had a chance to obtrude itself during the meal, and yet he managed to find out everything he wanted to know about his guest's private life and opinions. Liquefying helplessly in the genial warmth of Benny's hospitality, Mr Tombs became almost human. And Benny drew him on with unhurried mastery.

"I've always thought that insurance must be an interesting profession, Mr Tombs. You've got to be pretty wide awake for it too—I expect you always have clients who expect to take more out of you than they put in?"

Mr Tombs, who had never found his job interesting, and who would never have detected an attempted fraud unless another department had pointed it out to him, smiled non-committally.

"That kind of mixed morality has always interested me," said Benny, as if the point had only just occurred to him. "A man who wouldn't steal a sixpence from a man he met in the street hasn't any objection to stealing half-crowns from the Government by cutting down his income-tax return or smuggling home a bottle of brandy when he comes across from France. If he's looking for a partner in business he wouldn't dream of putting a false value on his assets, but if his house is burgled he doesn't mind what value he puts on his things when he's making out his insurance claim."

Mr Tombs shrugged.

"I suppose Governments and wealthy public companies are considered fair game," he hazarded.

"Well, probably there's a certain amount of lawlessness in the best of us," admitted Benny. "I've often wondered what I should do myself in certain circumstances. Suppose, for instance, you were going home in a taxi one night, and you found a wallet on the seat with a thousand pounds in it. Small notes that you could easily change. No name inside to show who the owner was. Wouldn't one be tempted to keep it?"

Mr Tombs twiddled a fork, hesitating only for a second or two. But the Simon Templar who stood behind his chair knew that that was the question on which Benny Lucek's future hung—the point that had been so casually and skilfully led up to, which would finally settle whether "Mr Tombs" was the kind of man Benny wanted to meet. And yet there was no trace of anxiety or watchfulness in Benny's frank open face. Benny tilted the last of the Liebfraumilch into Mr Tombs's glass, and Mr Tombs looked up.

"I suppose I should. It sounds dishonest, but I was trying to put myself in the position of being faced with the temptation, instead of theorizing about it. Face to face with a thousand pounds in cash, and needing money to take my wife abroad, I might easily . . . er . . . succumb. Not that I mean to imply—"

"My dear fellow, I'm not going to blame you," said Benny heartily. "I'd do the same thing myself. I'd reason it out that a man who carried a thousand pounds in cash about with him had plenty more in the bank. It's the old story of fair-game. We may be governed by plenty of laws, but our consciences are still very primitive when we've no fear of being caught."

There was a silence after that, in which Mr Tombs finished his last angel on horse-back, mopped the plate furtively with the last scrap of toast, and accepted a cigarette from Benny's platinum case. The pause gave him his first chance to remember that he was meeting the sympathetic Mr Lucek in order to hear about a business proposition—as Benny intended that it should. As a waiter approached with the bill, Mr Tombs said tentatively, "About your . . . um . . . advertisement . . ."

Benny scrawled his signature across the account, and pushed back his chair.

"Come up to my sitting room and we'll talk about it."

They went up in the lift, with Benny unconcernedly puffing Turkish cigarette-smoke, and down an expensively carpeted corridor. Benny had an instinctive sense of dramatic values. Without saying anything, and yet at the same time without giving the impression that he was being intentionally reticent, he opened the door of his suite and ushered Mr Tombs in.

The sitting room was small but cosily furnished. A large carelessly-opened brown-paper parcel littered the table in the centre, and there was a similar amount of litter in one of the chairs. Benny picked up an armful of it and dumped it on the floor in the corner.

"Know what these things are?" he asked off-handedly.

He took up a handful of the litter that remained on the chair and thrust it under Mr Tombs's nose. It was generally green in colour, as Mr Tombs blinked at it, words and patterns took shape on it, and he blinked still harder.

"Pound notes," said Benny. He pointed to the pile he had dumped in the corner. "More of 'em." He flattened the brown paper around the carelessly-opened parcel on the table, revealing neat stacks of treasure packed in thick uniform bundles. "Any amount of it. Help yourself."

Mr Tombs's blue eyes went wider and wider, with the lids blinking over them rapidly as if to dispel a hallucination.

"Are they . . . are they really all pound notes?"

"Every one of 'em."

"All yours?"

"I guess so. I made 'em, anyway."

"There must be thousands."

Benny flung himself into the cleared armchair.

"I'm about the richest man in the world, Mr Tombs," he said. "I guess I must be the richest, because I can make money as fast as I can turn a handle. I meant exactly what I said to you just now. I made those notes!"

Mr Tombs touched the pile with his finger-tips, as if he half expected them to bite him. His eyes were rounder and wider than ever.

"You don't mean—forgeries," he whispered.

"I don't," said Benny. "Take those notes round to the nearest bank—tell the cashier you have your doubts about them—and ask him to look them over. Take 'em to the Bank of England. There isn't a forgery in the whole lot—but I made 'em! Sit down and I'll tell you."

Mr Tombs sat down, stiffly. His eyes kept straying back to the heaps of wealth on the floor and the table, as though at each glance he would have been relieved rather than surprised if they had vanished.

"It's like this, Mr Tombs. I'm taking you into my confidence because I've known you a couple of hours and I've made up my mind about you. I like you. Those notes, Mr Tombs, were printed from a proof plate that was stolen out of the Bank of England itself by a fellow who worked there. He was in the engraving department, and when they were making the plates they made one more than they needed. It was given to him to destroy—and he didn't destroy it. He was like the man we were talking about—the man in the taxi. He had a genuine plate that would print genuine pound notes, and he could keep it for himself if he wanted to. All he had to do was to make an imitation plate that no one was going to examine closely—you can't tell a lot from a plate, just looking at it—and cut a couple of lines across it to cancel it. Then that would be locked up in the vaults and probably never looked at again, and he'd have the real one. He didn't even know quite what he'd do with the plate when he had it, but he kept it. And then he got scared about it being found out, and he ran away. He went over to New York, where I come from.

"He stopped in the place I lived at, over in Brooklyn. I got to know him a bit, though he was always very quiet and seemed to have something on his mind. I didn't ask what it was, and I didn't care. Then he got pneumonia.

"Nobody else had ever paid any attention to him, so it seemed to be up to me. I did what I could for him—it didn't amount to much, but he appreciated it. I paid some of the rent he owed. The doctor found he was half starved—he'd landed in New York with just a few pounds, and when those were gone he'd lived on the leavings he could beg from chop-houses. He was starving himself to death with a million pounds in his grip! But I didn't know that then. He got worse and worse, and then they had to give him oxygen one night, but the doctor said he wouldn't see the morning anyhow. He'd starved himself till he was too weak to get well again.

"He came round just before the end, and I was with him. He just looked at me and said, 'Thanks, Benny.' And then he told me all about himself and what he'd done. 'You keep the plate,' he said. 'It may be some good to you.'

"Well, he died in the morning, and the landlady told me to hurry up and get his things out of the way as there was another lodger coming in. I took 'em off to my own room. There wasn't much, but I found the plate.

"Maybe you can imagine what it meant to me, after I'd got it all figured out. I was just an odd-job man in a garage then, earning a few dollars a week. I was the man in the taxi again. But I had a few dollars saved up: I'd have to find the right paper, and get the notes printed—I didn't know anything about the technical side of it. It'd cost money, but if it went through all right that poor fellow's legacy would make me a millionaire. He'd starved to death because he was too scared to try it; had I got the guts?"

Benny Lucek closed his eyes momentarily, as if he were reliving the struggle with his conscience.

"You can see for yourself which way I decided," he said. "It took time and patience, but it was still the quickest way of making a million I'd ever heard of. That was six years ago. I don't know how much money I've got in the bank now, but I know it's more than I can ever spend. And it was like that all of three years ago.

"And then I started thinking about the other people who needed money, and I began to square my conscience by helping them, I was working over in the States then, of course, changing this English money in small packets at banks all over the continent. And I started giving it away—charities, down-and-outs, any good thing I could think of. That was all right so far as it went. But then I started thinking, that fellow who gave me the plate was English, and some of the money ought to go back to people in England who needed it. That's why I came across. Did I tell you that fellow left a wife behind when he ran away? It took me two months to find her with the best agents I could buy, but I located her at last serving in a tea-shop, and now I've set her on her feet for life, though she thinks it was an uncle she never had who died and left her the money. But if I can find any other fellow whose wife needs some money he can't earn for her," said Benny nobly, "I want to help him too."

Mr Tombs swallowed. Benny Lucek was a master of elocution among his other talents, and the manner of his recital was calculated to bring a lump into the throat of an impressionable listener.

"Would you like some money, Mr Tombs?" he inquired.

Mr Tombs coughed.

"I . . . er . . . well . . . I can't quite get over the story you've told me."

He picked up a handful of the notes, peered at them minutely, screwed them in his fingers, and put them down again rather abruptly and experimentally, as if he were trying to discover whether putting temptation from him would bring a glow of conscious virtue that would compensate for the worldly loss. Apparently the experiment was not very satisfactory, for his mouth puckered wistfully.

"You've told me all about yourself," said Benny. "And about your wife being delicate and needing to go away for a long sea voyage. I expect there's trouble about getting your children a proper education that you haven't mentioned at all. You're welcome to put all that right. You can buy just as many of those notes as you like, and twenty pounds per hundred is the price to you. That's exactly what they cost me in getting the special paper and inks and having them printed—the man I found to print 'em for me gets a big rake-off, of course. Four shillings each is the cost price, and you can make yourself a millionaire if you want to."

Mr Tombs gulped audibly.

"You're . . . you're not pulling my leg, are you?" he stammered pathetically.

"Of course I'm not. I'm glad to do it." Benny stood up and placed one hand affectionately on Mr Tombs's shoulders. "Look here, I know all this must have been a shock to you. It wants a bit of getting used to. Why don't you go away and think it over? Come and have lunch with me again tomorrow, if you want some of these notes, and bring the money with you to pay for them. Call me at seven o'clock and let me know if I'm to expect you." He picked up a small handful of money and stuffed it into Mr Tombs's pocket. "Here—take some samples with you and try them on a bank, just in case you still can't believe it."

Mr Tombs nodded, blinking.

"I'm the man in the taxi again," he said with a weak smile. "When you really do find the wallet—"

"Who loses by it?" asked Benny, with gently persuasive rhetoric. "The Bank of England, eventually. I never learnt any economics, but I suppose they'll have to meet the bill. But are they going to be any the worse off for the few thousands you'll take out of them? Why, it won't mean any more to them than a penny does to you now. Think it over."

"I will," said Mr Tombs, with a last lingering stare at the littered table.

"There's just one other thing," said Benny. "Not a word of what I've told you to any living soul—not even to your wife. I'm trusting you to treat it as confidentially as you'd treat anything in your insurance business. You can see why, can't you? A story like I've told you would spread like wild-fire, and once it got to the Bank of England there'd be no more money in it. They'd change the design of their notes and call in all the old ones as quick as I can say it."

"I understand, Mr Lucek," said Mr Tombs.

He understood perfectly—so well that the rapturous tale he told to Patricia Holm when he returned was almost incoherent. He told her while he was removing his make-up and changing back into his ordinary clothes, and when he had finished he was as immaculate and debonair as she had ever seen him. And finally he smoothed out the notes that Benny had given him at parting, and stowed them carefully in his wallet. He looked at his watch.

"Let's go and look at a non-stop show, darling," he said, "and then we'll buy a pailful of caviar between us and swill it down with a gallon of Cordon Rouge. Brother Benjamin will pay!"

"But are you sure these notes are perfect?" she asked, and the Saint laughed.

"My sweetheart, every one of those notes was printed by the Bank of England itself. The Green Goods game is nothing like that, though I've often wondered why it hasn't been worked before in this—*Gott in Himmel!*"

Simon Templar suddenly leapt into the air with a yell, and the startled girl stared at him.

"What in the name of—"

"Just an idea," explained the Saint. "They sometimes take me in the seat of the pants like that. This is rather a beauty."

He swept her off boisterously to the promised celebrations without telling her what the idea was that had made him spring like a young ram with loud foreign oaths, but at seven o'clock punctually he found time to telephone the Park Lane Hotel.

"I'm going to do what the man in the taxi would do, Mr Lucek," he said.

"Well, Mr Tombs, that's splendid news," responded Benny. "I'll expect you at one. By the way, how much will you be taking?"

"I'm afraid I can only manage to . . . um . . . raise three hundred pounds. That will buy fifteen hundred pounds' worth, won't it?"

"I'll make it two thousand pounds' worth to you, Mr Tombs," said Benny generously. "I'll have it all ready for you when you come."

Mr Tombs presented himself at five minutes to one, and although he wore the same suit of clothes as he had worn the previous day, there was a festive air about him to which a brand-new pair of white kid gloves and a carnation in his buttonhole colourfully contributed.

"I handed in my resignation at the office this morning," he said. "And I hope I never see the place again."

Benny was congratulatory but apologetic.

"I'm afraid we shall have to postpone our lunch," he said. "I've been investigating a lady who also answered my advertisement—a poor old widow living up in Derbyshire. Her husband deserted her twenty years ago, and her only son, who's been keeping her ever since, was killed in a motor accident yesterday. It seems as if she needs a fairy godfather quickly, and I'm going to dash up to Derbyshire in a special train and see what I can do."

Mr Tombs suppressed a perfunctory tear, and accompanied Benny to his suite. A couple of well-worn suitcases and a wardrobe trunk the size of a suburban villa, already stacked up and labelled, confirmed

Benny's avowed intentions. Only one of the parcels of currency was visible, pushed untidily to one end of the table.

"Did you bring the money, Mr Tombs?"

Mr Tombs took out his battered wallet and drew forth a sheaf of crisp new fivers with slightly unsteady hands. Benny took them, glanced over them casually, and dropped them on to the table with the carelessness befitting a millionaire. He waved Mr Tombs into an armchair with his back to the window, and himself sat down in a chair drawn up to the opposite side of the table.

"Two thousand one-pound notes are quite a lot to put in your pocket," he remarked. "I'll make them up into a parcel for you."

Under Mr Tombs's yearning eyes he flipped off the four top bundles from the piles and tossed them one by one into his guest's lap. Mr Tombs grabbed them and examined them hungrily, spraying the edges of each pack off his thumb so that pound notes whirred before his vision like the pictures on a toy cinematograph.

"You can count them if you like—there ought to be five hundred in each pack," said Benny, but Mr Tombs shook his head.

"I'll take your word for it, Mr Lucek. I can see they're all one-pound notes, and there must be a lot of them."

Benny smiled and held out his hand with a business-like air. Mr Tombs passed the bundles back to him, and Benny sat down again and arranged them in a neat cube on top of a sheet of brown paper. He turned the paper over the top and creased it down at the open ends with a rapid efficiency that would have done credit to any professional shop assistant, and Mr Tombs's covetous eyes watched every movement with the intenseness of a dumb but earnest audience trying to spot how a conjuring trick is done.

"Don't you think it would be a ghastly tragedy for a poor widow who put all her savings into these notes and found that she had been . . .

um . . . deceived?" said Mr Tombs morbidly, and Benny's dark eyes switched up to his face in sudden startlement.

"Eh?" said Benny. "What's that?"

But Mr Tombs's careworn face had the innocence of a patient sheep's.

"Just something I was thinking, Mr Lucek," he said.

Benny grinned his expansive display of pearly teeth, and continued with his packing. Mr Tombs's gaze continued to concentrate on him with an almost mesmeric effect, but Benny was not disturbed. He had spent nearly an hour that morning making and testing his preparations. The upper sash-cords of the window behind Mr Tombs's chair had been cut through all but the last thread, and the weight of the sash was carried on a small steep peg driven into the frame. From the steel peg a thin but very strong dark-coloured string ran down to the floor, pulleyed round a nail driven into the base of the wainscoting, and disappeared under the carpet; it pulleyed round another nail driven into the floor under the table, and came up through a hole in the carpet alongside one leg to loop conveniently over the handle of the drawer.

Benny completed the knots around his parcel, and searched around for something to trim off the loose ends.

"There you are, Mr Tombs," he said, and then, in his fumbling, he caught the convenient loop of string and tugged at it. The window fell with a crash.

And Mr Tombs did not look round.

It was the most flabbergasting thing that had ever happened in Benny Lucek's experience. It was supernatural—incredible. It was a phenomenon so astounding that Benny's mouth fell open involuntarily, while a balloon of incredulous stupefaction bulged up in the pit of his stomach and cramped his lungs. There came over him the feeling of preposterous injury that would have assailed a practised bus-jumper who, preparing to board a moving bus as it came by, saw it evade him by rising vertically into the air and soaring away over the house-tops. It was simply one of the things that did not happen.

And on this fantastic occasion it had happened. In the half-opened drawer that pressed against Benny's tummy, just below the level of the table and out of range of Mr Tombs's glassy stare, was another brown-paper parcel exactly similar in every respect to the one which Benny was finishing off. Outwardly, that is. Inside, there was a difference; for whereas inside the parcel which Benny had prepared before Mr Tombs's eyes there were undoubtedly two thousand authentic one-pound notes, inside the second parcel there was only a collection of old newspapers and magazines cut to precisely the same size. And never before in Benny's career, once the fish had taken the hook, had those two parcels failed to be successfully exchanged. That was what the providentially falling window was arranged for and it constituted the whole simple secret of the Green Goods game. The victim, when he got home and opened the parcel and discovered how he had been swindled, could not make a complaint to the police without admitting that he himself had been ready to aid and abet a fraud, and forty-nine times out of fifty he would decide that it was better to stand the loss and keep quiet about it. Elementary, but effective. And yet the whole structure could be scuppered by the unbelievable apathy of a victim who failed to react to the stimulus of a loud bang as any normal human being should have reacted.

"The . . . the window seems to have fallen down," Benny pointed out hoarsely, and felt like a hero of a melodrama who has just shot the villain in the appointed place at the end of the third act, and sees him smilingly declining to fall down and die according to the rehearsed script.

"Yes," agreed Mr Tombs cordially. "I heard it."

"The . . . the sash-cords must have broken."

"Probably that's what it was."

"Funny thing to happen so . . . so suddenly, wasn't it?"

"Very funny," assented Mr Tombs, keeping up the conversation politely.

Benny began to sweat. The substitute parcel was within six inches of his hovering hands: given only two seconds with the rapt stare of those unblinking eyes diverted from him, he could have rung the changes as easily as unbuttoning his shirt, but the chance was not given. It was an impasse that he had never even dreamed of, and the necessity of thinking up something to cope with it on the spur of the moment stampeded him to the borders of panic.

"Have you got a knife?" asked Benny, with perspiring heartiness. "Something to cut off this end of string?"

"Let me break it for you," said Mr Tombs.

He stood up and moved towards the table, and Benny shied like a horse.

"Don't bother, please, Mr Tombs," he gulped. "I'll . . . I'll . . ."

"No trouble at all," said Mr Tombs.

Benny grabbed the parcel, and dropped it. He was a very fine strategist and dramatic reciter, but he was not a man of violence—otherwise he might have been tempted to act differently. That grab and drop was the last artifice he could think of to save the day.

He pushed his chair back and bent down, groping for the fallen parcel with one hand and the substitute parcel with the other. In raising the fallen packet past the table the exchange might be made.

His left hand found the parcel on the floor. His right hand went on groping. It ran up and down the drawer, sensitively at first, then frantically. It plunged backwards and forwards. His fingernails scrabbled on the wood . . . He became aware that he couldn't stay in that position indefinitely, and began to straighten up slowly, with a cold sensation closing on his heart. And as his eyes came up to the level of the drawer he saw that the dummy parcel had somehow got pushed right away to the back: for all the use it would have been to him there it might have been in the middle of the Arizona desert.

Mr Tombs smiled blandly.

"It's quite easy, really," he said.

He took the parcel from Benny's nerveless hand, put it on the table, twisted the loose end of the string round his forefinger, and jerked. It snapped off clean and short.

"A little trick of mine," said Mr Tombs chattily. He picked up the parcel and held out his hand. "Well, Mr Lucek, you must know how grateful I am. You mustn't let me keep you any longer from your . . . um . . . widow. Goodbye, Mr Lucek."

He wrung Benny Lucek's limp fingers effusively, and retired towards the door. There was something almost sprightly in his gait, a twinkle in his blue eyes that had certainly not been there before, a seraphic benevolence about his smile that made Benny go hot and cold. It didn't belong to Mr Tombs of the insurance office . . .

"Hey—just a minute!" gasped Benny, but the door had closed. Benny jumped up, panting. "Hey, you—"

He flung open the door, and looked into the cherubic pink full-moon face of a very large gentleman in a superfluous overcoat and a bowler hat who stood on the threshold.

"Morning, Mr Lucek," said the large gentleman sedately. "May I come in?"

He took the permission for granted, and advanced into the sitting room. The parcel on the table attracted his attention first, and he took up a couple of bundles from the stack and looked them over. Only the top notes in each bundle were genuine pound notes, as the four whole bundles which departed with Mr Tombs had been: the rest of the thickness was made up with sheets of paper cut to the same size.

"Very interesting," remarked the large gentleman.

"Who the devil are you?" blustered Benny, and the round rosy face turned to him with a very sudden and authoritative directness.

"I am Chief Inspector Teal, of Scotland Yard, and I have information that you are in possession of quantities of forged banknotes."

Benny drew breath again hesitatingly.

"That's absurd, Mr Teal. You won't find any phoney stuff here," he said, and then the detective's cherubic gaze fell on the sheaf of five-pound notes that Mr Tombs had left behind in payment.

He picked them up and examined them casually, one by one.

"Hm—and not very good forgeries, either," he said, and called to the sergeant who was waiting in the corridor outside.

THE BLIND SPOT

It is rather trite to remark that the greatest and sublimest characters always have concealed in them somewhere a speck of human jelly that wobbles furtively behind the imposing armour-plate, as if Nature's sense of proportion refused to tolerate such a thing as a perfect superman. Achilles had his heel. The hard-boiled hoodlum of the Volstead Act weeps openly to the strains of a syncopated Mammy song. The learned judge gravely inquires: "What is a gooseberry?" The Cabinet Minister prances pontifically about the badminton court. The professor of theology knows the Saint Saga as well as the Epistle to the Ephesians. These things are familiar to every student of the popular newspapers.

But to Simon Templar they were more than mere curious facts, to be ranked with "Believe-it-or-not" strips of cigarette-cards describing the architectural principles of the igloo. They were the very practical psychology of his profession.

"Every man on earth has at least one blind spot somewhere," Simon used to say, "and once you've found that spot you've got him. There's always some simple little thing that'll undermine his resistance, or simple little trick that he's never heard of. A high-class cardsharper might never persuade him to play bridge for more than a halfpenny a hundred, and yet a three-card man at Brooklands might take a fiver off him in five minutes. Develop that into a complete technique, and you can live in luxury without running any risks of getting brain fever."

One of Simon Templar's minor weaknesses was an insatiable curiosity. He met Patricia at Charing Cross underground station one afternoon with a small brown bottle.

"A man at the Irving Statue sold me this for a shilling," he said.

The broad reach of pavement around the Irving Statue, at the junction of Green Street and Charing Cross Road, is one of the greatest open-air theatres in London. Every day, at lunch-time, idle crowds gather there in circles around the performers on the day's bill, who carry on their work simultaneously like a three-ring circus. There is the Anti-Socialist tub-thumper, the numerologist, the strong man, the negro selling outfits to enable you to do the three-card trick in your own home, the handcuff escape king, the patent medicine salesman, every kind of huckster and street showman takes up his pitch there on one day or another and holds his audience spellbound until the time comes for passing round the hat. Simon rarely passed there without pausing to inspect the day's offerings, but this was the first occasion on which he had been a buyer.

His bottle appeared to contain a colourless fluid like water, with a slight sediment of brownish particles.

"What is it?" asked Patricia.

"Chromium plating for the home," he said. "The greatest invention of the century—according to the salesman. Claimed to be the same outfit sold by mail-order firms for three bob. He was demonstrating it on a brass shell-case and an old Primus and brass door-knobs and what not, and it looked swell. Here, I'll show you."

He fished a penny out of his pocket, uncorked the bottle, and poured a drop of the liquid on to the coin. The tarnished copper cleared and silvered itself under her eyes, and when he rubbed it with his handkerchief it took a silvery polish like stainless steel.

"Boy, that's marvellous!" breathed Patricia dreamily. "You know that military sort of coat of mine, the one with the brass buttons? We were wanting to get them chromiumed—"

The Saint sighed.

"And that," he said, "is approximately what the cave woman thought of first when her battle-scarred Man dragged home a vanquished leopard. My darling, when will you realize that we are first and foremost a business organization?"

But at that moment he had no clear idea of the profitable purposes to which his purchase might be put. The Saint had an instinct and a collecting passion for facts and gadgets that "might come in useful," but at the times when he acquired them he could rarely have told you what use they were ever likely to be.

He corked the bottle and put it away in his pocket. The train they were waiting for was signalled, and the rumble of its approach could be felt underfoot. Down in the blackness of the tunnel its lights swept round a bend and drove towards the platform, and it was quite by chance that the Saint's wandering glance flickered over the shabbily-dressed elderly man who waited a yard away on his left, and fixed on him with a sudden razor-edged intentness that was more intuitive than logical. Or perhaps the elderly man's agitation was too transparent to be ordinary, his eyes too strained and haggard to be reassuring . . . Simon didn't know.

The leading draught of the train fanned on his face, and then the elderly man clenched his fists and jumped. A woman screamed. "You blithering idiot!" snapped the Saint, and jumped also.

His feet touched down neatly inside the track. By some brilliant fluke the shabby man's blind leap had missed the live rail, and he was simply cowering where he had landed with one arm covering his eyes. The train was hardly more than a yard away when the Saint picked him up and heaved him back on to the platform, flinging himself off the line in the opposite direction as he did so. The train whisked so close to him that it brushed his sleeve, and squeaked to a standstill with hissing brakes.

The Saint slid back the nearest door on his side, swung himself up from the track, and stepped through the coach to the platform. A small crowd had gathered round the object of his somewhat sensational rescue, and Simon shouldered a path through them unceremoniously. He knew that one of the many sublimely intelligent laws of England ordains that any person who attempts to take his own life shall, if he survives, be prosecuted and at the discretion of the Law imprisoned, in order that he may be helped to see that life is after all a very jolly business and thoroughly worth living; and such a flagrant case as the one Simon had just witnessed seemed to call for some distinctly prompt initiative.

"How d'you feel, old chap?" asked the Saint, dropping on one knee beside the man.

"I saw him do it," babbled a fat woman smugly. "With me own eyes I saw it. Jumped in front of the train as deliberate as you please. I saw him."

"I'm afraid you're mistaken, madam," said the Saint quietly. "This gentleman is a friend of mine. He's subject to rather bad fits, and one of them must have taken him just as the train was coming in. He was standing rather close to the edge of the platform, and he simply fell over."

"A very plucky effort of yours, sir, getting him out of the way," opined a white-whiskered retired colonel. "Very plucky, by Gad!"

Simon Templar, however, was not looking for bouquets. The shabby man was sitting motionlessly with his head in his hands: the desperation that had driven him into that spasmodic leap had left him, and he was trembling silently in a helpless reaction. Simon slipped an arm round him and lifted him to his feet, and as he did so the guard broke through the crowd.

"I shall 'ave to make a report of this business, sir," he said.

"Lord—I'm not going to be anybody's hero!" said the Saint. "My name's Abraham Lincoln, and this is my uncle, Mr Christopher Columbus. You can take it or leave it."

"But if the gentleman's going to make any claim against the company I shall 'ave to make a report, sir," pleaded the guard plaintively.

"There'll be no complaints except for wasting time, Ebenezer," said the Saint. "Let's go."

He helped his unresisting salvage into a compartment, and the crowd broke up. The District Railway resumed its day's work, and Simon Templar lighted a cigarette and glanced whimsically at Patricia.

"What d'you think we've picked up this time, old dear?" he murmured.

The girl's hand touched his arm, and she smiled.

"When you went after him I was wondering what I'd lost," she said.

The Saint's quick smile answered her, and he returned to a scrutiny of his acquisition. The shabby man was recovering himself slowly, and Simon thought it best to leave him to himself for a while. By the time they had reached Mark Lane Station he seemed to have become comparatively normal, and Simon stood up and jerked a thumb.

"C'mon, uncle. This is as far as I go."

The shabby man shook his head weakly.

"Really, I don't—"

"Step out," said the Saint.

The man obeyed listlessly, and Simon took his arm and piloted him towards the exit. They turned into a convenient café and found a deserted corner.

"I took a bit of trouble to pull you out of a mess, uncle, and the story of your life is the least you can give me in return."

"Are you a reporter?" asked the other wearily.

"I have a conscience," said the Saint. "What's your name, and what do you do?"

"Inwood. I'm a chemist and—a sort of inventor." The shabby man gazed apathetically at the cup of coffee which had been set before him. "I ought to thank you for saving my life, I suppose, but—"

"Take it as a gift," said the Saint breezily. "I was only thinking of our lines. I've got a few shares in the company, and your method of suicide makes such a mess. Now tell me why you did it."

Inwood looked up.

"Are you going to offer me charity?"

"I never do that. My charity begins at home, and stays on with Mother like a good girl."

"I suppose you've got some sort of right to an answer," said Inwood tiredly. "I'm a failure, that's all."

"And aren't we all?" said the Saint. "What did you fail at, uncle?"

"Inventing. I gave up a good job ten years ago to try and make a fortune on my own, and I've been living from hand to mouth ever since. My wife had a small income of her own, and I lived on that. I did one or two small things, but I didn't make much out of them. I suppose I'm not such a genius as I thought I was, but I believed in myself then. A month or so ago, when we were right at the end of our tether, I did make a little discovery."

The shabby man took from his pocket a small brass tube like a girl's lipstick case, and tossed it across the table. Simon removed the cap, and saw something like a crayon—it was white outside, with a pink core.

"Write something—with your pen, I mean," said Inwood.

Simon took out his fountain pen and scribbled a couple of words on the back of the menu. Inwood blew on it till it dried, and handed it back.

"Now rub it over with that crayon."

Simon did so, and the writing disappeared. It vanished quite smoothly and easily, at a couple of touches, without any hard rubbing, and the paper was left without a trace of discoloration or roughness.

"Just a useful thing for banks and offices," said Inwood. "There's nothing else like it. An ink eraser tears up the paper. You can buy a chemical bleacher, and several firms use it, but that's liquid—two reagents in separate bottles, and you have to put on drops of first one and then the other. That thing of mine is twice as simple and three times quicker."

Simon nodded.

"You're not likely to make a million out of it, but it ought to have quite a reasonable sale."

"I know that," said Inwood bitterly. "I didn't want a million. I'd have been glad to get a thousand. I've told you—I'm not such a genius as I thought I was. But a thousand pounds would have put us on our feet again—given me a chance to open a little shop or find a steady job or something. But I'm not going to get a penny out of it. It isn't my property—and I invented it! . . . We've been living on capital as well as income. This would have put us straight. It had to be protected." The old man's faded eyes blinked at the Saint pitifully. "I don't know anything about things like that. I saw a patent agent's advertisement in a cheap paper, and I took it to him. I gave him all my formulae—everything. That was a fortnight ago. He told me he'd have to make a search of the records before my patent could be taken out. I had a letter from him this morning, and he said that a similar specification had been filed three days ago."

The Saint said nothing, but his blue eyes were suddenly very clear and hard.

"You see what it was?" In his weakness the shabby inventor was almost sobbing. "He swindled me. He gave my specification to a friend of his and let him file them in his own name. I couldn't believe it. I went to the Patent Office myself this morning: a fellow I found there helped me to find what I wanted. Every figure in the specification was mine. It was my specification. The coincidence couldn't possibly have been so exact, even if somebody else had been working on the same idea at the same time as I was. But I can't prove anything. I haven't a shilling to fight with. D'you hear? He's ruined me—"

"Steady on, uncle," said the Saint gently. "Have you seen this bird again?"

"I'd just left his office when . . . when you saw me at Charing Cross," said Inwood shakily. "He threw me out. When he found he couldn't bluff me he didn't bother to deny anything. Told me to go and prove it, and be careful I didn't give him a chance to sue me for libel. There weren't any witnesses. He could say anything he liked—"

"Will you tell me his name?"

"Parnock."

"Thanks." Simon made a note on the back of an envelope. "Now will you do something else for me?"

"What is it?"

"Promise not to do anything drastic before Tuesday. I'm going away for the weekend, but Parnock won't be able to do anything very villainous either. I may be able to do something for you—I have quite a way with me," said the Saint bashfully.

This was on a Friday—a date that Simon Templar had never been superstitious about. He was on his way to Burnham for a weekend's bumping about in a ten-ton yawl, and the fact that Mr Inwood's misadventure had made him miss his train was a small fee for the introduction to Mr Parnock. He caught a later train with plenty of time to spare, but before he left the elderly chemist he obtained an address and a telephone number.

He had another surprise the next morning, for he was searching for a certain penny to convince his incredulous host and owner of the yawl about a statement he had made at the breakfast table, and he couldn't find it.

"You must have spent it," said Patricia.

"I know I haven't," said the Saint. "I paid our fares yesterday afternoon out of a pound note, and I bought a magazine for a bob—I didn't spend any coppers."

"What about those drinks at the pub last night?" said the host and owner, who was Monty Hayward.

"We had one round each, at two-and-a-tanner a lime. I changed a ten-bob note for my whack."

Monty shrugged.

"I expect you put it in a slot machine to look at rude pictures," he said.

Simon found his bottle and silvered another penny for demonstration purposes. It was left on a shelf in the saloon, and Simon thought no more about it until the following morning. He was looking for a box of matches after breakfast when he came across it and the sight of it made him scratch his head, for there was not a trace of silver on it.

"Is anyone being funny?" he demanded, and after he had explained himself there was a chorus of denial.

"Well, that's damned odd," said the Saint.

He plated a third penny on the spot, and put it away in his pocket with a piece of paper wrapped round it. He took it out at six o'clock that evening, and the plating had disappeared.

"Would you mind putting me ashore at Southend, Monty?" he said. "I've got some business I must do in London."

He saw Inwood that night, and after the chemist had sniffed at the bottle and tested its remarkable properties he told the Saint certain things which had been omitted from the syllabus of Simon Templar's variegated education. Simon paced the shabby inventor's shabby little lodging for nearly an hour afterwards, and went back to his own flat in a spirit of definite optimism.

At eleven o'clock the next morning he presented himself at Mr Parnock's office in the Strand. The inscription on the frosted-glass panel of the door informed him that Mr Parnock's baptismal name was Augustus, and an inspection of Mr Parnock himself showed that there had been at least one parent with a commendable prescience in the matter of names. Mr Parnock was so august a personage that it was impossible to think of anyone abbreviating him to "Gus." He was a large and very smooth man, with a smooth convex face and smooth clothes and smooth hair and a smooth voice—except for the voice, he reminded Simon of a well-groomed seal.

"Well, Mr . . . er . . ."

"Smith," said the Saint—he was wearing a brown tweed coat and creaseless grey flannel trousers, and he looked agitated. "Mr Parnock . . . I saw your advertisement in the *Inventor's Weekly* . . . is it true that you help inventors?"

"I'm always ready to give any assistance I can, Mr Smith," said Mr Parnock smoothly. "Won't you sit down?"

The Saint sat down.

"It's like this, Mr Parnock. I've invented a method of chromium plating in one process—you probably know that at present they have to nickel plate first. And my method's about fifty per cent cheaper than anything they've discovered up to the present. It's done by simple immersion, according to a special formula." The Saint ruffled his hair nervously. "I know you'll think it's just another of these crazy schemes that you must be turning down every day, but—Look here, will this convince you?"

He produced a letter and handed it across the desk. It bore the heading of one of the largest motor-car manufacturers in the country, and it was signed with the name of the managing director. Mr Parnock was not to know that among Simon Templar's most valued possessions were a portfolio containing samples of notepaper and envelopes from every important firm in the kingdom, surreptitiously acquired at considerable trouble and expense, and an autograph album in which could be found the signatures of nearly every Captain of Industry in Europe. The letter regretted that Mr Smith did not consider five thousand pounds a suitable offer for the rights of his invention, and invited him to lunch with the writer on the following Friday in the hope of coming to an agreement.

"You seem to be a very fortunate young man," said Mr Parnock enviously, returning the document. "I take it that the firm has already tested your discovery?"

"It doesn't need any tests," said the Saint. "I'll show it to you now."

He produced his little brown bottle, and borrowed Mr Parnock's brass ashtray for the experiment. Before Mr Parnock's eyes it was silvered all over in a few seconds.

"This bottle of stuff costs about a penny," said the Saint, and Mr Parnock was amazed.

"I don't wonder you refused five thousand for it, Mr Smith," he said, as smoothly as he could. "Now, if you had come to me in the first place and allowed me to act as your agent—"

"I want you to do even more than that."

Mr Parnock's eyebrows moved smoothly upwards for about an eighth of an inch.

"Between ourselves," said the Saint bluntly, "I'm in the hell of a mess."

The faintest gleam of expression flitted across Mr Parnock's smooth and fish-like eyes, and gave way to a gaze of expectant sympathy.

"Anything you wanted to tell me, Mr Smith, would of course be treated confidentially."

"I've been gambling—living beyond my means—doing all sorts of silly things. You can see for yourself that I'm pretty young. I suppose I ought to have known better . . . I've stopped all that now, but . . . two months ago I tried to get out of the mess. I gave a dud cheque. I tried to stay in hiding—I was working on this invention, and I knew I'd be able to pay everyone when I'd got it finished. But they found me last Friday. They've been pretty decent, in a way. They gave me till Wednesday noon to find the money. Otherwise—"

The Saint's voice broke, and he averted his face despairingly.

Mr Parnock gazed down at the silvered ashtray, then at the letter which was still spread open on his blotter, and rubbed his smooth chin thoughtfully. He cleared his throat.

"Come, come!" he said paternally. "It isn't as bad as all that. With an asset like this invention of yours, you ought to have nothing to worry about."

"I told them all about it. They were just polite. Wednesday noon or nothing, and hard cash—no promises. I suppose they're right. But it's all so wrong! It's unjust!"

Simon stood up and shook his fists frantically at the ceiling, and Mr Parnock coughed.

"Perhaps I could help," he suggested.

The Saint shook his head.

"That's what I came to see you about. It was just a desperate idea. I haven't got any friends who'd listen to me—I owe them all too much money. But now I've told you all about it, it all sounds so feeble and unconvincing. I wonder you don't send for the police right away."

He shrugged, and picked up his hat. Mr Parnock, a cumbersome man, moved rather hastily to take it away from him and pat him soothingly on the shoulder.

"My dear old chap, you mustn't say things like that. Now let's see what we can do for you. Sit down." He pressed the Saint back towards his chair. "Sit down, sit down. We can soon put this right. What's the value of this cheque?"

"A thousand pounds," said the Saint listlessly. "But it might as well be a million for all the chance I've got of finding the money."

"Fortunately that's an exaggeration," said Mr Parnock cheerfully. "Now this invention of yours—have you patented it?"

Simon snorted harshly.

"What with? I haven't had a shilling to call my own for weeks. I had to offer it to those people just as it stood, and trust them to give me a square deal."

Mr Parnock chuckled with great affability. He opened a drawer and took out his cheque-book.

"A thousand pounds, Mr Smith? And I expect you could do with a bit over for your expenses. Say twenty pounds . . . One thousand and twenty pounds." He inscribed the figures with a flourish. "I'll leave the cheque open so that you can go round to the bank and cash it at once. That'll take a load off your mind, won't it?"

"But how do you know you'll ever see it back, Mr Parnock?"

Mr Parnock appeared to ponder the point, but the appearance was illusory.

"Well, suppose you left me a copy of your formula? That'd be good enough security for me. Of course, I expect you'll let me act as your agent, so I'm not really running any risk. But just as a formality . . ."

The Saint reached for a piece of paper.

"Do you know anything about chemistry?"

"Nothing at all," confessed Mr Parnock. "But I have a friend who understands these things."

Simon wrote on the paper and passed it over. Mr Parnock studied it wisely, as he would have studied a Greek text.

$$Cu + Hg + HNO_3 + Bf = CuHgNO_3 + H_2O + NO_2$$

"Aha!" said Mr Parnock intelligently. He folded the paper and stowed it away in his pocket-book, and stood up with his smooth fruity chuckle. "Well, Mr Smith, you run along now and attend to your business, and come and have lunch with me on Thursday and let's see what we can do about your invention."

"I can't tell you how grateful I am to you, Mr Parnock," said the Saint almost tearfully as he shook the patent agent's smooth fat hand, but for once he was speaking nothing but the truth.

He went down to see Inwood again later that afternoon. He had one thousand pounds with him, in crisp new Bank of England notes, and the shabby old chemist's gratitude was worth all the trouble. Inwood swallowed several times, and blinked at the money dazedly.

"I couldn't possibly take it," he said.

"Of course you could, uncle," said the Saint. "And you will. It's only a fair price for your invention. Just do one thing for me in return."

"I'd do anything you asked me to," said the inventor.

"Then never forget," said Simon deliberately, "that I was with you the whole of this morning—from half-past-ten till one o'clock. That might be rather important." Simon lighted a cigarette and stretched himself luxuriously in his chair. "And when you've got that thoroughly settled into your memory, let us try to imagine what Augustus Parnock is doing right now."

It was at that precise moment, as a matter of history, that Mr Augustus Parnock and his friend who understood those things were staring at a brass ashtray on which no vestige of plating was visible.

"What's the joke, Gus?" demanded Mr Parnock's friend at length.

"I tell you it isn't a joke!" yelped Mr Parnock. "That ashtray was perfectly plated all over when I put it in my pocket at lunchtime. The fellow gave me his formula and everything. Look—here it is!"

The friend who understood those things studied the scrap of paper, and dabbed a stained forefinger on the various items.

"*Cu* is copper," he said. "*Hg* is mercury and HNO_2 is nitric acid. What it means is that you dissolve a little mercury in some weak nitric acid, and when you put it on copper the nitric acid eats a little of the copper, and the mercury forms an amalgam. $CuHgNO_3$ is the amalgam—it'd have a silvery look which might make you think the thing had been plated. The other constituents resolve themselves into H_2O, which is water, and NO_2, which is gas. Of course, the nitric acid goes on eating, and after a time it destroys the amalgam and the thing looks like copper again. That's all there is to it."

"But what about the Bf?" asked Mr Parnock querulously.

His friend shrugged.

"I can't make that out at all—it isn't any chemical symbol," he said, but it dawned on Mr Parnock later.

THE UNUSUAL ENDING

Simon Templar buttered a thin slice of toast and crunched happily.

"I have been going into our accounts," he said, "and the result of the investigation will amaze you."

It was half-past-eleven, and he had just finished breakfast. Breakfast with him was always a sober meal, to be eaten with a proper respect for the gastronomic virtues of grilled bacon and whatever delicacy was mated with it. On this morning it had been mushrooms, a dish that had its own unapproachable place in the Saint's ideal of a day's beginning, and he had dealt with them slowly and lusciously, as they deserved, with golden wafers of brown toast on their port side and an open newspaper propped up against the coffee-pot for scanning to starboard. All that had been done with the solemnity of a pleasant rite. And now the last slice of toast was buttered and marmaladed, the last cup of coffee poured out and sugared, the first cigarette lighted and the first deep cloud of fragrant smoke inhaled, and the time had come when Simon Templar was wont to touch on weighty matters in a mood of profound contentment.

"What is the result?" asked Patricia.

"Our running expenses have been pretty heavy," said the Saint, "and we haven't denied ourselves much in the way of good things. On the other hand, last year we had a couple of the breaks that only come once in a lifetime, which just helps to show how brilliant we are. Perrigo's illicit diamonds and dear old Dudolf's crown jewels." The Saint smiled reminiscently. "And this current year's sport and dalliance hasn't been run at a total loss. In fact, old darling, at this very moment we're worth three hundred thousand quid clear of all overhead, and if that isn't something like a record for a life of crime I'll eat my second-best hat. I'm referring, of course," said the Saint fastidiously, "to a life of honest crime. Company promoters and international financiers we don't profess to compete with."

Chief Inspector Claud Eustace Teal, on the same day, reviewed the same subject with less contentment, which was only natural. Besides, he had the Assistant Commissioner's peculiarly sarcastic and irritating sniff as an obbligato.

"I gather," said the Assistant Commissioner, in his precise and acidulated way, "that we are to wait until this man Templar has made himself a millionaire, when presumably he will have no further incentive to be dishonest."

"I wish I could believe that," said Teal funereally.

He had a definite feeling of injustice about that interview, for on the whole the past twelve months had been exceptionally peaceful. Simon Templar had actually been on the side of the Law in two different cases, whole-heartedly and without much financial profit, and his less lawful activities, during the period with which Teal's report dealt, were really little more than rumours. Undoubtedly the Saint had enriched himself, and done so by methods which would probably have emerged somewhat tattered from the close scrutiny of a jury of moralists, but there had been no official complaints from the afflicted parties—and that, Teal felt, was as much as his responsibility required. Admittedly, the afflicted parties might not have known whom to accuse, or, when they knew, might have thought it better not to complain lest worse befall them, but that was outside Teal's province. His job was to deal in an official manner with officially recognized crimes, and this he had been doing with no small measure of success. The fact that Simon Templar's head, on a charger, had not been included in his list of offerings, however, appeared to rankle with the exacting Commissioner, who sniffed his dissatisfied and exasperating sniff several times more before he allowed Mr Teal to withdraw from his sanctum.

It was depressing for Mr Teal, who had been minded to congratulate the Saint, unofficially, on the discretion with which he had lately contrived to avoid those demonstrations of brazen lawlessness which had in the past added so many grey hairs to Teal's thinning tally. In the privacy of his own office, Mr Teal unwrapped a fresh wafer of chewing-gum and meditated moodily, as he had done before, on the unkindness of a fate that had thrown such a man as Simon Templar across the path of a promising career. It removed nearly all his enthusiasm from the commonplace task of apprehending a fairly commonplace swindler, which was his scheduled duty for that day.

But none of these things could noticeably have saddened Simon Templar, even if he had known about them. Peter Quentin, intruding on the conclusion of the Saint's breakfast shortly afterwards, felt that the question, "Well, Simon, how's life?" was superfluous, but he asked it.

"Life keeps moving," said the Saint. "Another Royal Commission has been appointed, this time to discuss whether open-air restaurants would be likely to lower the moral tone of the nation. Another law has been passed to forbid something or other. A Metropolitan Policeman has won a first prize in the Irish Sweep. And you?"

Peter helped himself to a cigarette, and eyed the Saint's blue silk Cossack pyjamas with the unconscious and unreasonable smugness of a man who has dressed for breakfast and been about for hours.

"I can see that I haven't any real criminal instincts," he remarked. "I get up too early. And what are the initials for?"

Simon glanced down at the monogram embroidered on his breast pocket.

"In case I wake up in the middle of the night and can't remember who I am," he said. "What's new about Julian?"

"He skips today," said Peter. "Or perhaps tomorrow. Anyway, he's been to the bank already and drawn out more money than I've ever seen before in hard cash. That's why I thought I'd better knock off and tell you."

Mr Julian Lamantia should be no stranger to us. We have seen him being thrown into the Thames on a rainy night. We have seen him in his J. L. Investment Bureau, contributing to the capital required for buying a completely worthless block of shares.

If Mr Lamantia had restricted himself to such enterprises as those in which the Saint's attention had first been directed towards him, we might still have been able to speak of him in the present tense. He had, in his prime, been one of the astutest skimmers of the Law of his generation. Unfortunately for him he became greedy, as other men like him have become before, and in the current wave of general depression he found that the bucket-shop business was not what it was. His mind turned towards more dangerous but more profitable fields.

Out through the post, under the heading of the J. L. Investment Bureau, went many thousands of beautifully-printed pamphlets, in which was described the enormous profit that could be made on large short-term loans. The general public, said the pamphlet, was not in a position to supply the sums required for these loans, and therefore all these colossal profits gravitated exclusively into the pockets of a small circle of wealthy financial houses. Nevertheless, explained the pamphlet, as the hymnbook had done before it, little drops of water, little grains of sand, made the tiddly-tum-tum and the tumty-tum. It was accordingly mooted that, under the auspices of the J. L. Investment Bureau, sums of from five pounds to ten pounds might be raised from private investors and in the aggregate provide the means for making these great short-term loans, of which the profits would be generously and proportionately shared with the investors.

It was a scheme which, in one form or another, is as old as some of the younger hills and as perennially fruitful as a parson's wife. Helped on by the literary gifts of Mr Lamantia, it proceeded in this reincarnation as well as it always will. From the first issue of circulars thousands of pounds poured in, and after a very brief interval the first monthly dividend was announced at ten per cent and paid. In another thirty days the second month's dividend was announced at fifteen per cent—and paid. The third month's dividend was twenty per cent—"which," a second issue of circulars hoped, "should remain as a regular working profit"—and the money was pouring in almost as fast as it could be banked. The original investors increased their investments frantically, and told their friends, who also subscribed and spread the good news. The dividends, of course, were paid straight out of the investors' own capital and the new subscriptions that were continually flowing in, but any suspicion of such low duplicity was, as usual, far from the minds of the innocent suckers who in a few months built up Mr Julian Lamantia's bank balance to the amazing total of eighty-five thousand pounds.

Like all get-rich-quick schemes, it had its inevitable breaking-point, and this Mr Lamantia knew. "Clean up while it lasts, and get out," is the only possible motto for its promoter, but a certain fatal doubt has often existed about how long it may safely be expected to last. Mr Lamantia thought that he had gauged the duration to a nicety. On this morning whose events we have been following, Mr Lamantia drew out his balance from the bank, packed it neatly in a small leather bag, and called back at his office. Perhaps that was a foolish thing to do, but his new secretary was a very beautiful girl. It was Saturday, and the weekend would give him a long start on his getaway. He had a new passport in another name, his passage was booked from Southampton, his luggage was packed and gone, his moustache ready for moving: only one more thing was needed.

"Well," he said bluntly, "have you made up your mind?"

"I should like to come, Mr Lamantia."

"Julian," said Mr Lamantia attractively, "will do. Haven't you got a first name—Miss Allfield?"

"Kathleen," said the girl, with a smile. "Usually Kate."

The name meant nothing to Mr Lamantia, who did his best to hold aloof from ordinary criminal circles. He said he preferred Kathleen.

"When do we go?" she asked.

"This afternoon."

"But you told me—"

"I've had to change my plans. I had a cable from Buenos Aires at my hotel this morning—I must get there as soon as I possibly can."

He had not taken her into his confidence. That could be done later, by delicate and tactful stages, if he felt like prolonging the liaison. His projected journey to South America had been discussed as a purely business affair, in connexion with vague talk of a gigantic loan to the Argentine National Railways.

"It would be a wonderful trip for you," he said. "New places, new people, no end of new entertainments. Never mind about a lot of luggage. You can go home now and pack everything you want to take from London, and anything else you need you can buy at Lisbon."

She hesitated for a few moments, and then turned her deep brown eyes back to him.

"All right."

His gaze stripped her in quiet elation, but he did not try to make love to her. There would be plenty of time for that. He put on his hat again and went home to finish the last items of his packing, and when he had gone Kate Allfield picked up his private telephone and called the Saint's flat.

Peter Quentin answered it, and returned after a few minutes to the bathroom, where the Saint was washing his razor.

"It's today," he said. "The boat train leaves at two-thirty, and Kate is supposed to be meeting Julian for lunch at the Savoy first. Kate," said Peter reflectively, unaware that the same thought had struck Mr Lamantia, "isn't nearly so nice as Kathleen."

Simon turned off the taps that were filling his bath, threw off his pyjamas, and sank into the warm water.

"You have been seeing quite a lot of her lately, haven't you?" he murmured.

"Only on business," said Peter, with unnecessary clearness. "After she put us on to this stunt of Julian's, and volunteered to do the inside work—"

"And the new vocabulary, Peter? Did you get that out of a book?"

The Saint's mocking blue eyes swerved down from the ceiling and aimed directly at the other's face. Peter went red.

"I think I did get it from her," he said. "But that's nothing."

Simon picked up the soap and lathered his legs thoughtfully.

"In the preliminary palaver of that Star of Mandalay affair, she told me she was about to retire."

"I don't see why she shouldn't," said Peter, judicially.

"I don't see why anyone shouldn't retire," said the Saint, "when they've made a useful pile. Look at you."

"Why look at me?"

"You've done pretty well since we teamed up. About fifteen thousand quid, I make it."

These chronicles have only attempted a few incidents in the Saint's career that were distinguished by some odd twist of luck or circumstance or ingenuity. His crimes were always legion, and it is often hard for the historian to select the exploits which seem most worthy of commemoration.

"I owe you a lot," said Peter.

"Brickdust," said the Saint tersely.

He spread the lather over his arms and chest and shoulders, and submerged himself again. Then he said, "Peter, I let you come in with me because you wanted to and you'd lost your job and you had to live somehow. Now you've got fifteen thousand quid, nine hundred a year or more if you invest it skilfully, and you don't need a job. You don't need to run to seed in an office. You're not rich, but you can have all the fun in the world. You can go anywhere, do almost anything you like within reason. If I may talk to you like an uncle—don't be the pitcher that goes once too often to the well."

"You've never stopped," said Peter.

The Saint grinned.

"I never could. While I'm strong and alive, I've got to go on. When I stop crashing about the world and raising hell, I might as well die. Excitement, danger, living on tiptoe all the time—that's what life means to me. But it isn't the same for you."

"What will you do now?"

"I'm blowed if I know. I think I shall travel south, and put my trust in the Lord. Something's sure to happen. Something always does happen, if you go out and challenge it. Adventure never comes. You have to lug it in by the ears. You might settle down in a nice house in England for fifty years, and nothing would ever happen. A few people would die, a few people would get married, they might change over from auction to contract or back again, the man next door might run off with his wife's sister and the grocer's assistant might run off with the till—that's all. But you won't find adventure unless you look for it, and that means living dangerously. Sometimes when I hear fools complaining that life is dull, I want to advise them to knock their bank manager on the head and grab a handful of money and run. After a fortnight, if they could keep running that long, they'd know what life meant . . . I expect I shall do something like that, and the chase will start all over again. But somewhere in the south it will be, Peter. Do you know, when I woke up this morning it was cold enough for me to see my breath going up like steam, and when that happens I feel the old call of long days and sunshine and blue skies."

He stood up, twitched out the plug, and turned the tap of the cold shower. For a few seconds he stood under it, letting it stream down over him and laughing at the stinging brunt of it, rubbing the water over his arms and thighs and chest in a sheer pagan delight of hardiness, and then he climbed out and reached for a towel and cigarette, and his wet hand smote Peter between the shoulder-blades.

"And I feel like a million dollars on it," he said. "Come on—let's go and be rude to Julian!"

In a surprisingly short space of time he was dressed, immaculate and debonair as ever, and they walked up Piccadilly together.

"No alibi?" asked Peter.

"Why bother?" smiled the Saint. "If anything could possibly go wrong, Julian would have a swell job trying to explain exactly why he had the entire capital of the firm in a bag in his room, with a one-way passage booked to Buenos Aires—and I don't think he'd take it on."

He had a faultless sense of time, and Kate Allfield had also learned that in their profession punctuality may be more precious than many alibis. She had just paid off her taxi when they arrived at the Savoy, and Simon could understand the foolishness of Julian Lamantia no less than the foolishness of Peter Quentin. He had always thought her lovely, even at that first meeting on Croydon Aerodrome when he had only just discovered the hypnotic powers of her cigarettes in time, and the affair of the Star of Mandalay had shown him something else about her that he saluted in his own way. But it was Peter Quentin's hand that she touched first, and Simon knew that with this adventure one more adventurer came to an end.

They went in together, and Peter and Simon stood aside while the girl approached the hall porter and had her name telephoned up to Mr

Lamantia's room. The reply came back, as they had expected, that she was to be shown up, and the two men strolled along and joined her quite naturally as she was escorted to the lift.

They got out on the third floor, and she stopped the pageboy who accompanied them with a smile.

"I know the way," she said.

Simon slipped a half-crown into the midget's hand, and they brushed past him. In a few yards they had the corridor to themselves.

"You might wander downstairs and drift out, Kathleen," said the Saint. "Go to the Carlton. We'll join you there in about half an hour."

She nodded, and Peter's fingers slipped away from hers as they passed on.

They reached Mr Lamantia's room, and Simon lifted his hand and knocked.

Using our renowned gifts of vivid description, it would be possible for us to dilate upon Mr Lamantia's emotions at great length, but we have not the time. Neither, in point of fact, had Mr Lamantia. He suffered more or less what a happy bonfire would suffer if the bottom fell out of a reservoir suspended directly over it. With eighty-five thousand pounds in bank-notes of small denominations in his bag, an express service to the tall timber mapped out in front of him, and his aesthetic soul ripe with the remembered beauty and tacit acquiescence of the most beautiful girl he had ever seen, he opened his door with the vision of her face rising before his eyes, and saw the vision smashed into a whirling kaleidoscope of fragments that came together again as the lean smiling figure of the man who had once come striding through the wet night to drag him out of his car and immerse him in the Thames. His eyes bulged and his jaw dropped, and then the lean figure's hand pushed him kindly but firmly backwards and followed him on into the room, and Peter Quentin closed the door behind them and put his back to it.

"Well, Julian," said the Saint breezily, "how are all the little stocks and shares today?"

A tinge of colour squeezed slowly back into Mr Lamantia's ashen face. When he had first seen the figures of men outside his door he had had one dreadful instant of the fear that perhaps after all he had left his retirement too late.

"How did you get up here?" he stammered.

"We flew," said the Saint affably.

Suddenly his left fist shot over with the whole weight of his shoulder behind it. The upper knuckles came on the line of Mr Lamantia's twitching mouth, the lower knuckles on the point of his jaw-bone, clean and crisp in the horizontal centre on his face, and Mr Lamantia had a hazy feeling that his brain had been knocked off its moorings and was revolving slowly and painfully inside his skull. When it had settled down again to a rhythmic but stationary singing, he became aware that the automatic which he had been trying to pull from his hip pocket was gone.

"Tie him up, Peter," said the Saint calmly.

Peter Quentin came off the door and produced a coil of stout cord from under his coat. Mr Lamantia went down fighting, but Peter's muscular handling rapidly reduced him to mere verbal protest, which was largely biological in tone.

"I'll get you for this, you swine," was his only printable comment.

"And gag him," said the Saint.

The process was satisfactorily completed under the Saint's expert supervision. Simon had found Mr Lamantia's cigar-case, and while the knots were being tested he talked and smoked.

"I notice that the welkin hasn't rung with your shrieks for help, Julian. Can it be that you have something on your conscience? . . . I'm sorry about all these formalities, but we don't really want a disturbance, and in the heat of the moment you might have been tempted to do something rash which we should all regret. The staff are sure to find you in a year or two, and then you can explain that some pals did this on you for a joke. I'm sure you'll decide that's the best story to tell, but you need a little time to think it over."

He strolled round the room examining the items of Mr Lamantia's baggage, and eventually chose the smallest bag.

"Is this the one, Peter?"

"That's it."

Simon turned the lock with an instrument he had in his pocket, and glanced inside. The notes were there, in thick bundles, exactly as they had been passed across the counter of the bank. With a sigh of righteous satisfaction the Saint closed the attaché case again and picked it up.

"Let's go."

He bowed politely to the speechless man on the bed, replaced the excellent cigar between his teeth, and sauntered to the door. Without a care in the world he opened it—and looked straight into the face of Chief Inspector Claud Eustace Teal.

* * *

If there had been any competition for grades of paralysis in that doorway, it would have been a thankless task for the judge. Mr Lamantia had already given his own rendering of a man being kicked in the mid-section by an invisible mule, and now for two or three strung seconds Simon Templar and Chief Inspector Teal gazed at each other in an equally cataleptic immobility. Out in the great world around them, ordinary policemen scurried innocently about their beats, the London traffic dashed hither and thither at a rate of hundreds of yards an hour, the surface of the earth was rotating at five hundred miles every half-hour, whizzing round the sun at seventy-six miles a minute and tearing through space with the rest of the solar system at over twelve miles per second, but in the midst of all this bustle of cosmic activity those two historic antagonists stared at each other across a yard of empty air without the movement of a muscle.

On Mr Teal's rubicund features showed no visible emotion beyond the isolated, slow, incredulous expansion of his eyes; the Saint's tanned face was debonairly impassive, but behind the Saint's steady blue eyes his brain was covering ground at a speed that it had already been required to make before.

Once before, and once only, in Simon's hectic career, Teal had caught him red-handed, but then there had been a perfect alibi prepared, a grim challenge ready, and a clear getaway in the offing. At other times, of course, there had been close calls, but they had also been anticipated and legislated for in advance. And, with that alibi or getaway at hand, events had taken their natural course. Teal had been baited, defied, dared, punched in the tummy, or pulled by the nose: those were the rich rewards of foresight. But there was none of that now.

And the Saint smiled.

Teal's right hand was still poised in mid-air, raised for the official and peremptory knock that he had been about to deliver when the door opened so astonishingly in front of him he might have forgotten its existence. But the Saint reached out and drew it down and shook it, with that incomparable Saintly smile lighting his face again with as gay a carelessness as it had ever held.

"Come in, Claud," he said. "You're just in time."

And with that breaking of the silence Teal came back to earth with a jolt that closed his mouth almost with a snap. He advanced solidly into the room, and another burly man in plain clothes who was with him followed him in. They took in the scene in a couple of purposeful glances.

"Well?"

The interrogation broke from the detective's mouth with a curt bluntness that was as self-explanatory as a cannon-ball. The Saint's eyebrows flickered.

"This," he murmured, with the air of a Cook's guide conducting a tour, "is Mr Julian Lamantia, who recently revived the ancient game of inviting suckers to—"

"I know all that," said Teal thuddingly. "That's what I came here about. What I want to know is why you're here."

Simon's brow puckered.

"But did you really know all about it? Why, I thought I was doing you a good turn. In the course of my private and philanthropic investigations I happened to learn that the affairs of Julian were not all that they might be, so in order to protect his clients without risking a libel action I decided to have him watched. And this very morning my energetic agents informed me that he had drawn all the J. L. Investment Bureau's capital out of the bank and was preparing to skip with the simoleons—I mean abscond with the cash."

"Go on," said Teal dourly. "It sounds interesting."

The Saint hitched one leg on to the table and drew appreciatively on Mr Lamantia's cigar.

"It is interesting, Claud. We also learned that Julian was catching a boat train at two-thirty, so our time was limited. The only thing seemed to be for us to toddle along and grab him before he slipped away, and phone you to come round and collect him as soon as we had him trussed. I admit it may have been a bit rash of us to take the Law into our own hands like that but you must have a spot of excitement now and again in these dull days, and we were thinking of nothing but the public weal."

"And what have you got in that bag?"

"This?" Simon glanced down. "This contains the aforesaid simoleons, or mazuma. We were going to take it downstairs and ask the manager to stow it away in his safe till you arrived."

Mr Teal took the bag from the Saint's hand and opened it. He sniffed, reminding himself of the Assistant Commissioner.

"That's a great story," he said.

"It's a swell story," said the Saint quietly. "And it'll keep the Home Office guessing for a while. Remember that I'm a reformed character now, so far as the public are concerned, and any nasty suspicions you may have are like the flowers that bloom in the spring. They have nothing to do with the case. My reputation is as pure as the driven snow. Perhaps, as I admitted, we have been rash. The magistrate might rebuke me. He might even be rude." The Saint sighed. "Well, Claud, if you feel you must expose me to that tragic humiliation—if you must let the newspapers tell of the magistrate's severe criticism—"

"I don't want to hear any more of that," barked the detective.

"Just a word-picture," explained the Saint apologetically.

Teal bit down forcefully on his chewing-gum. He knew that the Saint was right—knew that the last useful word on the subject had been uttered—and the clear blue mocking eyes of the smiling Saint told him that Simon Templar also knew. The knowledge went down into Teal's stomach like gall, but in the days gone by he had learned a certain fatalistic wisdom. And this time, for the first time in the long duel, the honours were fairly even.

"If you're quite satisfied," murmured the Saint persuasively, "Peter and I have a date for lunch with a beautiful lady."

"That's your own business," said Mr Teal with all the restraint of which he was capable.

He turned his broad back on them and moved over to the bed, where his assistant was wrestling with the knots that held the empurpled Mr Lamantia, and Simon winked at Peter Quentin and removed himself from the table. They sauntered unopposed to the door, and from there, without a shadow on his face, Simon turned back for his irrepressibly gay farewell.

"Send my medal along by post, Claud," he said .

PUBLICATION HISTORY

As mentioned in the introduction, these stories were first published in a now defunct Sunday newspaper called the *Empire News* on a weekly basis at the tail end of 1932. The book was first published in February 1933 with an American edition following in August that year. Just eight years later, Hodder & Stoughton were on their sixteenth imprint, suggesting it was perhaps one of the bestselling volumes in the Saint's career. In 1951 this book was subsequently listed at number 86 in *Queen's Quorum*, a collection of the 125 best crime short stories published since 1845, by Ellery Queen.

The initial Spanish translation appeared in 1934 under the title of *Para pillo, pillo y medio* (published by regular Saint publisher Juventud) but in subsequent decades it was rechristened *El Santo en la jugada*, presumably following the English language logic of needing to include the Saint in the title. The Germans opted for *Der Heilige ist schlauer* in 1957, the Italians for *Un diavolo di bucaniere* in 1971, the Swedes for *Helgonet bland hårdkokta herrar* in 1955, and the Portuguese for the easily translatable *O Santo e o crime perfeito* in 1933.

"The Appalling Politician" was adapted by Norman Hudis as "The Imprudent Politician" for Roger Moore's version of *The Saint* and first aired on 6 December 1964. "The Export Trade" was adapted by Donald and Derek Ford with some help from Harry Junkin and aired as "A Double in Diamonds" on 5 May 1967, part of the first colour season for Roger Moore as The Saint.

ABOUT THE AUTHOR

I'm mad enough to believe in romance. And I'm sick and tired of this age—tired of the miserable little mildewed things that people racked their brains about, and wrote books about, and called life. I wanted something more elementary and honest—battle, murder, sudden death, with plenty of good beer and damsels in distress, and a complete callousness about blipping the ungodly over the beezer. It mayn't be life as we know it, but it ought to be.

—Leslie Charteris in a 1935 BBC radio interview

Leslie Charteris was born Leslie Charles Bowyer-Yin in Singapore on 12 May 1907.

He was the son of a Chinese doctor and his English wife, who'd met in London a few years earlier. Young Leslie found friends hard to come by in colonial Singapore. The English children had been told not to play with Eurasians, and the Chinese children had been told not to play with Europeans. Leslie was caught in between and took refuge in reading.

"I read a great many good books and enjoyed them because nobody had told me that they were classics. I also read a great many bad books which nobody told me not to read . . . I read a great many popular scientific articles and acquired from them an astonishing amount of general knowledge before I discovered that this acquisition was supposed to be a chore."[1]

One of his favourite things to read was a magazine called *Chums*. "The Best and Brightest Paper for Boys" (if you believe the adverts) was a monthly paper full of swashbuckling adventure stories aimed at boys, encouraging them to be honourable and moral and perhaps even "upright citizens with furled umbrellas."[2] Undoubtedly these types of stories would influence his later work.

When his parents split up shortly after the end of World War I, Charteris accompanied his mother and brother back to England, where he was sent to Rossall School in Fleetwood, Lancashire. Rossall was then a very stereotypical English public school, and it struggled to cope with this multilingual mixed-race boy just into his teens who'd already seen more of the world than many of his peers would see in their lifetimes. He was an outsider.

He left Rossall in 1924. Keen to pursue a creative career, he decided to study art in Paris—after all, that was where the great artists went—but soon found that the life of a literally starving artist didn't appeal. He continued writing, firing off speculative stories to magazines, and it was the sale of a short story to *Windsor Magazine* that saved him from penury.

He returned to London in 1925, as his parents—particularly his father—wanted him to become a lawyer, and he was sent to study law at Cambridge University. In the mid-1920s, Cambridge was full of Bright Young Things—aristocrats and bohemians somewhat typified in the Evelyn Waugh novel *Vile Bodies*—and again the mixed-race Bowyer-Yin found that he didn't fit in. He was an outsider who preferred to make his own way in the world and wasn't one of the privileged upper class. It didn't help that he found his studies boring and decided it was more fun contemplating ways to circumvent the law. This inspired him to write a novel, and when publishers Ward Lock & Co. offered him a three-book deal on the strength of it, he abandoned his studies to pursue a writing career.

When his father learnt of this, he was not impressed, as he considered writers to be "rogues and vagabonds." Charteris would later recall that "I wanted to be a writer, he wanted me to become a lawyer. I was stubborn, he said I would end up in the gutter. So I left home. Later on, when I had a little success, we were reconciled by letter, but I never saw him again."[3]

X Esquire, his first novel, appeared in April 1927. The lead character, X Esquire, is a mysterious hero, hunting down and killing the businessmen trying to wipe out Britain by distributing quantities of free poisoned cigarettes. His second novel, *The White Rider*, was published the following spring, and in one memorable scene shows the hero chasing after his damsel in distress, only for him to overtake the villains, leap into their car . . . and promptly faint.

These two plot highlights may go some way to explaining Charteris's comment on *Meet—the Tiger!*, published in September 1928, that "it was only the third book I'd written, and the best, I would say, for it was that the first two were even worse."[4]

Twenty-one-year-old authors are naturally self-critical. Despite reasonably good reviews, the Saint didn't set the world on fire, and Charteris moved on to a new hero for his next book. This was *The Bandit*, an adventure story featuring Ramon Francisco De Castilla y Espronceda Manrique, published in the summer of 1929 after its serialisation in the *Empire News*, a now long-forgotten Sunday newspaper. But sales of *The Bandit* were less than impressive, and Charteris began to question his choice of career. It was all very well writing—but if nobody wants to read what you write, what's the point?

"I had to succeed, because before me loomed the only alternative, the dreadful penalty of failure . . . the routine office hours, the five-day week . . . the lethal assimilation into the ranks of honest, hard-working, conformist, God-fearing pillars of the community."[5]

However his fortunes—and the Saint's—were about to change. In late 1928, Leslie had met Monty Haydon, a London-based editor who was looking for writers to pen stories for his new paper, *The Thriller*—"The Paper with a Thousand Thrills." Charteris later recalled that "he said he was starting a new magazine, had read one of my books and would like some stories from me. I couldn't have been more grateful, both from the point of view of vanity and finance!"[6]

The paper launched in early 1929, and Leslie's first work, "The Story of a Dead Man," featuring Jimmy Traill, appeared in issue 4 (published on 2 March 1929). That was followed just over a month later with "The Secret of Beacon Inn," starring Rameses "Pip" Smith. At the same time, Leslie finished writing another non-Saint novel, *Daredevil*, which would be published in late 1929. Storm Arden was the hero; more notably, the book saw the first introduction of a Scotland Yard inspector by the name of Claud Eustace Teal.

The Saint returned in the thirteenth issue of *The Thriller*. The byline proclaimed that the tale was "A Thrilling Complete Story of the Underworld"; the title was "The Five Kings," and it actually featured Four Kings and a Joker. Simon Templar, of course, was the Joker.

Charteris spent the rest of 1929 telling the adventures of the Five Kings in five subsequent *The Thriller* stories. "It was very hard work, for the pay was lousy, but Monty Haydon was a brilliant and stimulating editor, full of ideas. While he didn't actually help shape the Saint as a character, he did suggest story lines. He would take me out to lunch and say, 'What are you going to write about next?' I'd often say I was damned if I knew. And Monty would say, 'Well, I was reading something the other day . . .' He had a fund of ideas and we would talk them over, and then I would go away and write a story. He was a great creative editor."[7]

Charteris would have one more attempt at writing about a hero other than Simon Templar, in three novelettes published in *The Thriller* in early 1930, but he swiftly returned to the Saint. This was partly due to his self-confessed laziness—he wanted to write more stories for *The Thriller* and other magazines, and creating a new hero for every story was hard work—but mainly due to feedback from Monty Haydon. It seemed people wanted to read more adventures of the Saint . . .

Charteris would contribute over forty stories to *The Thriller* throughout the 1930s. Shortly after their debut, he persuaded publisher Hodder & Stoughton that if he collected some of these stories and rewrote them a little, they could publish them as a Saint book. *Enter the Saint* was first published in August 1930, and the reaction was good enough for the publishers to bring out another collection. And another . . .

Of the twenty Saint books published in the 1930s, almost all have their origins in those magazine stories.

Why was the Saint so popular throughout the decade? Aside from the charm and ability of Charteris's storytelling, the stories, particularly those published in the first half of the '30s, are full of energy and joie de vivre. With economic depression rampant throughout the period, the public at large seemed to want some escapism.

And Simon Templar's appeal was wide-ranging: he wasn't an upper-class hero like so many of the period. With no obvious background and no attachment to the Old School Tie, no friends in high places who could provide a get-out-of-jail-free card, the Saint was uniquely classless. Not unlike his creator.

Throughout Leslie's formative years, his heritage had been an issue. In his early days in Singapore, during his time at school, at Cambridge University or even just in everyday life, he couldn't avoid the fact that for many people his mixed parentage was a problem. He would later tell a story of how he was chased up the road by a stick-waving typical

English gent who took offence to his daughter being escorted around town by a foreigner.

Like the Saint, he was an outsider. And although he had spent a significant portion of his formative years in England, he couldn't settle.

As a young boy he had read of an America "peopled largely by Indians, and characters in fringed buckskin jackets who fought nobly against them. I spent a great deal of time day-dreaming about a visit to this prodigious and exciting country."[8]

It was time to realise this wish. Charteris and his first wife, Pauline, whom he'd met in London when they were both teenagers and married in 1931, set sail for the States in late 1932; the Saint had already made his debut in America courtesy of the publisher Doubleday. Charteris and his wife found a New York still experiencing the tail end of Prohibition, and times were tough at first. Despite sales to *The American Magazine* and others, it wasn't until a chance meeting with writer turned Hollywood executive Bartlett McCormack in their favourite speakeasy that Charteris's career stepped up a gear.

Soon Charteris was in Hollywood, working on what would become the 1933 movie *Midnight Club*. However, Hollywood's treatment of writers wasn't to Charteris's taste, and he began to yearn for home. Within a few months, he returned to the UK and began writing more Saint stories for Monty Haydon and Bill McElroy.

He also rewrote a story he'd sketched out whilst in the States, a version of which had been published in *The American Magazine* in September 1934. This new novel, *The Saint in New York*, published in 1935, was a significant advance for the Saint and Leslie Charteris. Gone were the high jinks and the badinage. The youthful exuberance evident in the Saint's early adventures had evolved into something a little darker, a little more hard-boiled. It was the next stage in development for the author and his creation, and readers loved it. It became a bestseller on both sides of the Atlantic.

Having spent his formative years in places as far apart as Singapore and England, with substantial travel in between, it should be no surprise that Leslie had a serious case of wanderlust. With a bestseller under his belt, he now had the means to see more of the world.

Nineteen thirty-six found him in Tenerife, researching another Saint adventure alongside translating the biography of Juan Belmonte, a well-known Spanish matador. Estranged for several months, Leslie and Pauline divorced in 1937. The following year, Leslie married an American, Barbara Meyer, who'd accompanied him to Tenerife. In early 1938, Charteris and his new bride set off in a trailer of his own design and spent eighteen months travelling round America and Canada.

The Saint in New York had reminded Hollywood of Charteris's talents, and film rights to the novel were sold prior to publication in 1935. Although the proposed 1935 film production was rejected by the Hays Office for its violent content, RKO's eventual 1938 production persuaded Charteris to try his luck once more in Hollywood.

New opportunities had opened up, and throughout the 1940s the Saint appeared not only in books and movies but in a newspaper strip, a comic-book series, and on radio.

Anyone wishing to adapt the character in any medium found a stern taskmaster in Charteris. He was never completely satisfied, nor was he shy of showing his displeasure. He did, however, ensure that copyright in any Saint adventure belonged to him, even if scripted by another writer—a contractual obligation that he was to insist on throughout his career.

Charteris was soon spread thin, overseeing movies, comics, newspapers, and radio versions of his creation, and this, along with his self-proclaimed laziness, meant that Saint books were becoming fewer and further between. However, he still enjoyed his creation: in 1941 he indulged himself in a spot of fun by playing the Saint—complete with monocle and moustache—in a photo story in *Life* magazine.

In July 1944, he started collaborating under a pseudonym on Sherlock Holmes radio scripts, subsequently writing more adventures for Holmes than Conan Doyle. Not all his ventures were successful—a screenplay he was hired to write for Deanna Durbin, "Lady on a Train," took him a year and ultimately bore little resemblance to the finished film. In the mid-1940s, Charteris successfully sued RKO Pictures for unfair competition after they launched a new series of films starring George Sanders as a debonair crime fighter known as the Falcon. But he kept faith with his original character, and the Saint novels continued to adapt to the times. The transatlantic Saint evolved into something of a private operator, working for the mysterious Hamilton and becoming, not unlike his creator, a world traveller, finding that adventure would seek him out.

"I have never been able to see why a fictional character should not grow up, mature, and develop, the same as anyone else. The same, if you like, as his biographer. The only adequate reason is that—so far as I know—no other fictional character in modern times has survived a sufficient number of years for these changes to be clearly observable. I must confess that a lot of my own selfish pleasure in the Saint has been in watching him grow up."[9]

Charteris maintained his love of travel and was soon to be found sailing round the West Indies with his good friend Gregory Peck. His forays abroad gave him even more material, and he began to write true-crime articles, as well as an occasional column in *Gourmet* magazine.

By the early '50s, Charteris himself was feeling strained. He'd divorced his second wife in 1943 and got together with a New York radio and nightclub singer called Betty Bryant Borst, whom he married in late 1943. That relationship had fallen apart acrimoniously towards the end of the decade, and he roamed the globe restlessly, rarely in one place for longer than a couple of months. He continued to maintain a firm grip on the exploitation of the Saint in various media but was writing little himself. The Saint had become an industry, and Charteris couldn't keep up. He began thinking seriously about an early retirement.

Then in 1951 he met a young actress called Audrey Long when they became next-door neighbours in Hollywood. Within a year they had married, a union that was to last the rest of Leslie's life.

He attacked life with a new vitality. They travelled—Nassau was a favoured escape spot—and he wrote. He struck an agreement with *The New York Herald Tribune* for a Saint comic strip, which would appear daily and be written by Charteris himself. The strip ran for thirteen years, with Charteris sending in his handwritten story lines from wherever he happened to be, relying on mail services around the world to continue the Saint's adventures. New Saint books began to appear, and Charteris reached a height of productivity not seen since his days as a struggling author trying to establish himself. As Leslie and Audrey travelled, so did the Saint, visiting locations just after his creator had been there.

By 1953 the Saint had already enjoyed twenty-five years of success, and *The Saint Detective Magazine* was launched. Charteris had become adept at exploiting his creation to the full, mixing new stories with repackaged older stories, sometimes rewritten, sometimes mixed up in "new" anthologies, sometimes adapted from radio scripts previously written by other writers.

Charteris had been approached several times over the years for television rights in the Saint and had expended much time and effort during the 1950s trying to get the Saint on TV, even going so far as to write sample scripts himself, but it wasn't to be. He finally agreed a deal in autumn 1961 with English film producers Robert S. Baker and Monty Berman. The first episode of *The Saint* television series, starring Roger Moore, went into production in June 1962. The series was an immediate success, though Charteris himself had his reservations. It reached second place in the ratings, but he commented that "in that distinction it was topped by wrestling, which only suggested to me that the competition may not have been so hot; but producers are generally cast in a less modest mould." He resented the implication that the TV series had finally made a success of the Saint after twenty-five years of literary obscurity.

As long as the series lasted, Charteris was not shy about voicing his criticisms both in public and in a constant stream of memos to the producers. "Regular followers of the Saint saga . . . must have noticed that I am almost incapable of simply writing a story and shutting up."[10] Nor was he shy about exploiting this new market by agreeing to a series of tie-in novelisations ghosted by other writers, which he would then rewrite before publication.

Charteris mellowed as the series developed and found elements to praise too. He developed a close friendship with producer Robert S. Baker, which would last until Charteris's death.

In the early '60s, on one of their frequent trips to England, Leslie and Audrey bought a house in Surrey, which became their permanent base. He explored the possibility of a Saint musical and began writing some of it himself.

Charteris no longer needed to work. Now in his sixties, he supervised the Saint from a distance whilst continuing to travel and indulge himself. He and Audrey made seasonal excursions to Ireland and the south of France, where they had residences. He began to write poetry and devised a new universal sign language, Paleneo, based on notes and symbols he used in his diaries. Once Paleneo was released, he decided enough was enough and announced, again, his retirement. This time he meant it.

The Saint continued regardless—there was a long-running Swedish comic strip, and new novels with other writers doing the bulk of the work were complemented in the 1970s with Bob Baker's revival of the TV series, *Return of the Saint*.

Ill-health began to take its toll. By the early 1980s, although he continued a healthy correspondence with the outside world, Charteris felt unable to keep up with the collaborative Saint books and pulled the plug on them.

To entertain himself, Leslie took to "trying to beat the bookies in predicting the relative speed of horses," a hobby which resulted in several of his local betting shops refusing to take "predictions" from him, as he was too successful for their liking.

He still received requests to publish his work abroad but had become completely cynical about further attempts to revive the Saint. A new Saint magazine only lasted three issues, and two TV productions—*The Saint in Manhattan*, with Tom Selleck look-alike Andrew Clarke, and *The Saint*, with Simon Dutton—left him bitterly disappointed. "I fully expect this series to lay eggs everywhere . . . the only satisfaction I have is in looking at my bank balance."[11]

In the early 1990s, Hollywood producers Robert Evans and William J. Macdonald approached him and made a deal for the Saint to return to cinema screens. Charteris still took great care of the Saint's reputation and wrote an outline entitled *The Return of the Saint* in which an older Saint would meet the son he didn't know he had.

Much of his time in his last few years was taken up with the movie. Several scripts were submitted to him—each moving further and further away from his original concept—but the screenwriter from 1940s Hollywood was thoroughly disheartened by the Hollywood of the '90s: "There is still no plot, no real story, no characterisations, no personal interaction, nothing but endless frantic violence . . ." Besides, with producer Bill Macdonald hitting the headlines for the most un-Saintly reasons, he was to add, "How can Bill Macdonald concentrate on my Saint movie when he has Sharon Stone in his bed?"

The Crime Writers' Association of Great Britain presented Leslie with a Lifetime Achievement award in 1992 in a special ceremony at the

House of Lords. Never one for associations and awards, and although visibly unwell, Leslie accepted the award with grace and humour ("I am now only waiting to be carbon-dated," he joked). He suffered a slight stroke in his final weeks, which did not prevent him from dining out locally with family and friends, before he finally passed away at the age of 85 on 15 April 1993.

His death severed one of the final links with the classic thriller genre of the 1930s and 1940s, but he left behind a legacy of nearly one hundred books, countless short stories, and TV, film, radio, and comic-strip adaptations of his work which will endure for generations to come.

> *I was always sure that there was a solid place in escape literature for a rambunctious adventurer such as I dreamed up in my youth, who really believed in the old-fashioned romantic ideals and was prepared to lay everything on the line to bring them to life. A joyous exuberance that could not find its fulfilment in pinball machines and pot. I had what may now seem a mad desire to spread the belief that there were worse, and wickeder, nut cases than Don Quixote.*
>
> *Even now, half a century later, when I should be old enough to know better, I still cling to that belief. That there will always be a public for the old-style hero, who had a clear idea of justice, and a more than technical approach to love, and the ability to have some fun with his crusades.*[12]

---

1 *A Letter from the Saint,* 30 August 1946

2 "The Last Word," *The First Saint Omnibus,* Doubleday Crime Club, 1939

3 *The Straits Times,* 29 June 1958, page 9

4 Introduction by Charteris to the September 1980 paperback reprint of *Meet—the Tiger!* (Charter), the last ever print edition.
5 *The Saint: A Complete History,* by Burl Barer (McFarland, 1993)
6 PR material from the 1970s series *Return of the Saint*
7 From "Return of the Saint: Comprehensive Information" issued to help publicise the 1970s TV show
8 *A Letter from the Saint,* 26 July 1946
9 Introduction to "The Million Pound Day," in *The First Saint Omnibus*
10 *A Letter from the Saint,* 12 April 1946
11 Letter from LC to sometime Saint collaborator Peter Bloxsom, 2 August 1989
12 Introduction by Charteris to the September 1980 paperback reprint of *Meet—the Tiger!* (Charter).

WATCH FOR THE SIGN
OF THE SAINT!

THE SAINT CLUB

And so, my friends, dear bookworms, most noble fellow drinkers, frustrated burglars, affronted policemen, upright citizens with furled umbrellas and secret buccaneering dreams that seems to be very nearly all for now. It has been nice having you with us, and we hope you will come again, not once, but many times.

Only because of our great love for you, we would like to take this parting opportunity of mentioning one small matter which we have very much at heart . . .

—Leslie Charteris, The First Saint Omnibus *(1939)*

Leslie Charteris founded The Saint Club in 1936 with the aim of providing a constructive fanbase for Saint devotees. Before the War, it donated profits to a London hospital where, for several years, a Saint ward was maintained. With the nationalisation of hospitals, profits were, for many years, donated to the Arbour Youth Centre in Stepney, London.

In the twenty-first century, we've carried on this tradition but have also donated to the Red Cross and a number of different children's charities.

The club acts as a focal point for anyone interested in the adventures of Leslie Charteris and the work of Simon Templar, and offers merchandise that includes DVDs of the old TV series and various Saint-related publications, through to its own exclusive range of notepaper, pin badges, and polo shirts. All profits are donated to charity. The club also maintains two popular websites and supports many more Saint-related sites.

After Leslie Charteris's death, the club recruited three new vice-presidents—Roger Moore, Ian Ogilvy, and Simon Dutton have all pledged their support, whilst Audrey and Patricia Charteris have been retained as Saints-in-Chief. But some things do not change, for the back of the membership card still mischievously proclaims that . . .

> *The bearer of this card is probably a person of hideous antecedents and low moral character, and upon apprehension for any cause should be immediately released in order to save other prisoners from contamination.*

To join . . .

Membership costs £3.50 (or US$7) per year, or £30 (US$60) for life. Find us online at www.lesliecharteris.com for full details.

Made in the USA
Monee, IL
01 September 2022

12994040R00171